A DRUG KING AND HIS DIAMOND

Nicole Goosby

.

Lock Down Publications and Ca$h
Presents

A Drug King and His Diamond
A Novel by *Nicole Goosby*

Nicole Goosby

Lock Down Publications
P.O. Box 870494
Mesquite, Tx 75187

Copyright 2018 by A Drug King and His Diamond

Lock Down Publications
Like our page on Facebook: Lock Down Publications @
www.facebook.com/lockdownpublications.ldp
Cover design and layout by: **Dynasty Cover Me**
Book interior design by: **Shawn Walker**
Edited by: Kiera Northington

4

Stay Connected with Us!

Text **LOCKDOWN** to 22828 to stay
up-to-date with new releases, sneak peaks,
contests and more…

Thank you!

Submission Guideline.

Submit the first three chapters of your completed manuscript to ldpsubmissions@gmail.com, subject line: Your book's title. The manuscript must be in a .doc file and sent as an attachment. Document should be in Times New Roman, double spaced and in size 12 font. Also, provide your synopsis and full contact information. If sending multiple submissions, they must each be in a separate email.

Have a story but no way to send it electronically? You can still submit to LDP/Ca$h Presents. Send in the first three chapters, written or typed, of your completed manuscript to:

LDP: Submissions Dept
Po Box 870494
Mesquite, Tx 75187

DO NOT send original manuscript. Must be a duplicate.

Provide your synopsis and a cover letter containing your full contact information.

Thanks for considering LDP and Ca$h Presents.

Acknowledgements

I don't write for my struggles. I write for a purpose, which is a gift from God. Without my past, I will not have my future. Some people look at you and think you're doing great. I'm doing great because I have a gift from God. My grandmother, Pepper, you have always been my rock. You never question my actions. You never judge my flaws, of which I do have aplenty. Nickolvien, you're my angel with wings, just know I'm always running the race for you. Renetta Clifton Jones, you grew to be more than a friend to me; you support me in everything I do. I appreciate your husband, Quinn. I appreciate your hearing and reading everything that I write.

My BFF, Demia Brown, you're my pillar, my ride-or-die friend, you always keep me encouraged. My sisters, Erica and Lolo, I love and cherish you. Cory Walker, you are my every-thing. I couldn't ask for nothing else in the world. J-boy, keep putting your CD's out; it's going to pay off one day. Concepcion, I know I work your nerves, you like me to work your nerves. Without you, I don't know what I would do. Nuel Uyi, you are my second pair of eyes, you go back and double-check my work and edit. I know I work your nerves, and I thank you for hanging out with me. KP and Silvia, shout out to you for letting me use your name.

Mama, you always tell me to shake them haters off and that's what I've been doing. Lol! Roslyn Long, my sister from another mother, Ced Reed A.K.A. King, I don't know anything about that Florida life, welcome to Texas! I really enjoyed playing with the King. He's one of my favorite characters in the book. Thank you, Ced, for giving me the idea. My #LDP family, you're very support-ive. I appreciate everyone for having my back. Cash, you're the best. My readers, you're the reason why I write. Thank you for all the feedback, negative and positive. Without you, I could never grow. Thank you for supporting my first novel, A Dopeman's Riches: Money Rules the World. You can always catch me on Fa-cebook. Much love to my readers. I'm going to keep doing what I do best; that is, write, write and write!

Nicole Goosby

Prologue

Chanel McClendon hated the four-hour drive it took to get to the federal facility located outside San Antonio, TX. However, the luxury of the Rolls Royce Phantom not only comforted her trip, but allowed her to do other things rather than stare at the passing landscapes and the other people traveling to various locations themselves. This was a trip she made monthly, and although she'd been doing it for the past six months, she had yet to tell her brother what she was planning.

Her brother, Antonio, had been committed to a fifteen-year imprisonment, as well as a life sentence for a conspiracy to commit murder and the Continuing Criminal Enterprise charge, known as CCE, he was convicted of over seven months ago. He'd been head of the "Circle" for over ten years, and the drug game had been a very lucrative one for himself and his associates. Being ten years her senior and the only guardian she had, the life he afforded her was one she wasn't willing to relinquish. He made sure she had the best of everything, enjoyed the best of anything.

Chanel was reclined in the soft leather chairs in the rear of the Rolls Royce, watching a movie and enjoying the surround sound in the cabin of the hundred and seventy-five-thousand-dollar automobile offered her, when Chris, who doubled as her driver and bodyguard, told her, "We'll be there in five minutes, Diamond."

That was the name given to her by her brother, because of her metamorphosis from rough gem into a beauty queen over the years. Kids the same age as Diamond considered her a tomboy, because sports had become a part of her life. It was what they identified her by and having been to countless football games, courtside at All-Star signings and three Super Bowls, being looked at as such had its rewards.

It wasn't until her twentieth birthday when Antonio began to notice how beautiful his sister was. He'd surrounded himself with beautiful women, and whenever he heard them compliment her on her natural features, he began seeing new potential in her, to say nothing of how other men regarded her as well. They pushed her into the modeling world. At twenty years of age, Chanel stood five foot nine and weighed one hundred and forty-five pounds. Her coconut complexion, sharp features, thin nose, flawless skin tone, slim build, long legs and enviable cheekbones were reminiscent of the model, Cynthia Bailey, in her younger days. And after being introduced to nightly cleanses, morning exfoliations and weekly treatments, Chanel became a much sought-after beauty.

In her world, she felt she knew all there was and if she had a say in it, the drug game was something she'd choose over any hustle or any other career. After using the remote to end the movie, she straightened her seat, unfolded the mirror in the console beside her, applied a coat of lipstick to her lips and combed her naturally long lashes. She always admired her almond-colored eyes and their shape. It was a must she looked good for her brother, knowing full well how he loved to boast about her being a model. Today, she wore a tan Le Peria dress and some Rossi heels, her signature Chanel shades and a Hermes ankle bracelet on her left leg. Her hair was neatly done in a Chinese bow, with feather-soft hair aligning her temples. She would definitely turn a few heads for her brother.

Seconds after the car stopped, she attempted to open the door like always, but Chris was sure to beat her to it. He had never given her cause to question his loyalty, and that loyalty was because of her brother.

"You needn't bother trying to open the door yourself. That's why you have me, Diamond."

"Yeah, yeah, I remember," she said, while accepting his hand and being pulled out of the car.

"If word got back out to your brother that you were being treated anything less than a lady, he'd trip and you know this."

Diamond adjusted her Chanel shades while looking around at the other people there to visit their loved ones. She even nodded at a few. "Damn, I hope these hoes ain't crowded," she told Chris.

"I doubt it, 'cause we're earlier than most." Chris escorted her into the building.

The inside of the Three Rivers Facility was cooler than it had been in the past, and she was now hoping she wouldn't freeze once inside the visitation room. After being directed through a set of electronic doors and one sliding entryway, she and Chris were led into a single-leveled visiting room. Once their paperwork was verified and they were properly searched, Diamond was given an alphabet, telling her which table she'd be seated at. Knowing her brother would like a few items from the vending machines, she ventured that way. After selecting a carrot cake, two root beers and three deli sandwiches, she walked them back to the table where Chris waited.

"What?" he asked, upon seeing him roll his eyes at her.

"I didn't say anything to you." Chris looked at the many faces around and smiled at a few of the ones he recognized.

"You didn't have to. You're over there rolling your eyes like a queen or something." She began placing the items on the table before him. "Well, look who's here." Diamond saw her brother walk through the doors. He headed their way. She took in the attire he wore. His khakis were starched without wrinkles, the gray shirt stiff all the way, his shoes shined. He might have not been clad in his usual Italian and linen attire, but she did find him presentable. Diamond gave him an ecstatic smile before jumping into his embrace. Diamond loved the security and comfort she felt while hugging him, and she let him know it. "Is that how tight you can squeeze a bitch?"

Antonio kissed his sister's forehead. "What did I tell you about referring to yourself as 'a bitch'?" He held her at arm's length, shook his head and kissed her again. "I hope you're well." He pushed her chair under her as she sat, then walked over to Chris, and hugged him. "Love you, boy."

"I'm super good, what's up with you?" she said in her attempt to regain his attention.

"You know I'm more than a conqueror," he assured her. There was never a visit where he worried her about the things that went on inside the prison that sheltered him. Even though he was in prison, Antonio McClendon lived like a king. He got whatever he wanted, whenever he wanted. With a light sixty thousand dollars wired at his discretion to his account from various accounts, and over seven and a half million on the outside, he didn't have a care in the world. His only concern was his sister. "What are the agents talking about?" he asked in respect of her modeling plans, knowing it was about time she stepped on somebody's runway.

Diamond smiled, gave Chris a subtle glance and told Antonio, "Them hoes, I mean, they ain't talking about nothing I want to hear, so I just decided to give it a break for a while."

Antonio looked over at Chris, as if he needed him to contribute to the topic, but Chris shrugged, giving the impression he had no say in the matter. "What about the people I hooked you up with?" Antonio asked his sister with a hint of suspicion in his voice.

Diamond sighed. She hated lying to her brother just as she disliked fighting with him, and since she was there to tell him of her future plans, she told him, "I'm just not feeling that modeling shit, bro. I be having shit, I mean, I want to do what I want to do, man."

"Like what, Chanel? What's got you so caught up that you can't think about your future, huh?" He watched her struggle with an answer, and said, "Bullshit, you out there bullshitting, Chanel. You…"

It had been ages since he called her by her first name when he was disappointed at her. At times when he was downright mad at her, he called her full name. "I'm doing what I got to do to stay on top, bro. This shit ain't the same without you." She pouted.

Seeing his sister play the "pout" role hadn't worked on him since the day she pouted about wanting to hang out with her girlfriends, but was found on the other side of town with some guy six years older than she was. "What the hell you mean by that?" He watched her grab one of the deli sandwiches and slide him the other. When seeing her toss the last towards Chris, he knew then he'd most likely missed his cue for the conversation. "I know you're not broke, so…" He watched her with an incredulous expression.

"I just feel like I'm leeching from you and what you got going on, bro. These niggas are only respecting me because of you. I want to make my own way. I need to."

"You need to be doing something else with your life, girl. I'm not sitting in this place for nothing. I sacrificed enough for us already, and it was done so you wouldn't have to toil, Diamond. I wanted you to have better opportunities, and I need for you to do the right thing, sis. Come on now." He reached for one of the root beer drinks and opened it for her.

With her second attempt to change the subject, she asked, "What's up with your appeal?"

"Don't worry about that, Diamond. I'm straight on that end. I just need you to be alright until I get back out there."

"Somebody set you up, bro. Ain't no way you were supposed to—"

Antonio cut her off. "Diamond, stop. Don't sweat that shit. If a nigga did set me up and cross me out, that's a part of the game when you getting money. And we've been blessed to still have some, so fuck them niggas. You hear me? Fuck them niggas, Diamond."

"The shit just doesn't sit well with me and I'm not like you, I'm not letting shit slide."

Antonio took a long swig of root beer and sat the can on the table. He watched his sister before saying, "So, what now? You gonna break me out of jail or something?" He regarded his sister intently. He refused to believe she was lost. As many people as he put around her to help her with the decisions she was to make, it was becoming harder to believe she was in control of her life. Her inability to look at life the way he saw it was his fault, and it was now he regretted it. She never had a job, any obligations other than doing what she wanted, when she wanted and answering to no one. Now that she was to own these responsibilities, he knew he'd have to paint a better picture for her. "So, what do you suggest, Diamond?"

"I want to take your place on the Circle," she told him in an even tone.

He looked at Chris, then back to his sister, whose lips were moving without words.

"Hold up, sis, what did you just say?"

"I'm telling you, bro, I can do this shit. Me and Chris—"

"You and Chris what?" Antonio's brows met at the center of his forehead. He was questioning her, but looking at Chris.

And for the first time since their arrival, Chris spoke. He had to. "I ain't done shit, big homie. She's the one who came up with that idea."

"Snitching ass," she mumbled, eyeing Chris.

"What the hell is wrong with you, Chanel McClendon?"

There it was, but she wasn't backing down. "That nigga can't hold shit. He's supposed to be riding with me on whatever I choose to do."

"And who told you that lie?" Antonio asked her. "He's supposed to look out for you when you can't, not run off the same cliff you're willing to dive from." He sat back in his seat and just looked at her. She was a beautiful young woman, and he'd been trying to get her to see that.

"Just put me on, bro. Let me do what I've got to do."

He thought back to the days when he found it funny to see her rock-up ounces, weigh quarter-kilos and do small deals with the drugs he gave her. He couldn't help but remember the words he spoke over his sister's life. She was going to be a queen pin, and she was going to be richer than he ever was. Those were the words he spoke just a few years ago, and today he was regretting it in the worst way.

"So you really want to play the game, huh?"

"Hell yeah, that is what you groomed me to do."

"No, I didn't. I groomed you to be the gem you are, and to shine like you're supposed to, but it seems you want something different for yourself." His tone was unenthusiastic.

"You see where I'm at, Diamond?" He looked around them. "You want this shit? Is this how you want to live? You're twenty-five years old, sis, take advantage of that, 'cause you can't get it back once time passes you by."

"You gave me the blueprint, bro, and with Chris running point, we win!"

Her zeal tugged at Antonio's heart. He sensed that whether he OK'd her decisions or not, she'd do it without him, and the last thing he needed was for his only sister to get caught up, chewed up and spat out in the dog-eat-dog game of the streets.

"I'm serious, bro. Tell them motherfuckers I'm in." Diamond reached for his hand and subtly placed the folded paper into his palm. She'd made sure that during the course of visiting, she'd slipped him a little cash. Seeing him accept the money and his frown fade, she knew it was only a matter of seconds before she was flooding a section of the region she lived. "Buy yourself some pussy or something."

"You know I don't need your money, Diamond," he told her, as he did during every visit of hers.

"I wish I could say the same, bro."

Nicole Goosby

Chapter One
Six months later

Camille checked her rearview mirror. She accelerated as if she was being pursued. With two million dollars in the trunk of her platinum Audi R8, she had to hurry. She'd already called Kengyon to let him know that things went according to plan on her end, and as always, she was about to make the two-hour trip as quick as she could. In the game she played, speed was of the essence, and with interstate patrolmen on her payroll, she rarely obeyed the traffic lights, and considered every light green.

At twenty-eight years of age, she was the boss of many people, and when she wanted something moved, or someone stepped on, it was just a call away. She'd been in the drug trade for over five years, and had developed an instinct that kept both her and her team above the waters that drowned many of the competitors she knew. That instinct also placed her off the radars of the FBI or any other agency that threatened their livelihood.

As she maneuvered the sports car through stretches of traffic, she peered at the speedometer. Seeing she'd reached a speed of one hundred sixty mph, she smiled. Between her Audi R8 and her Porsche 911, she still couldn't choose a favorite. One thing Camille loved was speed, whether it was the fast life she lived, or the speed her cars were capable of. Standing five foot six and weighing one hundred and sixty five pounds, she had a bigger stature than most of the guys she supplied in the game. She was not only Kengyon's right-hand man, but also a gangster. Her soft facial features, light complexion, hazel-green eyes and full lips gave her a gentle exterior that caused most people she dealt with to underestimate her, and that alone was the reason she had six bodies under her belt, and another handful if push came to shove.

Hearing the chime of her iPhone, she lowered the volume of the radio and answered the phone. "Yeah?"

"Where you at?" The voice that greeted her was deep, menacing and comforting at the same time.

After checking her rearview for the umpteenth time, she smiled to herself.

"Damn near there," she told him upon seeing the Dallas exit coming up. "You need to get rid of that slow ass truck anyway," she added, before ending her call.

Buddy was the owner of the comforting voice on the other end of her phone. When she made a trip, he was that menacing presence one was sure to see when she did arrive. Buddy had been a part of her team since high school. With him standing six foot five and weighing three hundred and fifty pounds of solid muscle, she had no inhibitions about her small stature. He was a neatly groomed monster of a man, and sent chills up the spines of many of the people he met. Not only was he always there for Camille. He was also the one that carried out the orders she gave, and if it came down to it, he'd lay down his life for the woman he referred to as "Boss Lady".

He adjusted himself and sunk lower into the captain chairs of the black 3500 Chevy Dually he was driving, and once the cruise control was set at eighty mph, he selected the tunes of Marvin Gaye's "Distant Lover" and sang along with him. This trip alone would reward him around two hundred thousand dollars, and with nothing and no one to spend it on, it would be put up with the rest of the cash he'd been saving for five years.

Kengyon Johnson lowered his phone and smiled. He'd been anticipating Camille's call for the last hour, and having heard things were as they should be, his anxiety disappeared. She'd come to him and proposed a possible venture that could expand the distribution he and his team so desperately needed. Seven months ago, a known kingpin by the name of Antonio McClendon took some heat, and was rumored to have received a life sentence for his part in a drug ring that stretched from Dallas to San Antonio, TX, and supplied the cities and counties in between. With McClendon out of the picture and the trade, Kengyon did think about a possible expansion into those areas, but decided against it, not wanting a war with the many players that felt the areas were theirs for the taking. That was when Camille assured him the move was feasible, and she'd oversee the operation, notwithstanding any possible threat. Against his better judgment, he allowed her to spread her wings and began pushing their products further out towards Kansas. The San Antonio deal she had made was not only what pushed their profit margins upward, but was her way to make their presence known in the face of the players that overlooked her in the beginning.

He'd heard many tales and rumors of the notorious Antonio McClendon and the so-called "Circle", but never really took interest in their team because he and his own crew were doing very well. For the past three years, he and his team had been moving one hundred and fifty kilos of flake a month, which provided them plush and lavish lifestyles. But, now that Camille's expansion was without blemish, they were able to push a hundred and seventy-five as well as score two hundred from their Columbian plug. He wasn't trying to take on any additional drama. His system had been working and he hoped his latest move wouldn't be considered greedy. This was why he was on edge every time Camille went off to do her thing.

Kengyon descended the spiral staircase of his bi-leveled home, located on Ravinia Drive in West Oak Cliff. This was one of his homes he frequented, because not only was it tucked off in its own little wooded area with all the security features one could want, but his neighbors were cops, lawyers, judges and city councilmen. The landscaping business he used was the perfect façade, and with over twenty volunteers working that entity, his reputation in the hoods was unblemished. He walked out on his patio and looked up at the rays of sun that peeked through the clearing provided by the trees around his home. They'd had a successful run in the game and as always, he couldn't help but think about the days and the reasons it all ended. He'd not too long ago celebrated his twenty-ninth birthday, counted over three million dollars in cash, and promised himself those numbers would not only double but triple, and if he had to partake of this life for the rest of his life, that was what he'd do. To him, there was no other life to live.

After walking back inside, he crossed his dining area, increased the volume on his one hundred and thirty thousand dollars' worth entertainment system, fell onto the suede and leather trimmed sectional and closed his eyes. He thought about his recent break-up. For some reason, he couldn't dismiss the idea of Camille having something to do with it. He had no reason to believe she was jealous of any relationship he found himself in, but when she disapproved of the women he found interest in, things happened and people disappeared forever.

To think that Camille could perform such a task was too far-fetched to him, but when it came to the monster of a man that ran wherever she pointed, Kengyon's thoughts ran amuck. For the past three years, he'd been with many women, but his last relationship was one he thought would last. The morning he awoke and found the note on the pillow, stating she no longer wanted to live in his shadows and she deserved more, something died inside his heart. He felt that way because they had gotten very close, yet she never voiced anything other than the love they shared with one another. What broadened his suspicions was that she took over one hundred and seventy-five thousand dollars from the hallway safe, but left the two hundred and fifty thousand dollars he'd given her as a gift.

Besides the missing money, there'd been a note left behind, and he knew it wasn't written in her script at all. These were the things he kept to himself until he knew for sure that Camille really did make the woman run away or something.

He hinted at a possible engagement, and while hoping Camille would offer him ideas and suggestions of romantic evenings and settings, she only pointed out the flaws she felt the woman had. "That broke bitch don't give a damn about us, King. All she wants is what you spoil her with, and when the bitch finds better, she's gone." King would never forget Camille's words when it came to the women he chose, and he could never forget the things that mysteriously happened to them either. He knew Camille was a killer, having seen her put in the work personally—but never once thought she'd be the reason he didn't find a love of his own.

King was the only child of a single mother, who'd had a fling with a Nigerian prince, who felt his child should be born where his royalty was. Once she refused to be on the same page with him and leave all that mattered to her, he went back home without her, leaving her to raise and care for Kengyon herself. With most people mispronouncing his birth name and refusing to believe he descended from a royal bloodline, she called him King, the son of a prince.

***

Silvia Bates had owned and operated the Totally Awesome Hair Salon for the past five years and had become a sought-out name when it came to getting some of the more expensive hairdos and better treatments. She and her beauticians specialized in a bevy of hairstyles, ranging from virgin hair to front-laced wigs, shampoo and set to crème serums.

Silvia once hustled drugs for her cousin, and after falling on hard times with several failed businesses and unpaid loan debts, she felt she had no choice. Once she'd saved enough money to pull her out of the debt she owed and opened the salon, she found a couple of friends and associates to help her push it to unexpected heights. Not only was Antonio McClendon her first cousin, but they were best friends. Doing whatever he needed was never questioned, and when he started washing his money through her salon and other legit businesses, there was nothing to discuss. With her and Antonio being ten years older than Chanel, there was a certain responsibility she had to her youngest cousin. Despite not being Chanel's mother, Silvia was still that go-to person when it came to the womanly things they shared.

Silvia was on the chubby side, but beautiful. She was five foot six with naturally green eyes. Her redbone complexion and bi-racial features told a story as confusing as the one she gave when explaining her nationality. Her high-arched eyebrows, thin lips, naturally long lashes and blown-out curls with blonde highlights screamed albino or Creole, but she was a black woman in every sense of the word. With enough money in the bank from her salon and the kickback she received from her kingpin cousin, she was able to snatch

21

the silver BMW Roadster and buy her first home in Forest Hills, a prominent community in Fort Worth, TX.

She married her long-time boyfriend, KP, who was a freelance contractor, but she was known to step out every now and again. It wasn't that she didn't love her husband, or he wasn't faithful to her. It was just something she'd gotten used to doing.

"Has anyone heard from Diamond and Chris yet?" she asked her co-workers, believing they should have returned from visiting Antonio by now.

"They're probably laying up somewhere in some high-dollar hotel, thinking of a lie to tell when they get back," said Somolia. Painting wild and vivid pictures of everyone else's relationship was something she had no problem doing, and when it came to Chanel McClendon and Datrina's boyfriend, Chris, those were paintings she hung everywhere. Somolia stood five foot four and was heavyset, with full thick lips and a wide nose. Her chubby cheeks and dimples, slanted eyes and outspoken character got her likes and dislikes from people. She was a bronze beauty, but the way she hated everyone with a seemingly successful relationship or marriage, created that double-edged sword people used to judge her.

"Whatever, bitch," Datrina told her, knowing Somolia had indirectly meant that statement for her. She and Chris had been an item since college, and the only time she could say he might have stepped out on her was when Chanel McClendon was mentioned. It was just something about the way he treated the other girl that raised suspicions. Silvia tried to assure her time and time again there was nothing between Diamond and Chris, and if it hadn't been for the fact that Silvia was Chanel's cousin, Silvia herself might have believed it.

Not only did Somolia have a way of casting doubt when it came to the so-called platonic friendship between Chris and Diamond, she also had the habit of spreading rumors about them. It was true that Chanel McClendon was what all the guys wanted because not only was she rich, the woman got whatever and whoever she wanted. On top of all the things she couldn't see past was that whenever Chanel did call Chris, he ran as fast as he could to her, even if it meant leaving Datrina at that moment.

At first, Datrina thought it was because of Chanel's beauty, but when she looked in the mirror at herself, she realized her chocolate complexion, curvaceous body, thick thighs and height alone had men peeping into their workplace, just to get a glimpse of her. Besides, Chris promised her millions of times that Chanel was like a sister to him, and he was the only one that could keep her in check.

"Well then, where are they?" Somolia asked her while setting the temperature to the barreled curling irons she was heating.

"They went to go see her brother, Somolia, and Chris drove her. Is there a problem with that?" Silvia asked her, knowing Datrina was easily irked when Somolia began giving visuals of what she thought was happening.

"He texted me not too long ago and said they were on the road now," Datrina told them unenthusiastically.

"Every month, they disappear together. Why can't she go see her brother herself? She's a grown-up, Silvia. Chris ain't got to drive that woman around like he does. When you see her, you see Datrina's man. When you see her leaving, Datrina's man leaves also." Somolia shook her head.

Datrina retorted, "Don't get me started. Please don't, Somolia."

"While you over there looking crazy, Datrina, you need to be telling Chanel to be careful with your man."

Datrina eyed Somolia.

Silvia spoke to Datrina without looking at her. "It's none of your business, Somolia."

Chris had worked for Antonio before Antonio's incarceration and was now on Chanel's payroll. The money he showered on Datrina gave her the good things of life. The convertible Pontiac Datrina drove and an all-expenses-paid loft in Echo Heights caused her to wonder about the nature of his service to Diamond. For now, she had to believe the things they told her. "I trust my man, Somolia. It might not seem like it at times, but I do. Besides, I think he has too much respect for Antonio to mess with his little sister." Datrina gave a weak smile.

"That nigga got a life sentence, girl. What the hell can he do if he finds she's fucking one of his workers?" Somolia pointed the curling iron at her. "Huh?"

"Shut up, Somolia," said Datrina. "Diamond is not fucking Chris. End of story."

Silvia sprayed her station's mirrors and prepared for the day's work. She looked up and noticed she had only minutes before her first appointment was to arrive. Today was Saturday, and this was about to be the first of the five heads she had lined up to work on.

For the past six months, she knew about the business between Diamond and Chris, and worried like hell about her cousin. After being assured by Antonio that he still had a hold on Diamond, Silvia agreed to sit back and let her cousin do her thing. Not only did Silvia know about the drugs Diamond and Chris were pushing, she also knew the youngster held a seat in the same circle Antonio had been a part of for years.

***

"Don't you think you need to slow down a bit?" Chris asked Diamond, when she made their vehicle blow past other cars as if there was no tomorrow.

"Man, fuck these snail-ass people!" Diamond yelled, pushing her brand new Bentley Coupe to its limits. She hoped her brother would increase her package, considering she and Chris were peddling just the twenty-five kilos. Having to wait until the next month before she was given anything else, dampened the plans she had for herself and Chris. They'd just left the facility, having concluded the visit to her brother, and she was scheduled to make another drop the same day. She needed to stop by her home, then she had to drop Chris off at the salon so he could get his car and follow her. There weren't enough hours in the day for her and as optimistic as she was, she still didn't have enough product for her endeavors.

"They just don't want you to rush things, Diamond. These niggas been doing this shit for a minute and they know how to move and when to move." Chris tried to get her to see reason. But, like always, he had to fight her first.

"We've been doing this shit our way for six months now, nigga. You think I don't know how to move?" Diamond sped through a couple of eighteen-wheelers, which caused the car to sway in the draft.

"Just chill, Diamond. They gonna raise out shit eventually. Just chill."

"I need my shit now, nigga! I'm tired of waiting on these secretive-ass niggas. I was thinking about going to holler at Dell and Raymond myself."

To hear her speak of going behind her brother's back and getting at the head niggas didn't sit well with Chris, because word would eventually get back to Antonio, and there was no way he'd understand or even want to hear that her doing so was a decision she made alone. Chris's job was to make sure she stayed in line.

"Just trust me, Diamond. Don't go to them niggas. If ya brother finds out some shit like that, I'm dead. And you know it." He leaned back, placed his ankle on his knee and folded his arms, hoping she'd listen.

"That nigga ain't going to do shit to you. I got him. You gonna trust me or what?"

"Yeah, you're a boss bitch, but even bosses got to have a listening ear and heed advice as well, and in this situation, it's me asking you to."

Diamond looked over at Chris and rolled her eyes. She knew he was right. One thing they promised was that they were in it together and neither would make a move without the other. "I hope you know your shit, nigga. I really do." Her voice trailed off when the volume to her stereo increased. This time she would chill, and since it was Chris that asked her, it would be something she enjoyed.

"Stop by the shop first, since we're damn near there. I know Datrina is worried."

"Call her, nigga. Let her know you're alright."

"I don't feel like answering a million questions, Diamond, and I damn sure ain't trying to hear what them hoes at that salon is talking about."

Diamond laughed. She knew personally what that talk consisted of, but as long as they were talking about the things they thought they knew and not what was really going on, then there was no harm in it, even if it did cause fights between Chris and his girlfriend. Diamond only laughed when asked about the nature of her relationship with Chris and to get tongues wagging, she would even snuggle up to him, hold his hand at various places and post selfies on her Facebook of the two of them at different games and such. "You probably do want to fuck me, Chris."

"Whatever. You ain't black enough for me, though."

"The pussy ain't ever black, nigga."

Chris laughed. "My girl's is."

Diamond smiled. One thing she loved about Chris was that he was loyal to her and faithful to Datrina. Even when they did end up spending the night at hotels, he never once came on to her, and even when she'd walk out of the shower naked and fall across the same bed he was in, he never looked at her as anything other than the sister she wanted to be to him. Their relationship alone taught her it was never about the sex and when money was made, it couldn't be. "It's me and you, nigga," she told him without thought.

"And me and you," he responded.

"I'm telling you, Chris, we can move fifty by ourselves," she assured him.

Chris could tell that she was contemplating numbers, and even when he couldn't see as far as she could, he knew she was accurate in her calculations. Not only did it have an undeniable appeal, there was still a certain risk they were sure to take with the responsibility of an expansion. Ever since the first drop six months ago, Chris had pocketed half a million dollars himself and knew that if he was given the chance, he'd also profit double what he was making now. The only thing Antonio made him promise was that they paid their dues to the Circle.

"We'll cross that bridge when we get there, Diamond. Until then, let's play this shit by ear."

Diamond pulled into the salon's parking lot and pulled in beside her cousin Silvia's new BMW Roadster. She checked herself in the visor's mirror. Satisfied that her appearance was flawless, she climbed from behind the wheel and followed Chris inside.

"Hey, Cuz!" Diamond yelled upon entering. "What's up, Datrina? Somolia?"

"Hey, girl, how was the visit?" Somolia asked the two of them.

"What visit?" Diamond acted as if she knew nothing of it, but when she saw Datrina turn to face her and Chris, she laughed and said, "As always. He seems to be doing well, if that answers anything."

"Did he get my pictures?" Silvia asked.

"Yeah. He also said something about you needing a vacation of some sort."

Diamond walked over and looked at herself in the floor-length mirror. The need to change clothing appealed to her. As always, she'd dressed the part for the visit and she was dying to slip into something more comfortable. The silk jumpsuit, peep-toe booties and the bangle bracelets she wore accented the make-up she had on and the French braid she pinned up, but what she wanted to do now was change both attire and hair-dos.

"I want some curved cornrows," she told no one in particular.

"Girl, leave your hair alone. You just got it done yesterday, Diamond." Silvia walked over and examined the 'do. "You're tripping."

"I got fifteen hundred dollars for a chair right now," she told them before looking towards Chris, who was now shaking his head.

All those present knew the money was nothing to the youngster, and knew she didn't mean it as a cap at them. It was her outlandish spending that caused them to look askance at her.

"Your hair is beautiful, Diamond. Why mess it up or even change it, for that matter?"

"I just got this shit done for the visit." She half-turned in front of the mirror, posing as she did. "Do I have to spend my money elsewhere?"

"Girl, go sit down," Somolia told her. Not only was she going to accept the money, she was also going to push back her first appointment. "I need that money."

Nicole Goosby

Chapter Two

It had been two weeks since she visited her brother and requested a raise in the products they were issuing her. It was the end of the month and she was missing out on several lucrative deals, having to wait for the first.

She even shared with Chris their need to step out on their own, to ensure that they'd be able to make moves of their own when they needed to. Despite being given a green light on the deals she did and the six hundred thousand dollars she made personally in the past six months, there was still a need for her to step from under the shadow of the Circle, to step from under the leash they held her with.

"We need our own plug, Chris," she told him, before throwing him the black duffle that contained her last five kilos.

Chris had been down this road with her for the past few days and hoped Antonio would come through for them. Diamond had expressly told Antonio that if she didn't get what she wanted, she and Chris would make a move of their own, and if there were repercussions or a tax, then that's something they'd deal with when the time came.

"Who did you have in mind?" he asked her, knowing there weren't too many people able to do what the Circle was doing for them.

"Not sure yet. I sometimes think about the risk that comes with the game."

"Oh, you're scared to make some moves now?"

Diamond was standing at the fridge door, filling her glass with ice when those words hit her. She knew Chris feared no one, but it was time to push him into action and what better way to move him than playing on his emotions and ego?

"You forgot how to hold your own dick, nigga? I think it's you who really wants to chicken out."

"Don't start, Diamond. It ain't going to work."

"That's some shit a nigga say when he knows he can't make shit happen." She chunked one of the ice cubes at him and popped one into her mouth. "We've been paying these niggas over sixty thousand dollars a month for dues and we can't even get our shit when we need it. What the fuck is that money for?"

"We pay dues because we're a part of something. Something your brother put together years ago." Chris checked the content of the duffle and dialed a number into his phone. This would be a deal made with some associates of the guys he'd been dealing with for a while, a possible outlet for them for when they did get their raise. The way they saw it, it was better to do good business with everyone and if they pointed you in the direction of other associates of theirs, then good business would be done with them also.

Chris watched the text and as soon as the location was dialed in, he looked at Diamond and said, "You're ready?"

"I was born ready, nigga."

Since this would be a deal made within the city, there was no need for the luxury of the Rolls Royce or her Bentley Coupe, and after deciding against driving her brother's pride and joy, the pearl blue Camaro Convertible, she grabbed the keys of her brand new Benz instead. Today she wore a camo halter top and pants and some custom Jordan shoes. She was feeling every bit of the tomboy she was. And once they'd pulled out of the multi-car garage of the McClendon estate, they were on their way.

***

Camille was lounging by the pool, sipping on a citrus mimosa when King approached her. He'd wanted to run some things by her for a couple of days and now that she was there, it was now or never. "Hey, babe, how are you feeling?" he asked her, but was looking at Buddy, who was watching him as if it was his first time seeing them interact.

She lowered her Gucci shades and smiled at him, her hazel-green eyes boring into his soul. "Like a little trouble, can you help me with that?"

"Well, yeah, but first I need to holler at you about some-thing."

"What is it, King?"

"Have you heard anything about Nava?" he asked, knowing if word got back about the whereabouts of the woman that had disappeared and left him, it would have been something Camille knew of first. He made sure he paid attention to the monster of a man sitting across from her, and saw no reaction from him, not even a glance in Camille's direction. He looked back into Camille's eyes.

"No, she hasn't called me, King, and I'm more than certain she won't." Camille lowered her shades and continued reading the novel she held, then added, "It's not like we were the best of friends anyway."

"It just doesn't sit well with me that she would just leave without a trace, Camille. We were supposed to get engaged and everything." He adjusted himself in the outdoor chair and looked out over the waters of the pool.

She told him without looking up from her book, "There are always other fish in the water, Kengyon, and no fish is the be-all and end-all of a man's catch. Another fish will land in your net sometime. Have faith."

Hearing those words along with his birth name told him that this was a conversation she wasn't trying to have at the moment, and instead of begging her for a lie or a truth he wasn't willing to accept, he changed the subject. "Let's go to Miami next weekend."

Camille lowered her shades for the second time and asked him, "For what?"

King shrugged. "Change of scenery, I guess." The words he spoke were true, but Miami was also where Nava was from and he felt the trip was overdue. Besides, there were too many unanswered questions when it came to her just up and leaving.

"Why Miami, King? And what kind of scene are you looking for?"

King pushed himself from the seat he was sitting in and told her, "I'm trying to find that out, so get your shit in order because we're going." Instead of waiting for a response from her, he walked off, making sure he met eyes with Buddy, so the fella also knew the trip was in order.

31

Camille knew what the trip was about. She was also sure of one thing. No matter what King did or said, if he did find Nava, the babe wouldn't be coming back. That was the promise Camille had forced her to give in exchange for her life.

"You hear that, Buddy? We're going to Miami."

"I'm already packed, Boss Lady," he told her while patting the pistol under his left armpit.

"Good, 'cause I'd hate for a bitch to break a promise." Camille turned the page of the book she was holding, raised her leg and lost herself in yet another world, a world she found herself characterized in.

***

After the subtle transaction in the Sonic eatery, Diamond walked across the lot and climbed into the Camaro, where Chris awaited her. With it only being five kilos of work, there was no need for both of them conducting the deal and exposing the hands they had. It was also her idea that she do it alone, by way of showing the guys that she was not only capable of coming through, but that she was more than just another pretty face. The fact that she was Antonio McClendon's sister wasn't something she wanted known, and when asked about her social ties, she only left them with the name she wanted to be known by, Diamond.

As soon as she climbed into the car, Chris watched the other guy pull out of the lot and speed off into traffic. "You're straight?" he asked her.

Yeah, that wasn't shit, nigga. Five punk-ass birds. He was acting as if that was the most he scored in his life." Diamond was putting her car in gear when Chris began looking through the duffle bag she was given. "I already checked the money, nigga. Hell, these niggas ain't built like that."

"You'd be surprised, Diamond." He pulled out every stack of cash and immediately tore the bands off of them. There was supposed to be either twenty-three stacks of five thousand dollars, or eleven-and-a-half stacks of ten thousand dollars. When he saw the thick bundles, he separated them by halves. It took Chris seconds to see that the cash was there, but the hundred-dollar bills that should have been there were fives, tens, and twenties. He at first started to laugh, but stopped laughing when he saw Diamond's expression. Instead, he told her, "Always check your shit, Diamond, always."

"You got to be shitting me, nigga?" She looked, still disbelieving what her eyes were showing her.

"Fuck it, Diamond. It wasn't anything but five birds. Charge that shit to the game." Those were the words told to him years ago, and now that he was seeing the game being played as it always had been, he hoped it taught Diamond a very valuable lesson.

"Yeah, I'm going to charge a nigga's ass alright," she told him, before making a wild turn at the intersection and speeding off in the direction the guy went she'd just dealt with.

"Fuck that shit, Diamond. It just shows you who you can and can't fuck with, out here." Chris threw the duffle bag into the back seat and smiled at her. "This is the game we in now, sis."

"I'm also about to show a motherfucker who he shouldn't have fucked with."

Diamond sped through traffic and seeing the familiar Suburban way up ahead, she ran a light and jumped a curb.

"What the fuck are you tripping on, Diamond?" Chris then looked around for the cops and when he noticed her pulling alongside the guy's Suburban, he asked her, "Are you serious?"

"Kill that hoe, Chris." Diamond looked over at Chris and demanded, "Kill him, Chris!"

"You're tripping, Diamond. That shit was crumbs to us. You're going to drop a nigga over some crumbs now?"

Instead of answering a question he knew the answer to, Diamond crashed her brand-new car into the side of the truck.

"Dammit, Diamond!" Knowing there would definitely be a reaction from the guy she hit, Chris reached for his Glock, fired inside the driver's door and window. Once they stopped, he jumped out. He climbed into the back of the truck and grabbed the duffle bag Diamond had exchanged with the guy traded him.

Seeing the guy's blood and brain matter sprayed over the passenger seat and door, Chris knew his duty had been fulfilled. "Let's go!" he told her after slamming the door. This wasn't the first time he put in some work, but it was the first time it was done without thought.

"When you let niggas pull their dicks out on you, one is gonna piss, and I'll be damned if a nigga pulls his dick out and piss on me." Diamond checked her rearview until they were blocks away and when she was sure they were in the clear, she told him, "This car ain't about shit anyway."

Chris watched her. As beautiful as she was, he knew that if he hadn't put in the work, she would have done it herself. Before he allowed her to fall victim to some guy's pistol, he'd be that beast they'd have to take down first. And, he felt there was no turning back. "Goddammit, Diamond!"

***

Silvia busied herself with the hair she was doing, but continued to look up at the clock in her office. Diamond always called her at a certain time of the day. Since she was over an hour late, Silvia began to worry. "Hold on right quick. I have to make a call," she told her client. Lord, please let this girl be alright. Silvia said the quiet prayer before dialing Diamond's phone number. Just then, she heard her voice in the lobby of her salon. Silvia headed that way.

"Hey, cuz, what's up?" Diamond said as soon as her gaze met Silvia's.

Silvia peered out of the window of her shop and asked, "Where's your car, Diamond?"

"I wrecked it."

"You did what?" Silvia walked towards her. Seeing nothing out of the ordinary, she looked towards Chris, who was now hugging Datrina and feigning ignorance of her talk with Diamond.

"I'll get another one tomorrow. Don't sweat it, cuz."

Silvia shook her head at Diamond and Chris, and then headed back into her office. There were things that needn't be said. Looking back to the days of her past, she couldn't help but feel there was more to the story Diamond had concocted. In an attempt to get a true picture of things, she yelled, "Chris, come help me move this cabinet!"

Somolia had been watching Diamond and Chris ever since they walked in the building. When she saw the hush-toned conversations they held and the way Diamond glanced in his direction when he hugged Datrina, she knew there was something neither of them was telling. There was just something about the way they looked at each other that Somolia could see past, and since she recognized it, everyone else had to as well. "Where have the two of you been all day?" she asked, looking from Diamond to Chris.

"Having fun," Diamond answered her before Chris could form the words. And when she heard Silvia call out to him, Diamond whispered to him, "Mind what you discuss with her, nigga."

Datrina smiled like she'd just received a personal invite to the Hair Symposium in Paris, and Chris was the reason for her smile. He might have been with Diamond most of his days, but when he did show himself around his girl, she had his undivided attention and affection. "Thanks, Diamond."

"For what?" Diamond took a seat behind the receptionist's desk and looked back at her.

"For keeping Chris out of trouble. I know that as long as he's around you, he won't be doing something untoward."

Instead of answering and responding to that statement, Diamond only smiled. This was a game where sacrifices had to be made and promises had to be kept, and when it came to her and Chris, it was them against the world.

Silvia was standing in the entrance of her supply closet away from both the patrons that walked around her shop and the ears of those close to her office when Chris rounded the corner. He knew this was coming and if he could help it at all, he'd appease her and allay her suspicions of them. "How many lies do I have to hear in one day, Chris?"

Chris lowered his head and subtly looked behind him, making sure Diamond hadn't walked up. Not only was he loyal to Antonio, but he owed Silvia no lies as well. He just didn't like seeing her worrying her about things. Since this was the very first time Diamond wrecked a brand-new car, it alarmed Silvia.

"What are you talking about, Silvia?"

"I expect it from the women that walk in and out of these doors, but when my family lies to me, I take offense and I hate being offended, Chris. What's going on with you two?" Silvia walked him into the supply closet and leaned against the fully stocked shelf.

"She wasn't lying about that part, Silvia, she did wreck the car," he answered her.

"And?"

"And now I've got a possible murder case." He filled her in on the things that transpired during the deal Diamond had made in her attempt to expand her business frontiers and explained that she'd done so because of the Circle's reluctance at giving her more than they had ever given her.

As much as Chris wanted to believe they'd take the leash off of Diamond, he now knew he needed help and the only person able to do that besides Antonio was Silvia.

"We can move sixty a month easily, Silvia, and she knows it. She's already talking about finding a supplier of our own and she's serious as hell about it."

"Sixty?" Silvia asked, knowing most guys she was acquainted with didn't move sixty kilos of cocaine a year. "Who the hell are you both dealing with, Chris?"

"We're rolling, Silvia," was all he said, hoping it would suffice.

Silvia peeked out of the door and told him, "Let me make a couple of calls, Chris." She placed her hand on her head and massaged her temples. "Shit!"

"Don't worry. I've got her back, and you know that." Chris reached out and grabbed her arm, pulling her to him. "I'm not going to let anything happen to Diamond."

"That girl just can't see past this game shit. I told Antonio a long time ago that she was going to be trouble. I at first thought she was going to be gay, but truth is, I would rather she were gay than see her as some…" Silvia looked for the words that evaded her, and finding none, she said, "Boss bitch."

"She found the game on a high level, Silvia, and now she feels as if she has to be her brother's replacement."

"Antonio fucked that girl up. Why can't she find some young man and sit her ass down somewhere? Has she even had sex yet, Chris?"

As far as he knew, the only times she got with a guy was to exchange packages, and those packages had been filled with cash. "You might have to ask her that, Silvia. I'm not in her business like that."

"Hell, you're with her every day, very close to her, Chris. You know something."

Seeing tears form in the corners of Silvia's eyes, he wrapped his arms around her. "I got her. Just trust me on this."

Somolia had been watching the play even before it went down, and when she'd seen Silvia walk past her office and yelling for Chris to help her move a cabinet that wasn't there, her nose began twitching. She waited every bit of five minutes. When she saw Datrina and Diamond in their hushed exchange, she'd made her way to the back.

She peeked inside of Silvia's office, saw only her client, and figured Silvia and Chris most likely went to the back. After rounding the corner and walking towards the supply closet, she saw Chris hugging her friend. Instead of walking away, she told them, "Oh, I didn't know you two were back here. I just came to get a couple of things."

"Yeah, whatever, tramp. Ya ass just wants to be nosey." Silvia half-laughed at her friend's antics. Somolia always found her way into other people's business and this was something everyone had gotten used to. Silvia wiped the corners of her eyes and told Chris, "We need to find Somolia a man so she can have a dick to suck."

Chris laughed.

"If I wrapped these lips of mine around any man's dick, even Chris's dick, they would surrender and lose control within seconds." She looked Chris square in the face and said to him, "A trial will convince you."

Chris looked away from Somolia and spoke to Silvia, "Well, I have to go." He walked past the short, heavyset Somolia, who was rumored to have the best B.J. skills in Fort Worth. "Excuse me, Somolia." He was careful not to rub himself against any parts of her, knowing it would have gone the wrong way and gotten back to Datrina in the worst way.

"I'll catch up with you later then, Chris," Somolia called after him. Silvia smiled at her friend, shook her head and said, "You need a man badly and we know it."

Diamond eyed Chris as soon as he came from the back. Having entertained his girl with a couple of lies and several truths, she was ready to hear what Chris had to say about his meeting with Silvia. Besides, it was time for them to go and since she now needed a ride back to the house, he would be the one to give it.

"How many cabinets did you have to move, nigga?" she asked him, not waiting for the questions he was sure to ask.

"You know how Silvia is when she wants something, she—"

"Yeah, I do," Diamond told him, rolling her eyes. Then, she headed back into her cousin's office. "Be ready to go once I finish talking with her, 'cause we have things to do," she told him before disappearing into Silvia's office.

***

Raymond had been looking over several papers when the knock on his office door redirected his attention. He'd spoken with Antonio on several occasions, yet felt he'd failed to explain the importance of sending a reliable infiltrator into the camps of their competition. One particular competitor they found them-selves up against was Kengyon Johnson. Ever since Antonio's incarceration, they hadn't had a solid footing in the San Antonio region and were missing out on the millions it promised.

To crown it all, Raymond wholeheartedly felt Kengyon had something to do with the charges filed against this closest friend. Antonio assured him that all was good, and that the lawyers were taking care of things they couldn't. But Raymond still felt there was something he could do to eradicate the charges against Antonio. He knew personally what the heads of the competition liked. Seeing the Young Diamond shine, he knew their chance was now. The only thing about it was getting Antonio to approve of the move.

"Come in," Raymond told his visitor.

Dell walked in, crossed the office space and took a seat in the armchair adjacent Raymond. Dell was the third associate of the Circle and made sure distribution was as it should be, and that dues were collected and invested to where they'd receive the best return. Ever since Antonio was replaced by his younger sister, he knew he had to make sure everything was spot-on in their operations.

"Just got a text from Silvia and she's also asking for Diamond's raise." He crossed his leg over the other, exposing the silk fabric of his socks and the highly polished shine on his Italian loafers. "Antonio said no, so that's a non-issue." Raymond went back to looking over the papers on his desk. Dell went on, "We can use her to dip into the expansion and—"

Raymond cut him off. "No, it's too risky and she doesn't have the team to do so. That's why Antonio's holding her back."

"Let's put her on King then. She wants to play the game, so let her play."

Raymond thought about those words longer than he should have. Considering it was something he wanted himself, he looked for reassurance. "This is not going to sit well with Antonio. You know that, right?"

"Diamond has more than the potential and when she starts seeing that, even we won't be able to stop her. It's best we put her in play now, then to allow her to play it alone. This way, we get rid of Kengyon and his team, as well as enjoy the millions of dollars they're playing with."

Raymond watched the way Dell closed his eyes when he spoke of the money they could be making. Instead of listening to the tone behind his words, Raymond couldn't help but hear his own. This move would definitely have potential, deadly potential at that, he thought.

"This shit is about to get ugly, Dell," Raymond told him, sure of it.

Dell stood, straightened his cuffs and reminded his associate, "Dead people ain't never been pretty, Raymond."

Chapter Three

Kengyon and Camille pulled up in the plush Lexus truck ahead of the shipment that was soon to arrive. They'd taken the trip to Austin personally and with a half-million dollars cash to be made for the twenty-five kilos they promised, it just seemed the thing to do. He also wanted to set Camille up for future endeavors in case he was unable to take the trip himself. These were guys he dealt with on a regular basis. But, in the game King played, it was never cool to get comfortable with the people he dealt with. "You got it?" he asked Camille, before they drove past the security gates of the estate in the Westlake Hills Community.

The guy they were meeting had been scoring work from King for over two years and Camille saw firsthand, how the man prospered. It even crossed her mind to make the move to Austin for gains of her own, but as Kengyon pointed out to her, he needed her in Dallas. He needed her close to him.

"Don't I always?" she asked him before checking herself in the visor's mirror. Camille wore a mint green mini dress that showed off her small curves and a pair of silver peep-toe booties. She complimented her outfit with every bit of one hundred and fifty thousand dollars' worth of jewelry, which consisted of a canary yellow diamond choker, six platinum bangles and several multi-carat diamonds that adorned the piercings in each of her ears. She wanted the guys she supplied to know exactly what they were dealing with as well as how beautiful she was.

"The way you're looking, they might be willing to pay for more than some work," he told her with an approving nod

"We're here for business, King." Camille applied a silver matte lipstick, made sure not a strand of hair was misplaced, and looked over at him. "My pleasure comes with counting millions, not orgasms."

Kengyon admired the bi-leveled home as he did his own. Rounding the rear of the cobblestoned driveway and parking several feet from the yard fountain, he knew money was being made as well as spent.

Knowing it was his part to play, he parked and jumped out of the driver's side of the truck and ran around to open the rear door for Camille. "Boss Lady," he addressed her as she exited the truck.

He followed Camille through a walkway and into a foyer that led into the home. Once they were escorted into yet another living area, they were offered drinks, which Camille politely declined.

"Ms. Camille, it is so nice to see you again."

After being seated at the edge of the loveseat, Camille crossed her legs at the ankles, crossed her hands over her knees and told him, "As it is to see you also, Blake."

Blake, she knew, had a penchant for underage women. He didn't seem to have a thing for a more mature woman, at least having judged his disinterest at making a move on her whenever they were together, her seductiveness notwithstanding. Camille had more money than most, so treating her to luxury less than anything she could provide for herself wasn't rewarding, and with her being his supplier, the intimidation was there.

"Now that all parties are present, shall we?" Blake then signaled for his guy to retrieve the cash he had for her, along with the counters.

Camille watched Kengyon check the time on his watch continuously. To ease his mind, she placed a hand over his wrist while he stood. She knew the importance of being punctual and also knew it wasn't good business to have the money counted and without a product for the exchange. As if on cue, Blake was paged.

"Hey, boss, I have a big-ass black guy at the main gate in a big-ass Dually looking at me as if I fucked his wife."

"Let him through." Blake laughed and told Camille, "Sorry about that. He's new."

"Well, then, let's get this over with. I have other places to be." Camille commanded the attention of everyone there and when she moved, so did the eyes of every man.

Before the counters stopped, Buddy walked into the room carrying a huge duffle bag over his shoulder as if it was a preschooler's back pack, and instead of watching them load the cash into the other bags, he kept his eyes trained on Camille. Any sudden sight of discomfort from her, he'd spring into action and more than anything, he was ready.

Camille could only look in Buddy's direction because to look into his eyes would be the signal used when things were about to go south, and now that everything was as it should have been, there was no need.

Once the packages were checked and the money was bagged, Buddy slung the two duffle bags of cash over his shoulder and headed for his truck. Like always, he'd take his trips alone and follow whatever automobile Camille was in.

"How about we do dinner sometime, Camille?" Blake asked, upon seeing Kengyon open the back-passenger door for her.

"How about you spend some more money first? The niggas I eat with spend one point five million dollars and better," she told him, before allowing Kengyon to close her door. She lowered the heavily tinted window and continued. "Mountains are meant to be climbed, Blake, not looked at."

Kengyon took the on-ramp and pointed the Lexus truck south. He loved the way Camille handled her business and if he could help it, she'd conduct plenty of more of it. One of Kengyon's strongest suits was that he didn't trip on the power Camille had. There were plenty of guys around that wanted everyone to know they were the man, but with him, he cared not that Camille's was the face they dealt with and spent their money on. He paid her handsomely just for the perception alone, and now that she had her own businesses to handle, more money was coming into his hands. "You speak with Terry yet?"

"Haven't really felt pressed to do so," she told him before texting Buddy.

"I need for him to put things on pause once we make the trip, Camille." Kengyon knew she'd get uncomfortable when he spoke of the trip to Miami, and was more than sure why. She'd been talking around his idea for the past couple of days and he was starting to see anxiety in her.

"I'm more than sure he's capable of doing nothing, King. It's not like he's making any trips in our stead."

"He's the one we need to stay outside of the box, Camille. We can't all fall when the pins get hit."

"Consider yourself a pin if you will. As for me, I'll be that bitch standing when you do."

Buddy wasn't certain at first, but when he saw the tinted Caprice the second time, he decided to see if his instincts were right. He crossed over into the far lane as if he was about to exit, and when he saw the driver of the Caprice do the same, he took the nearest exit. The last thing he wanted to do was show the Boss Lady that he was incapable of handling whatever came his way. And, if stepping on his tail in the process was what he had to do, then so be it. Buddy knew how the game went, and if they felt they'd have an easy win with him, then they were about to have a rude awakening. Leading them to any stash spot, safe house or even lounging place was something he hadn't done and wasn't about to do.

Buddy pulled into the Flying 3 truck stop and parked around the rear of the building. He noticed two guys behind the tint. As subtly as he could, he climbed out as if none the wiser. Buddy walked inside, just to make sure there were no patrolmen in the area. Knowing a camera was somewhere in the store, he went to make a purchase of a family-sized bag of Doritos, a six-pack of Sprite and he grabbed a pack of spearmint gum.

"Paper or plastic, sir?"

"Double up on the paper," he told the clerk in a tone that had the lad fumbling with a task as simple as that.

Before exiting the building, Buddy discarded all the items from the paper sacks into the restroom's trash and replaced them with the MAC-11 he concealed under his left arm. Once outside the store, he spied the same car sitting two cars over, and it was then he realized they were playing for more than the money he had in the truck at the time. Either they wanted more or they wanted Camille, and while giving too much thought to the whole scenario, he was determined no such thing was going to happen.

Buddy acted as if he was about to walk past the Caprice, but as soon as he cleared the car beside it and was out of the view of the camera at the corner of the store, he pulled the MAC-11 from the bag and pointed it at the head of the driver.

"How far did you think we were going?"

Buddy let off a series of silenced rounds into both their faces, before either of them could grasp the realization that prey had become predator. He then grabbed the phone sitting between them and when he noticed Blake was the last person contacted, he smiled and pressed the dial.

"Where they at?" Blake asked.

Buddy recognized the voice off straight away and told him, "Dead." He ended the call immediately.

With a half-million in cash in the back of his truck and a place to be shortly, he pointed the nose of his Dually southbound.

***

Kevin Pierson thought of something special he could do and give Silvia. Their three-year anniversary was right around the corner and he wasn't about to wait until the last minute to put things together. He'd been an independent contractor for the longest and his thing was making sure everything in her world was straight. At first, he wanted to take her on a cruise, but decided against it when he remembered the fear she had of the ship being so far from shore for so long. He then thought about the fact that she could afford just about anything she wanted, considering her cousin was one of the richest people he knew personally.

KP, as they liked to call him, was depositing a company check of thirty-three thousand dollars for the work his crew did for the construction company that built and reconstructed plazas and small offices. Most of the crew he employed was paid cash, by way of not wanting to provide the health care or social security benefits they'd be entitled to if they were on a payroll. And, with this level of tax evasion nowhere near the crimes of those he was employed by, it would be something he thrived from.

He wasn't the fittest guy around, but neither was he the one person would consider to be in need of a workout. KP was short, dark-skinned, with gray eyes and wore nothing but cornrows in his hair. His wife, Silvia, made sure his hair stayed tight. He was funny. People always complimented him on his humor and often told him he should have done stand-up comedy, but he begged to differ. As long as he was able to make his wife laugh, he was cool, and this was the reason he was pulling out of that bank's drive-through and heading to the mall.

"Where we headed now?" Q asked, having been paid his fee for the work they'd done.

"I need to stop by the mall so I can grab Silvia something right quick." Q only shook his head. Now that they'd just gotten paid, his friend was already talking about spending his money on his wife.

"Nigga, you got plenty of time for that shit. Let's go by the liquor store and get something strong and dark." Q pushed himself back into the seat and looked on with disgust.

"We need to be stopping by the dentist so we can get you something white, with them dark-ass teeth you got." KP looked over at his friend and smiled. "When was the last time you kissed a bitch?"

"Fuck you, nigga."

KP stopped at the intersection, looked across the street and pointed. "Isn't that Diamond's car?"

Q leaned forward so he could see well. The once brand-new Camaro was fender-less and the passenger side door was scratched beyond repair. They watched as the wrecker driver pulled it onto the flatbed truck. "Looks like it, but she just bought hers the other day."

"It can't be hers, huh?"

"I doubt it. The bitch is rich, but I doubt if she would just leave something like that on the side of the street." Q looked behind them and towards the end of the street. There were no cops in sight and by the way the wrecker driver was trying to hurry and clear the car, Q could tell he was doing something illegal. And, when the driver of the wrecker truck covered it with the car cloth, his suspicions were confirmed. "That shit don't look right to me, man."

"Well, whatever the case, I'm more than sure it will be taken care of."

As soon as the light changed, they drove past the truck and instead of asking questions they were sure the driver wouldn't be able to answer, they headed for the mall.

***

Diamond had awaited the call from the dealership ever since she'd wrecked and had the newly bought Camaro towed and scrapped. She even made sure that no parts of it would ever touch the streets again, and after paying the guy twenty thousand dollars more than he'd asked, she was sure of his promise.

She and Chris arrived by taxi and as soon as they pulled into the lot, several of the salesmen recognized her. "Good evening, Ms. McClendon, back so soon?"

Instead of walking across the lot in search for the next best thing, she and Chris walked straight to the showroom.

"Ms. McClendon, what brings you back so soon?" the guy asked again. He was the same youngster who accepted the seventy-five thousand dollars cash payment for the Camaro days before, and hoping things were still good between them, he told them, "Camaro troubling you already?"

"Not at all, not at all," she told him, before walking over to where several high-end Corvettes sat.

Would you be interested in a trade?" the salesman asked while following her through the lobby.

Diamond walked towards the cyber-black Coupe and told him, "I want this one."

Knowing she'd just spent a heavy sum days before, he threw subtle hints that the car she had just shown interest in, had a price tag far above the one she saw when she purchased the Camaro. "Um, this is the Callaway Coupe. Only a few hundred in production and this particular one is the supercharged special edition. We..." He began pointing in the direction of the lower-priced Corvettes, but held himself back when he saw her walk towards yet another showcased beauty.

"Is this the same kind of Corvette?" Diamond looked over the side of the convertible and smiled.

"Yes, they have the same engines, but the only difference is that this is the convertible and that's a coupe. Both cost around—"

"I'll take both," she told him before looking back at Chris, who was now shaking his head as if he disapproved.

"Diamond, really?" Chris asked her.

"Yeah. The coupe is for me, and the convertible is for you."

The salesman figured this was his chance to inform her about the price of each and when doing so, he told her, "I might need to tell you the price of each, Ms. McClendon."

"I'll give you two hundred thousand dollars for both of them, and I'll throw in an extra twenty-five thousand dollars for your commission, if you can have everything ready in under an hour." She then looked at the time on her diamond-glazed watch.

"Same as the other day, Ms. McClendon?" he asked, sure of his next assignment.

"Yeah, put it in Silvia Pierson's name."

***

Diamond and Chris pulled up at the salon. Before either of them could park, Silvia and half of the staff came out to greet them. Seeing Silvia's expression of dismay and other faces in awe, it was apparent the greetings differed.

"Chanel McClendon, what the hell are you doing?" Silvia said with a frown and pointed accusingly at Chris with a brush she was holding.

Diamond replied, "It's nothing. Don't make such a fuss about it, Silvia. I'm on my way to the house to get the money now."

"It has nothing to do with the money, Diamond. Do you even think about the things you do before you do them?"

Not the one to answer questions or be embarrassed in front of people, Diamond walked past Silvia and told her, "I don't have to ask a bunch of niggas if and when I can spend my money. I'm my own boss."

Silvia only watched her as she walked past. Once Diamond was out of view, Silvia went off on Chris. "When she trips out, you trip out and buy a brand-new car also?"

Chris shook his head. "She bought both of them, Silvia. I tried to stop her, but you know how she is."

"I'm beginning to question your loyalty now, Chris." Silvia turned on her heels and went to catch up with her cousin.

"You mean she bought you another car, Chris?" Somolia asked, knowing it would be something Datrina failed to ask.

"Yep."

Somolia looked at Datrina, expecting her to say anything by way of reacting, but Datrina kept a straight face, her expression unreadable. "I have a bevy of friends, but not one of them has ever bought me a car, let alone a convertible."

"Yeah, well, you don't have friends like Diamond." Chris grabbed his girlfriend's hand and led her inside.

Silvia closed her office door behind Diamond and said, "I got a call from my bank, Diamond, and transactions such as the one you just made raises all kinds of red flags. And in the game we play, we can't afford the challenges."

"Maybe you need to start playing a different game. You ever thought about that?"

"Save the attitude, Chanel. Before you bring my shit down, I promise you, you will fall. You're acting as if you know how to play this shit, but you're turning people against you. You're supposed to move in silence, Diamond. You never let—"

Diamond cut her off, "That's the way y'all played it. When I move, a motherfucker is going to know I'm coming and they ain't going to be able to do shit about it."

"You got it all figured out, huh?"

"Most of it."

Silvia closed her eyes, shook her head and pointed. "Get out of my office, Chanel. I think it's time I visited your brother."

Before clearing the doorway to her cousin's office, Diamond turned and told her, "A new boss is in town, cuz, and she's starting from the bottom."

As soon as Diamond closed the door to Silvia's office, she felt a buzz inside her pocket, and pulled out her phone. Upon seeing Dell's contact, she frowned. She knew Chris paid their dues. For Dell to be calling her there must have been something wrong. "What's up, Dell?" She walked back into the lobby where Chris and Datrina awaited. She signaled for Chris to come over.

Dell couldn't help but smile when he heard the voice of the woman he was about to use.

"Diamond?"

What the fuck you want, Dell?"

"You still insist on raising your package?" He knew these were the words she wanted to hear.

"Yeah, what's up?"

"Meet me tomorrow at the house around noon."

"I can meet you right now."

"Tomorrow, Diamond." Dell hung up the phone and looked over at the clock on the wall adjacent to his desk. It was only a matter of time before he was counting the millions of dollars his ideas promised.

"You hear that, nigga?" she asked Chris with more excitement than she should have. "These niggas see we're serious about our shit and now they want to push play." Diamond faced Datrina and smiled. "They're gonna really be talking about us now."

Chris opened his arms and gave her a big squeeze. He'd promised they'd see the game from their end and now that Dell was calling, they were about to make it happen.

"Me and you, my nigga!" Diamond said.

Somolia watched the small celebration taking place, and as happy as Datrina was about the deal, she felt a bit uneasy with the way Chris embraced Diamond. It wasn't as if this was the first time she'd seen them embrace, but she felt the onset of jealousy this time. All the same, she smiled in order to veil her true feelings.

Silvia had been listening the entire time and heard Dell's voice on the other end of Diamond's phone. She hoped there would be something he'd tell her to enable her to gain a different perspective on the game they were playing, as well as the modus operandi. The way she saw things, Diamond would either end up all the way on top, or all the way under, and the latter was looking more promising.

Nicole Goosby

Chapter Four

The following morning, Diamond was at Chris and Datrina's home before either of them expected. When they heard the knock on their door, along with the instructions to open up, Datrina looked over at Chris.

"We got something to take care of early, babe," he told her, before unlatching the locks on the door.

As soon as the door was opened, Diamond entered and told him, "When are you going to buy a house, nigga? I'm tired of seeing you cooped up in this small-ass loft."

"We're good, Diamond. We have more than enough space and I like it here." Chris closed the door behind her and began walking to his bedroom. He could tell Datrina was uneasy because he had nothing on but a pair of silk boxers, a sight that ought to be for her eyes only, yet Diamond was taking it in there and then. Datrina had covered herself with a robe now, but still couldn't help the way she viewed the situation. Hearing Diamond comment on Chris's physique, she looked at her.

"What?" Diamond's brows rose slightly. "The nigga is fine." She knew what she was doing and as long as Datrina was insecure about the relationship she had with her man, Diamond would play on it.

"Don't pay that girl any mind, babe!" Chris yelled from the back room.

"I'm not!" Datrina smiled.

"You know I'm fucking with you, girl. You don't ever have to worry about me doing it with Chris."

Datrina offered Diamond a drink and when the two of them were seated in the breakfast nook, she asked her, "Diamond, why aren't you modeling or something? You are beautiful."

Diamond noticed Datrina was a little closer than she should have been and was staring her directly in her eyes. She leaned back slightly "Girl, what you tripping on?"

"I'm serious, Diamond. You could actually make it out there." Datrina reached for Diamond's chin.

"You're tripping, girl." Considering Datrina was both a hair stylist and make-up artist, Diamond didn't take offense and instead of pulling back from her grasp, Diamond allowed her to turn her face.

"Your skin is flawless too and your teeth. You're perfect, Diamond." Chris returned from the room. He was in dressed in a denim unit that had cost him a thousand dollars. He slowed his step when he saw Diamond and Datrina looking as if there was a kiss about to happen. He smiled. "I knew y'all were some freaks," he said.

Datrina released Diamond's face and told him, "Boy, there wasn't no one doing nothing."

"I see now I'm going to have to watch the two of you from now on," said Chris. He knew better than anyone nothing was going on between Datrina and Diamond, but still had the cap to shoot at both of them.

"Nigga, please." Diamond stood, looked down at Datrina and told her, "A nigga would love to see some shit like that."

"I just might have, had I stayed back there a few more minutes," he told Diamond.

"How about you just might need a foot in the crack of your ass, Chris?"

"Don't be getting mad at me. I'm just going off of what I saw." Chris leaned over and kissed Datrina's dark lips. "Umm, your lips taste like chocolate."

"Come on, nigga, we got shit to do and I don't need ya dick sticking out in the car with me." Diamond walked towards the door. "Let's go see what those niggas talking about."

***

Dell lowered his phone and thought about the words Antonio spoke just seconds before. He got weekly calls from Antonio. With Diamond's latest stunt and negligent transactions, this call came unexpected. He started to tell Antonio of his plans to put Diamond in the middle of the King ring in a possible take-over, but when he heard Antonio emphasize the constant need to rein the young woman in, Dell only agreed. He couldn't understand they could be making millions of more dollars, as well as expanding into areas that promised them even more in the near future, and all they had to do was put their newest member of the Circle in play. Yet, her brother was against that.

Dell was sitting in his pitted den with the glass doors of the patio ajar, when he heard the deep growl of the Corvette Diamond bought just the day before, pull around the rear of the house. He stood, walked out onto the second-story terrace and watched as she parked. He silently admired the way she rolled, and nodded his approval. He understood Diamond's stance and against his better judgment, he was going to use that to his advantage.

"Come on up, you two." He watched her climb from behind the wheel of the coupe and told her, "You'd look better in the Lambo, Diamond."

"I'll look even better when I can afford to buy it," she shot back. Chris followed her through a black marbled foyer, up a staircase and into the pitted den area.

He looked towards the huge grand piano, and immediately noticed the huge duffle bags sitting atop it and smiled. He'd been to Raymond's home many times, but this was the first at Dell's new home.

"Damn, Dell, what kind of numbers it took to get this one?" Chris spun around the room, walked over to the open patio doors and looked down at the turquoise waters of the pool below.

"They wanted four point six million dollars, but I got it for four million." Dell prided himself on the easy purchase.

Chris knew these guys were making money, but when looking out over the selection of cars and trucks Dell had parked around his home, it painted a totally different picture for him.

"Where is everyone?" Chris asked in his attempt to confirm a certain suspicion.

"What do you mean?" Dell asked him, before pouring the two of them glasses of darkened liquor.

"All the cars out there."

"Oh." Dell chuckled. "I just got a few lying around to make it look as if I've got company, that's all."

"What's up, Dell? I know we ain't over here to brag about the shit we buying." Diamond wanted to get straight to the point, just in case she had to bend a few corners and make a few moves.

"So anxious, huh?" Dell walked the drinks to where they stood and handed one to Chris, knowing well that Diamond did not drink.

"I'm just ready to take care of my shit," said Diamond. "No harm in that, is there?"

Dell looked deep into the eyes of the woman standing before him and could see her brother inside of her, and something else he couldn't identify. This is one dangerous woman, he thought. He was feeling the vibes she exuded, the woman many only knew as "Boss Lady". And, he found her beauty captivating.

"We're giving you thirty-five more, Diamond. You think you can handle that?"

"You sounding as if you handing over a hundred," Diamond replied, looking toward Chris, then back to Dell, who was now looking at his watch as if he had something else to attend to.

"Now, here's something I want you to know, Diamond." He smiled at her and nodded at Chris. "But, this stays here."

"What's up?" Diamond could tell this was something he hadn't even let her brother know, and she liked it that way.

"We got word that Kengyon Johnson may have had something to do with the case built against your brother and I need you to look into it, and into the ring he has going on. This move could be the one you need, as well as expand your dealings into Kansas, Oklahoma, and San Antonio."

Diamond only smiled. This was something she wanted for herself and here he was, handing it to her on a silver platter. Hearing the guy who set her brother up could be possibly touched, she was ready to be the arrowhead in the attack aimed at bringing Kengyon down from grace to grass.

"There's millions to be made here, Diamond. Millions."

"And, I'm supposed to do this with sixty kilos of work?"

"Hell, no!" Dell walked over, stood inches in front of her and said, "You help us remove Kengyon, then you not only get the win we get from him, but I'll personally see to it you get two hundred with it."

***

After throwing the duffle bag into the trunk of the Corvette, Chris climbed into the car and looked over at Diamond. "I don't know about this shit, sis."

"This is what I've been dreaming of, Chris. This is our time, nigga." She looked at him with determined eyes and unwavering nerve. "We make or break right here, Chris."

"You really want to do this, Diamond? 'Cause when we start pushing niggas, they are going to push back."

"That means we can't let up, bro. Regardless of what happens, we can't let up."

Chris closed his eyes and exhaled fully. There was one component they needed, because in the game they played, it always took a team. "We need a team, Diamond. We need some mother-fuckers we can trust no matter what, and more than anything, we need some motherfuckers that are willing to die."

"Correction, Chris, we need motherfuckers willing to kill and that's got to be something done without thought."

***

Dell thought about the move he was making, and while thinking about Antonio McClendon, he told himself, "That nigga got a life sentence. He should be glad we're keeping this shit on top." With a couple of calls to make and a plan to devise, he grabbed his linen sports coat and after selecting the keys to his cobalt blue Bentley Continental, he headed down the stairs.

***

Kengyon walked around the Lexus truck for the third time. He wanted to make sure there was nothing out of place, nothing missing or kaput, because of the trip Camille was about to make alone. She'd been summoned to Houston for a deal that promised the sale of fifty kilos, and it was one she wasn't about to pass up. He normally went on these expeditions, but because he had some business to attend to himself, this would be one of the few times they went separate ways.

"You're sure you can't wait until I take care of this other issue first?" said Kengyon.

Camille only looked at him as if he wasn't standing there. This was something she looked forward to doing, and for him to question her certainty, as he always did, she found it best to just ignore him.

"Are you even listening to me?" he asked when seeing her busy herself with the papers she taken out of the glove compartment.

"Don't you have things to do, King?" she said. Camille pulled at the driver's door, hoping King would move, but when she saw him continue to keep her from it, she said, "Yes, King, I am listening to you." She lowered her shades and looked into his eyes.

"As soon as you take care of this, come home. These moves are going to set us up for a minute, and by the time we get back from Miami—"

Camille cut him off. "Enough said, King." She knew he was continually mentioning Miami as his way of accusing her of some misdeed. She'd been through this before with him, and as clean as she made the breaks between King and the women he found interest in, she now realized that he was onto her. "Move, Kengyon." After closing her door, she lowered the tinted window and told him, "I've always had your best interest at heart, and for you to continually question my loyalty, that makes me wonder where your trust is."

King laughed. These were the words Camille used when trying to undermine him, and now that they were being used, he knew he was that much closer to the truth he was seeking. "Really, Camille? Well then, I guess our little trip to Miami will tell us both some things we don't know, huh?"

Instead of answering the question they both knew the answer to, Camille placed the truck in gear and smiled. "The things we do for the people we love, huh?"

King's smile faded as soon as she pulled off, and when he saw the huge Dually Buddy drove seconds behind her, he found himself saying a silent prayer. For a reason he couldn't under-stand, he always thought of Buddy wronging her in some fashion. It was a thought he couldn't shake.

With a couple other thoughts he couldn't seem to dismiss, he dialed the familiar number and when the dial sent straight his call to voicemail, he couldn't help but think he'd never see her again.

Camille checked her rearview mirror every so often, and when seeing Buddy's truck several cars back, she relaxed a little more. If need be, she'd send Buddy to Miami in front of them to ensure she and King didn't run across the tramp of a woman he knew as Nava.

Hoping to have things over and done with within the hours, Camille adjusted the A/C and set the truck's setting on cruise control. Knowing she'd be one million, one hundred and fifty thousand dollars richer if things went accordingly, she sat back and rode.

***

As soon as Diamond left the salon, Silvia cancelled the remaining appointments she had earlier scheduled. The two duffle bags, containing the two hundred thousand dollars cash Diamond dropped on her seat behind her desk were still there, and had become the topic of a discussion she didn't care for. She couldn't shake off the feeling that Diamond was going haywire.

"How much is it?" KP asked when he saw the reasons his wife's mood had dampened.

"That's two hundred thousand dollars. The thing I am tripping on is that she just got the work this morning. She's making a hell of a lot more than I had first thought."

Silvia kicked the duffle bag closed and placed it in her office closet. It would take her a couple of days to filter it, but she'd make it happen. Feeling the weight of the bags reminded her of the days

Antonio used to do the same things. The same ways he began the game was the exact same way Diamond was starting.

"Maybe it's time to call your contact, baby." KP could see the worry on his wife's face.

Even though he knew how sensitive the subject was for her, he still felt it was something that would bring resolve to her dilemma.

"I haven't talked to Orlando in years, ever since Antonio needed me to." Silvia thought back to the day when she and Orlando spent nights together in various suites, while KP and the rest of the crew were enjoying the festivities thousands of miles away. Orlando was the one many thought she'd marry, but when hard times came, he was the first to make a run for higher ground. He had even tried to get Silvia to move to Miami with him. At that time, she and KP had not only gotten closer, but became engaged.

Silvia had been contemplating speaking with Antonio about the way his sister was spiraling out of control, but decided against it for the sake of not wanting to get too far into their disagreements. She also promised Chris that she would make a couple of calls, and with money and drugs being the only things that seemed to hold Diamond's attention, she felt bound to make the overdue call. "Let me make this call right quick," she told her husband, before looking through her contacts.

"Oh, you need me to step out or something?" KP asked, seeing her look at him before dialing.

"Do you mind?" Silvia took a seat behind her desk and watched him.

"Um, I guess not."

"You're the one that suggested it, Kevin." Silvia placed both her elbows on her desk.

Once KP walked out, she inhaled deeply. "Here goes nothing," she said, while waiting to see if the number was still in service. By the fifth ring, she was certain it had been changed or owned by another person. Just before she ended the call, she heard a voice.

"Hello, Silvia?"

"Uh-huh. Orlando?"

"Yeah, how's it going beautiful?"

Silvia was taken aback by his voice alone. It had been a while. "Can you talk?"

"What's on your mind, Silvia? You know I always have time for you."

"Hey, well, I need you to talk numbers right now."

"Where's Antonio?"

"Three Rivers."

"Kidding me?"

"No kidding." She could hear the surprise in his tone and decided to make a play on it. "You're on or what?"

"I'm in the middle of something at the moment, but I'm more than sure if I don't have it, I can get it."

"Let's make this long-term for me. I need my own deal." Silvia knew the game and she also knew that in order to sit at the table with certain guys and women, the price tag would matter.

"Whoa! You know it's going to take nothing less than seven figures for that, don't you?"

"Make it happen."

"Seriously, Antonio must have set you up real nice."

"I'm ready to spend if that's what you're asking." Silvia looked towards her office door. Seeing Somolia standing there, she held up a finger.

"Let me open a window for you. I'll be in touch."

"Hey," she called out before he could hang up.

"Yeah?"

"I'll need one hundred and fifty and I'll be picking it up." She knew that not only did the price fall with the more you purchased, but she knew that if you incurred your own pick-up, it would fall even more. Silvia didn't necessarily know what kind of numbers Diamond was sitting on, but she did know that if she really wanted the plug herself, then she'd have to come up with it.

"I'll make sure they play nice, since it's you, Silvia."

The game wasn't for those that didn't know the rules and for him to tell her that he'd make sure they played nice, it meant both the business they conducted and the product they bought would be as it should.

Somolia was sure she knew the nature of the call, because KP had walked into the lobby and busied himself with an outdated Essence mag and when she asked him why he was there, his only reply was, "Silvia's on the phone with one of her boyfriends."

"What's up, Somolia?" said Silvia.

"You got this clown in here looking like he just walked in on you giving a nigga some head or something." Somolia took a seat in front of Silvia's desk and watched her.

"You know how dramatic that man is, Somolia. I had to make a call and I needed it to be a private one."

"Yeah, well, you might need to suck his dick or something, because it's obvious he's feeling strange about it."

"I'll handle it, Somolia, unless you want to." Silvia knew that would be the way to conclude the little meeting Somolia thought they were having, and when she saw her stand, Silvia felt a slight relief.

"Seems you don't plan on being married that long, 'cause I know once he—"

Silvia cut her off with a laugh. "Bye, Somolia, with your messy ass."

Once Somolia had talked her way out, Silvia dwelled in her thoughts. I hope I don't regret the decision I just made. With more than enough money to cover the shipment herself, Silvia hoped she didn't have to pay more than half. While thinking Diamond might need to bend a few corners, she dialed her number.

Diamond had been wired ever since her conversation with Dell. The sixty kilos she was given was accounted for. Just to show what she and Chris were capable of, she made the deals she promised that much sweeter. The more they bought, the cheaper it was. To make it all the better, she promised to deliver, and this alone was the reason she and Chris were headed to Dallas now.

"You're sure you want to move it all in one day, Diamond?" Chris was making sure the rear seats in his Dodge Durango looked as they would have, had they not been filled with over fifty kilos of cocaine.

"I wished I was moving this shit in one deal," she told him before walking past him.

"One day, Diamond." Chris closed the rear door of the truck and walked around it. He was satisfied. Since they'd already promised the work, all they had to do now was collect their money and pray no one pulled a stunt like the one attempted just days before.

Diamond walked back into the storage-like garage and headed for the Calloway Coupe. She looked over at Chris and said, "Let's get it, nigga."

Just as she was about to climb into the cyber-black coupe, her phone rang. Seeing it was Silvia, she sighed before answering. "Hey, cousin, what's up?"

"I got something for you."

"Like what?" Diamond leaned against the door of the coupe and waved Chris over.

"A price tag you'll like and your own plug out of Miami."

"Whatcha say?"

"Yeah, you heard me. You want to play the game, so let's see what you made of. These people ain't even sitting down if you ain't spending a million or more. You think you're ready for that?"

"How long I got?" Diamond asked her, before pushing herself from the coupe and walking away off from Chris.

"One week," Silvia told her, thinking it would be more than the initiative needed for her to move.

"I'll have that for you tomorrow," Diamond assured her as if it was nothing.

"Make it happen, then."

Diamond slid her phone in her pocket and smiled at Chris, who was now looking at her with questioning eyes.

"Silvia got us a plug, nigga. She's talking about bringing her a million."

"Damn! Who's she fucking with?"

Diamond shrugged. "The hell if I know. As long as they're good business, we're good business."

"That's a helluva lot of money, Diamond. If anything goes wrong, it's going to be hard for us."

"Then let's make sure nothing does." Diamond climbed into the Calloway 'Vette, fingered her remote and raised the garage door.

Once her shades were pulled down over her eyes and Kendrick Lamar's "DNA" was booming through the stereo, she pulled out. If everything did go right, they'd be returning with well over the million Silvia called her on.

Chapter Five

Kengyon concluded his call with the travel agent, threw his phone onto the marbled counter and lapsed into thinking. Lately, his only thoughts were of Nava and her sudden disappearance. There was so much promise between the two of them, and even though they came from different backgrounds and lived totally different lives, they had so much in common. One of Camille's open dislikes was that King had met the girl while she was stripping and that she only saw him as the trick he was, instead of him being a guy that wanted her out of a bad situation. The thing King loved about Nava was that she was real and had been through her share of hard times.

He checked his messages once more. When he saw the thumbs-up sign from Camille, he fell onto the sectional and closed his eyes. Money was being made and his lifestyle was classy, but the only thing King was missing was true love. More than anything, he was praying his trip to Miami would have its reward.

**

Dell was sitting in his Bentley, looking over a few investments when Silvia climbed in. He called her earlier and since he really needed to speak with her privately, he'd made his way to her shop.

"What's going on, Dell?"

"Oh, I'm just checking on you to make sure you were straight," he told her.

"You could have said this on the phone." Silvia looked to-wards the shop to see who might have been trained on them. She already knew KP was looking at them and since it was a known fact that she and Dell once messed around, it would be something she was questioned about when she did return.

"I've got a little bonus for you," he told her while handing her a brown envelope.

"What's this?" Silvia, at one time, liked the way Dell surprised her with gifts. But, when he started surprising her in front of her husband, in his attempt to show the things he could afford and the things KP couldn't, it became a problem Antonio had to weigh in on. "It's just a little something from an investment we made." Dell smiled when seeing her frown.

"And what investment would that be?" she asked upon seeing the one-hundred-and-fifty-thousand-dollar check.

"I also wanted to tell you that I spoke with Diamond about her raise."

"Yeah, I appreciate that."

"Um, has she told you anything other than the fact that it was raised by thirty-five?"

"Not that I can recall." Silvia thought about their last conversation and shrugged. "What happened now?"

"We're looking at a possible expansion and we're thinking of putting her in a very promising position."

"Have you spoken with Antonio about it?" Silvia asked, knowing the play Dell was running.

"I, um, was hoping I didn't have to."

By the time Silvia climbed out of Dell's Bentley, she was sure of two things. First, Dell was fishing for help on her end. Second, the investment Dell spoke of was one she really knew nothing about. She told Diamond a visit to see her brother was in order, but that was about to be done sooner than later.

***

Camille completed her text to King as soon as she pulled into the River Oaks mansion. It took her and Buddy less than two hours to make the trip and as comfortable as the ride was, she still needed to stretch her legs. She climbed out, smoothed the wrinkles on the slacks of her silk jumper and pulled off her shades. Before she was able to make a step, she was greeted by two older white guys that looked to be in their late forties, early fifties even. From the selection of automobiles around the compound, she knew people had been awaiting her arrival. The amount alone told her this would be a combined purchase and with a possible future to it, she made sure all bases were covered.

"The lovely Camille arrives," the slim white guy said, before shaking her hand.

"It's always a pleasure," she told him, before being escorted to a pool area and then into the palatial estate.

"How's business these days?" he asked, making small talk.

Camille looked from one of the guys to the other and fought to recall where she knew a couple of them from. "Better than expected. And yours?"

"I've been partying more than ever but hey, that's why we do it, right?"

He offered Camille a drink and told her, "I've made several arrangements for both of us and I'm more than sure you'll agree to the terms we came up with."

"And these terms consist of?" Camille sat on the antique sofa and crossed her legs at the ankles. With as much money as they were spending, she'd stay as long as it took.

"I have a couple of guests visiting next month and I would like for you to host the gathering and," he took a sip of his drink and continued "bring at least fifty more and being that we were so generous with this purchase, I was hoping we could get each for twenty thousand dollars instead of twenty-three thousand dollars." He looked around at the men present and smiled.

Camille's smile failed to touch her eyes, because she knew he was really telling her what he'd be willing to pay for his next shipment. By the looks of all those in attendance, she could also tell they were users and not distributors. Quiet as it's kept, she had no problem with the one hundred and fifty thousand dollars' loss, but what she did have a problem with was the way they were shaking her down. Camille knew drugs and she also knew drug addicts and with this being her business venture she told him, "I'll tell you what. Since we're making arrangements, I'll give you that, but there will be no delivery. My guys prosper from their deliveries and if you'd like to try a hand in a game, then I'm all for it."

As if on cue, Buddy walked into the room and nodded. The exchange had been made.

"Well, um, how much would that be, if we paid your guys to deliver?"

Camille stood. "I'll be in touch."

Seeing the discomfort in the room, she felt it was best to leave that conversation in the air. She was more than sure she'd have the last say, and now that they felt she was to be toyed with, that price would be included.

***

Diamond stood and watched the counters as they hurried. This was their third stop and was worth a whopping two hundred and forty thousand dollars. The twelve kilos delivered was sure to be distributed to the surrounding area, and that was something she took into consideration when deciding against dealing with the people she dealt with on an individual basis. As long as they were scoring under twenty, her prices would remain the same.

One of the things that surprised Diamond was that they were doing the deal at an apartment complex in North Dallas in the Skillman area. She'd gotten used to visiting homes and estates, but kind of liked the idea of something less attractive.

"What's up with the timeline?" she asked the guy that was apparently in charge.

"Give us a month and we'll be right back on point."

How about I give you two weeks, because I have people pushing more than this in a week and when they come, I have to be ready. The way I see it, when you start moving, the numbers do too, and I'm really not supposed to be dealing with it, if it's under twenty. I just did this because it's you." Her lie wasn't obvious to the guy.

"Um, well, let me see what I can do and I'll get back to you."

Diamond followed Chris to the Durango and once the money was loaded, she told the guy she was dealing with, "I need you to make it happen, I really do."

"If I'm to wholesale, Diamond, I need a better price. I'm not out here trying to spin my wheels and I'm more than sure you can understand that," he told her.

"I'll tell you what, if you're ready in two weeks, I'll give you twelve for twenty thousand dollars and I'll front you another twelve at twenty-two thousand dollars."

"Where in the hell am I supposed to move all this shit, Diamond? 'Cause I'd hate to just be sitting on your shit."

"You've gotta step outside the box one day, baby." Diamond climbed into the 'Vette and smiled at him. "I might even have a job for you in the future, near future at that."

"Let me see what I can do, Diamond. You got a nigga out here taking a hell of a loss, just for you."

"Don't look at it that way, baby, you've got to see the long-term of it."

Diamond pulled out of the Friargate complex, pulled past Chris and hit the highway. Her next stop was Oak Cliff, TX.

***

KP had been watching his wife, ever since she told him about her conversation with Dell. His insecurities were getting the better of him, and this was something he felt he shouldn't have been dealing with. He didn't like his wife running out and sitting in a car with a guy that at one time did everything for her. He followed her into her office and sat in the same seat he sat in just minutes ago.

"Everything straight?"

"Yeah, why wouldn't they be?"

"What's he talking about now?" he asked, recalling the scene he just witnessed minutes ago.

"Oh, nothing, he just wanted to give me my bonus for some investments he got returns from." Silvia handed him the envelope and continued to sort out the papers she had on her desk. She knew he was about to trip, because this was the first time in a long time that Dell showed up at her job to give her a check.

"One hundred and fifty thousand dollars!" he said with an incredulous expression.

"Is there something wrong with that?"

KP thought about the check he cashed earlier and to think that he was able to bring something to the table worthwhile, boosted his ego in the best way, but now that he was holding a check given to his wife with an amount that dwarfed some of his best efforts, he was feeling strange. "What kind of investment gives a return like this?"

"If you must know, it's for Antonio," she told him, hoping that would close the case against her. And seeing him place the check on her desk and standing, she told him, "I need to go see him anyway."

"Yeah, alright."

Somolia walked into Silvia's office, just as KP was walking out and when seeing his expression, she allowed his passage without question. She walked in and stood at the corner of Silvia's desk before looking back towards the door. "What the hell's wrong with him?" she asked and when noticing the check on the desk, she picked it up.

"Damn! You're nosey, Somolia."

"Dell's back to his old tricks, huh?" Somolia knew their history and was no stranger to the way Dell propositioned and spoiled women.

"That's a return on some investment he's made."

"Hell, that nigga's getting returns like that? You need to let me get at him. I start sucking his dick, then we'll be getting a check like this weekly."

"Shut up, Somolia." Silvia stood, walked around the desk and placed the papers she was sorting out in the file cabinet by her office window.

"Just give me the green light and I'll have his dick in my mouth tonight."

Silvia laughed. She knew Somolia was crazy, but that would definitely prove it.

"Do your thing then, girl."

Somolia looked askance at Silvia. "You're serious, aren't you?"

"Get that nigga for everything he got, if you can." Silvia smiled at her. "You need me to help you or what?"

"Hell naw, that nigga been wanting me for the longest any-way," Somolia lied and when seeing Silvia laugh, she laughed also. "He just don't know it yet."

***

KP couldn't help but think of the possibility that Dell was trying to get at his wife again. The only thing he wasn't able to compete with against Dell was the money he was making. How could he compete with a millionaire? Hoping that things weren't as they seemed to be, he made a mental note to get at Dell the first chance he got.

***

Camille had just made it back to Kengyon's Ravinia home and helping Buddy with the duffle bags, when her phone began vibrat-ing. Since King was gone when they arrived, she was expecting it to be him and this was the reason she didn't check the caller ID before answering. "Money's in the bank, King."

"Camille?"

Not recognizing the voice on the other end of the line, she corrected herself.

"May I ask who's calling?"

"Yes, this is Dell."

"Dell?" Camille tried to put a face with the voice but couldn't, and since he called her name, it was evident he knew of her at least.

"Yes, we met a few years ago in Cabo San Lucas."

Camille held the door for Buddy and once all the bags were inside, she ventured off towards the pool area. "Um, are you sure?"

"Am I sure? How could I ever forget about you, your beauty and the impression you left me with."

"And yet you contact me years later?" Camille slowly began remembering the man named Dell. The egotistical man that felt as if his money was supposed to buy him love.

"I've been wanting to get at you long before now, but I was in a relationship of my own during this time. Is there any way we can talk?"

"I believe we're doing that now." Camille stood beside the pool's ladder and smiled. It had been a while since she was approached or even allowed herself to be, and when remembering the guy that spoke of such lucrative investments, she decided to see just how lucrative it could be to her.

"I'm talking breakfast, a light lunch or even dinner."

"Where are you?" she asked.

"I'm downtown at the moment and if need be, I'll forward you when and where." Camille concluded her call and smiled at the monster of a man that was now standing a few feet in front of her. "I have a luncheon date tomorrow, Buddy."

"Do I need to be ready also?"

"Not right off the top, baby. Let me see what it's all about first." She then looked out over the landscape of King's home and thought, it might be about time I got my own.

Dell concluded his call and looked towards Raymond, who'd been listening intently. "Only a matter of time now."

"Does she even remember you?" Raymond still wasn't sure this was the route for them to be taking

"Yeah, she remembers a nigga!" Dell crossed ankle over the knee and took a sip of the cognac he was drinking.

Raymond sighed. There were things about Dell's plan that didn't really sit right with him, but since the card had been played, it was too late to pull money from the table. "If she thinks for one minute that—"

Dell cut him off. "Let me handle this, nigga. A bitch can't out-think me! And she damn sure can't play a nigga out of shit!"

Raymond sat his drink on the tinted glass table before him, leaned backwards and rubbed his chin. The possibility of getting Diamond hurt or even killed stained his thoughts and when thinking of Antonio McClendon and what he would do, the thought unsettled him. "If this shit don't work, we gonna fall. You know, right?" He looked over at Dell, who was lost in thoughts or his own. "You know that, right?"

***

Diamond had been through Oak Cliff more than a few times, but today she was going through the hood with over one million, one hundred and ten thousand dollars cash in her possession. Even though she passed up the invite to hang out at the Palace, a top-notch upscale club, she made no hurry to get the money safely home. Chris had been against the idea of them hanging out instead of conducting business, but since she was in charge, whatever she chose to do was considered business.

They'd just delivered twenty kilos to José and his associates, with the promise that they'd be back with her in as short as two weeks and she was looking forward to it. If things went as promised, she'd be supplying the Oak Cliff Cartel and they'd been looking for a better product and price. When inquiring about the supplier they now had, they only referred to her as Boss Lady.

Diamond was sitting at the intersection of Illinois and Westmoreland Road. She was looking through her contacts when the black and platinum Audi R8 pulled alongside of her, and for the first time in a long time, she did a double take. It was the man she saw first but when seeing the car he was driving, she looked again and smiled. She once entertained the idea of buying herself an R8, but for reasons of her own, she stayed loyal to the Chevrolet brand. Diamond admired the small hardtop with an approving nod and by the way the guy was looking at her, she knew there was about to be a conversation of some kind.

***

Kengyon had personally driven to Terry's home, laid out the plans he had for the next two weeks, and even made sure he had something to do until they got back from Miami. The only part of their meeting that dampened things was that their Oak Cliff buyers were complaining about having to pay the same price for the work they'd been scoring for the longest, and the threat of going elsewhere was in the air. Kengyon was thinking about these very things while driving and as big an issue it was, he forgot all about it when he thought he saw her. He'd pulled to the light, looked around and immediately noticed the Calloway Corvette in the lane next to him. He knew Nava's profile anywhere and was certain he was meeting her, until the woman driving the sports car looked at him and began looking over Camille's Audi.

He could feel his heart palpitating and realized he was holding his breath, hoping the woman he was seeing was his fiancée. The way her face was structured, the skin tone and her lips reminded him so much of the woman that had walked out of his life. The only difference between his Nava and the woman in the Corvette next to him was that Nava's eyes were hazel and the woman's next to him were a mixture of hazel and green. With this being his only chance to make sure he wasn't seeing ghost of some kind, he hit the horn and waved at her.

When hearing the small horn of the Audi, Diamond checked her rearview to find Chris smiling at her. She knew what he was smiling about and to say the least, she was sure her 'Vette would take the R8, easily. Instead of waving back, Diamond only nodded. There was nothing to talk about and as soon as the light changed, he made the left turn and she continued straight. Even if he would have called her out in a street race, Diamond had other things to do at the moment. Seeing the caller on her phone, she pressed speaker. "What?"

"It was apparent the nigga liked what he saw. Niggas ain't pulling up on bitches, waving just to be waving."

Diamond thought about the way she was being looked at and shrugged it off.

"Hell naw, that nigga had better keep it moving."

"Look like he had a little money, Diamond. You might have let a good one get away."

After pressing "end call", she smiled. Men had continually pulled up on her, but this was the first time ever a man pulled up on her and waved.

"The nigga might have even been gay," she told herself before flooring the Corvette.

***

Kengyon pulled into his driveway, thinking about the woman he just ran across. As bad as he wanted it to be Nava, she wasn't and it was now that he wished he'd asked her name. He then thought about the way she was rolling, 'cause not everyone was pushing a limited edition Calloway Corvette. Whoever she was, she had to have some money or was involved with someone who did.

Camille met him at the stairs and told him, "I have a luncheon date tomorrow. Is that cool with you?"

"Who is he?" King climbed out of the R8 and smiled.

"An old acquaintance of mine and what's up with the shit eating smile?" she asked, knowing something was off with him.

"Guess who I saw today?" King walked past her and she followed.

"Who did you see, King?" she asked, not wanting to play the game.

"Nava."

"Really?" Camille looked from King to Buddy who by now had stood and was looking at both of them as if shots were about to be fired.

Kengyon laughed. The picture before him explained a million things as well as answered a thousand questions. "Well, she looked just like you."

"And you saw her in Dallas?"

"Yeah, she was driving a posh Corvette and had cornrows in her hair."

"Cornrows?" Camille asked, knowing Nava was too high-maintenance for the do.

"I could have sworn it was her, but turns out it wasn't."

Camille watched the way King's entire posture slumped when he spoke of it not being her. She hated the things he was putting himself through, but one thing she wasn't about to regret was not allowing him to go through it with a gold digger like Nava Munez.

Chapter Six

Silvia never doubted for one minute that Diamond would come through as soon as she claimed, but she was at least hoping it would stall her in her efforts and when seeing Diamond pulling up in her brother's Bentley Coupe and Chris driving his Escalade truck, she knew they were about their business. Instead of waiting for them in her lobby, she walked back into her office and waited. She was hoping to have heard from Orlando by the end of the week and now that Diamond was there waiting for them in her next move, Silvia planned to do a little negotiating herself.

Diamond and Chris walked through the doors of the Totally Awesome Hair Salon and was welcomed by both staff and clients. Their closeness was something people couldn't ignore, despite the affection and attention he showered Datrina when he did come around.

"What's up, everybody?" Diamond spoke, before heading back to her cousin's office.

"You're looking good, Diamond," Somolia said, knowing she was the doer of the hairstyle Diamond wore.

"Thanks, Somolia and I need my shit done over. Visit this weekend."

"I might need to be doing Chris's also, because I know he's going with you," Somolia shot back, wanting the rest of the women to realize what she felt she already knew.

"Yeah, you might as well. You know I need my man looking good," Diamond added, knowing the effect of her statement.

"Will there ever be a day when I can come in here and be left out of the things y'all say?" Chris asked, knowing his girl must have been feeling some kind of way.

"You tell me." Somolia spun her client so she could see both Chris and Datrina through her work station's mirror.

"I would have you know that me and Diamond are business consultants and we're about to open a new venture soon," he lied, knowing this would paint a totally different picture than they were used to seeing.

"As much as the two of you are together, I would have sworn a business of some sort was already up and running." Somolia looked at Datrina, because this had been the topic of many of their conversations. The way she saw it, if Chris was really as loyal and faithful as she claimed he was, she wouldn't be working at a friend's salon, she'd have her own.

The truth of it was that Datrina never cared to own her own shop and it wasn't because Chris hadn't proposed the idea. It was because she was doing something she wanted to do. The cars she drove, the clothes she wore and the things she was able to do at any given notice were because she didn't have any extra obligations.

"It's a slow process, Somolia. You have to cross all your t's and dot all your i's when stepping into unchartered waters, especially in the field we are in."

Chris wrapped his arms around Datrina and kissed her dark lips. "Besides, my babe needs me around."

"So, what's up for the weekend?" Datrina asked him.

"Let me see what Diamond had planned first, cause we're about to make a major move soon."

Seeing Chris walk around them and into Silvia's office, Somolia stopped and just looked at Datrina, who was now busying herself with the chemicals she was mixing. "I don't see how you do it, girl."

"Nothing has happened, nothing is happening and nothing ever will," Datrina told her, sure of the promises her man made

Diamond sat in the chair adjacent to Silvia's desk and picked up the magazine she saw. "I got the mil in the truck right now, what's up?"

"I'm waiting on a call now, so until then, we wait."

"Wait? I told you I was going to have that today, Silvia."

Silvia pulled herself to the end of her chair and rest her elbows on the red oak desk. "Being that patient isn't one of your best attributes, it will become one that fights you. This game requires you to sit and think, and when your every move is as spontaneous as the thoughts you have, then you turn whichever way the wind blows.

Appreciate the fact that you are able to put something together and better prepare your next step."

Silvia watched her cousin to make sure she was paying attention and when seeing she was, she continued. "It's time to play chess now, Chanel. Jumping all over the board not only gets you fucked off, but your whole team as well. Your brother fell alone because he played chess, Diamond, he was able to think, and not only that, he's still thinking and he's still making moves."

Diamond, at first, started to voice her opinion but decided against it when seeing the seriousness in Silvia's demeanor and posture. One thing Antonio taught her was that when a person's posture stood out, their outlook on the things discussed wasn't to be taken lightly. She looked Silvia straight in her eyes and saw unblinking resolve. Not only that, but during her talks with Chris, he also told her that Silvia had more game than she thought and that if it wasn't for her part, Antonio couldn't have risen in the game he played. The way Chris explained it, Silvia was able to make the call because she always kept business relations good and open, despite the feelings others had about it. She was her own woman, and if Silvia did choose to play the game, she would definitely be a boss.

Diamond said, "I'm trying to be bigger than that, Silvia. I'm trying to take this shit to a whole other level."

"That's not for you to decide, Diamond. Your best efforts can get you killed faster than anything and when you in it solo, there's no respect from the other players that play. It's your team that positions you. It's your team that holds you up in victory or hides you in surrender. Your next move is going to determine the position you end up in next."

"I need better prices, Silvia."

"No, what you need is better players. I can only give you so much, but the level you're trying to get to is beyond the game I have and I'm not going to fool you into thinking I know the direction you're going. I didn't choose that life, Diamond." Silvia looked around her office and told her, "I'm doing what I love right here, right now. It's only two ways that lifestyle ends, Diamond and you need to be aware of it."

"Yeah, locked up or in the grave. I know." Diamond lowered her head for the first time.

"Raise your head up and look at me. Despite the consequences, you still choose to play it, so embrace it. You've got to become that person, Diamond, and the feeling you have about people can't follow, and this is what most fail to understand."

Chris walked into the office at the end of what was said and when seeing Diamond's attentive gaze on Silvia, he knew she was soaking up the game from a more experienced player. He and Silvia spoke as often as they could and if Chris knew or felt something amiss, Silvia most likely weighed in on it.

"Is everything alright?"

"Yeah, close the door right quick," Silvia told him.

Chris backed against the door until it closed and crossed his arms. "What up?"

"I'm making the arrangements needed for us to go to Miami. This is going to be the biggest move you two have made this far and it's going to be crucial."

Diamond looked from Silvia to Chris. "We're ready."

"We're going to have to drive ourselves."

"How about we rent a jet, Silvia?" Diamond leaned back, crossed her ankle over knee and watched her. "I'll just tell Dell we need to make a trip and commercial ain't going to do it," she told them with resolve.

"Make the call then," Silvia told her, realizing this was her chance to get a better hold on Dell. "This stays here, you two."

Diamond stood and turned and added, "I'll even send the 'Vette and the EXT ahead of us, so we'll have a way to get around."

"That is so ghetto, Diamond. You want to be a boss, you make moves like one. When we get there, I'm more than sure we can rent something for us to enjoy. We're going to have fun."

"Mix a little business with pleasure?" Chris chimed in.

"Just say we're going to be enjoying the business we do." Silvia stood and walked them both back to the lobby and when seeing Diamond's gangster lean, she told her, "That tomboy shit ain't going to do it, Diamond, and a shopping spree is overdue."

A Drug King and His Diamond

***

Dell had been waiting at the doors of the Hyatt Regency Hotel for his luncheon date for every bit of twenty minutes, and was growing tired of the wait. He checked the time on his platinum on gold Rolex every other minute and was about to call to make sure he was at the right location when the huge gray CTS pulled under the canopy. He prayed this was her and as soon as the driver ran around to open the rear door, he began walking towards them. It had been years since he last saw her and even though it was done in passing, he never forgot how beautiful the queen pin was.

Camille was pulled out of the rear of the sedan by none other than Buddy. Even the valets present stepped back seeing the three hundred and fifty pound guy doing the job they were supposed to be doing. And seeing her themselves, they knew she was someone of both prestige and wealth.

Camille wore a silver satin blouse, a pair of flared trousers with silver and blue pinstripes, with a pair of blue platform sandals. The blue floppy hat and designer shades completed the ensemble and the only other accessory she had was her iPhone.

"Camille, your beauty is unmatched." Dell stepped forward to intercept her from the huge man by presenting his left arm. "It's been too long."

Camille smiled, reached for his arm and told him, "Thank you, and it has."

She silently admired Dell's style of dress and the gentleman he was portraying himself to be. The Italian suit and loafers he wore screamed success, but it was his neatly manicured facial hair, augmented eyebrows, and dark eyes that captivated her. And the cologne he was wearing shot through her sense of smell. The man was more than she expected, and much more than she remembered.

Dell led her straight to the table he had reserved and pulled her chair out and once she'd seated herself, he did the same. "I'm so grateful that our schedules allow the reunion."

"Um, is this reunion business or pleasure?" Camille was known to get straight to the point and just because she was impressed on many levels, didn't mean her principles changed.

"Um, just say we're enjoying the business about it," he told her, making the familiar saying his own.

"The last time we spoke, you were a part of an investment firm, are you still active with that?" Camille summoned the waiter.

"I'm afraid I have my own investment firm these days. You looking to spend some money?"

"No, I'm looking to invest in me another home."

"Where?" Dell never took his eyes off her and when seeing her avoid his gaze, he knew the roles played was understood.

"Does that matter?" she asked, knowing the game he was trying to play, but deciding to play one of her own. She leaned forward in her seat, straightened her posture and added, "Where would you have me?" She looked him dead in the eyes and smiled.

"Um, I would um, put you wherever you wanted to be," he stammered.

Camille had been entertained by a variety of men and she knew how to create that level of uncomforting, and now that she had, she continued her push.

"I thought we were having lunch, not conversation about my investments but now that we are I'd like to hear promise."

"Um, well, would you be interested in commercial or personal properties?"

"Both."

"How much are you willing to play with?" Dell smiled, this was his area of expertise. As well as his way of fingering the idea of how much money could possibly be in play.

"I don't play with my money. I'd rather play with a life." Again, she smiled.

Dell knew exactly what she was implying and to say the least, he would also. He matched her gaze and told her, "Likewise."

"Let's open the door with half a mill." Camille thanked the waiter for her salad and sides and placed her napkin in her lap.

"I'm beyond those numbers now, the properties I oversee are well into the seven-digit figure spectrum," he told her, knowing that if she and Kengyon had upped their game, it would be easily agreed to.

"I meant that as the payment I'd pay you."

"Oh, um, yeah, we can definitely do that."

"Let's say a palatial estate on the outskirts of Dallas, multi-car garage, tinted glass, eleven room bi-level with an outdoor pool. I'm more than sure I'm leaving out a this or that, but for the most part, I need something gated with surveillance."

Hearing the list go on, Dell knew they were playing with every bit of what he figured and to make it all the better, he told her, "Give me a quarter million dollars deposited and we'll go from there."

"Which bank do you frequent?" Dell pulled out his phone, typed an entry and signaled the waiter.

"Let's do cash, make it a little interesting."

By the time Camille climbed back into the Cadillac sedan, numbers were exchanged, and promises made. He'd also gotten a pretty good outline on the draft he was about to make, because not only was he sure they were sitting on something nice, their distribution expanded more than he thought, at first.

To hear she owned properties in Oklahoma, Kansas, Dallas, and San Antonio, brought more than a smile to his face, it was downright bliss. And the half a mill she was to deliver began that promise. Dell even entertained the idea of being with a woman like Camille, but that was short-lived because he knew if it came down to it, she'd give her life before she gave her money and he didn't have the slightest problem with it.

King walked from his kitchen area and out onto the pools patio. He was expecting to hear from Camille soon and instead of interrupting her date with silly questions and hints of what could easily be misconstrued as jealousy, he looked through his contacts, saw Nava's old number and pressed dial. The face of both Nava and the woman he ran across just yesterday stood side by side in his thoughts. It was now that he regretted not doing anything more than waving at the look-alike. King held his breath, hoping Nava would pick up and hearing the phone service telling him what he'd heard so many times, he exhaled and closed his eyes. There had to be an explanation for her sudden departure and there had to be a name for the woman that now filled his every thought.

He knew he was tripping when thinking about the fact that there weren't too many people pushing one hundred thousand dollars' worth of Corvettes and if only he could narrow it down, then he'd most likely find the driver of the cyber-black one he ran across yesterday. By the looks of the car, it had to have been brand-new, or at least well stored. After looking through a few apps on his phone and googling the address of the Chevrolet dealership he called the service center. There was no way he was about to pass up this chance, and if he ever did get to see her again, she'd definitely know how much she stayed in his thoughts.

"Dan Merring Chevrolet of Dallas, how may I direct your call?"

King started to hang up but decided the hell with it. "Sales, please."

"One moment, sir."

For the first time in a long while, he felt there was a piece of hope when locating the woman he ran across, and once the sales rep came online, he went into his spiel.

"Yes, I was calling to inquire about the new supercharged Calloway Corvettes you're selling and just wanted to know how many are on the streets. I don't like the idea of having the same car so many people have."

King could hear the keys of the computer on the other end of the phone as well as feel his heart beating harder than it should have.

"Um, sir?"

"Yes, I'm still here."

"Neither of our Dallas locations show any sale of the Calloway Corvettes."

King closed his eyes and cursed himself for his stunt, but before he could thank the service woman for wasting her time, she told him, "But our Fort Worth branch just sold two of them three days ago."

"Fort Worth?"

"Yes, sir."

Feeling that hope resurface, he asked her, "Could you by chance tell me who bought them?"

"Um, our information doesn't show that, sir. That's undisclosed information for us."

King concluded the call with a ton of thank you's and compliments for a job well done. And as soon as he finished, he grabbed the keys to Camille's 911 Porsche and headed for Fort Worth.

***

Raymond dialed Silvia's number for the third time and right when it began to ring, he hung up. The moves Dell was making definitely called for questions since they needed to get to the bottom of the ordeal concerning Antonio. He felt it was a move that had to be made. The thing he didn't like was the fact that Diamond could possibly be in danger. Hoping that things would fall into place without him interfering, he lowered the phone and sighed.

Somolia had been the one to answer the phone the last couple of times and was now upset at the idea of someone toying with her. They'd let the phone ring once and hang up and she was now frustrated by it. As soon as she picked up for the fourth time, she went off. "Punk-ass motherfucker, stop calling here!" She slammed the landline phone down and smiled at the rest of the women that were watching her. "Hell, y'all would have done the same thing."

"Just press star sixty-nine, crazy woman," Datrina told her while shaking her head.

"Oh," Somolia frowned and asked her, "they still got shit?"

"Just dial it."

Raymond was just about to reach for his briefcase when the ringing phone startled him. He looked towards the door then down at the ringing Samsung.

"Global Investing. How may I help you?" he answered.

"I would appreciate it if you'd call like everybody else and at least ask a question or two, instead of just hanging up!"

"I beg your pardon?" Raymond only heard pieces of the rant she spilled.

"You heard me, motherfucker! Who do you want anyway?"

Raymond knew there was no need in hanging up and instead of making a bad situation worse, he said, "Please excuse that, my line hasn't been connecting lately."

"Yeah, well, who you trying to reach?"

"Um, is Silvia around?"

"Yeah, hold on."

Somolia transferred the line and hung up. The caller was more than likely another friend of Silvia's, and by the picture Somolia was able to paint, he was probably another so-called associate of hers.

Silvia and KP were sitting in her office discussing the plan concerning the trip when her desk phone began ringing. Their conversation was far from over because of the fact that this was a call she made without her husband, and the last time she made an unexpected trip, it was to accompany a man he never thought would go behind his back to be with his wife.

"I'm serious, Silvia. I don't want you going to Miami," he told her.

"That's not a decision of yours to make, Kevin. I have to make the trip, because I'm the one that put it together for her." She spoke her piece, and answered her phone, "Silvia Pierson speaking."

"Hey, Silvia, it's Raymond. We need to talk."

Silvia looked at KP and by the expression he wore he could tell that a man was on the other end of the conversation and in her attempt to show him that there was nothing for him to trip on, she said, "Haven't heard from you in a minute, Raymond. What's up?"

"I'll be up there to get you. We're going to see your cousin."

"When?"

"Tomorrow. Attorney visit."

"Um, okay, what time?" Silvia frowned. She'd been meaning to get at her cousin for a minute, but now that Raymond was voicing the same things, something wasn't right at all.

"I'll be there before ten a.m., so cancel whatever," he told her before ending the call.

"I don't want you getting dragged back into that shit, Silvia. I'm serious." KP walked out before she could respond and she knew why. She was just hoping he would understand the reasons she had to and the reasons he would also.

Nicole Goosby

Chapter Seven

Diamond looked through several magazines and profiles before selecting the floral braid up-do. She handed Somolia the catalogue and sat back in the swiveling chair. She was going to visit her brother the next morning and wanted to look her best.

"Why is it that the day before visiting Antonio you spend hundreds of dollars on your hair and shortly afterwards you undo it by spending whatever else to do so?" Somolia pulled out a series of combs and sprays and aligned them on her station.

"Coz he's up there telling everyone I'm a model and I just continue to play the part."

Datrina walked past the two on her way to the back and told her, "He knows you're not doing any modeling, Diamond."

"That doesn't mean I can't look good for him, does it?" Diamond adjusted herself in the chair and leaned back. The game was being good to her and if things went according to plan during their visit to Miami, they'd be that much closer to the freedom she wanted.

"So, where did Chris go?" Somolia asked Diamond, knowing she'd know instead of his own girlfriend.

"He went to get the Phantom detailed and serviced."

"So, he's driving you tomorrow?" Somolia wasn't letting up.

"Well, you know how he is when it comes to me. That man treats me like a queen." Diamond laughed when seeing Somolia roll her eyes. This was the game she loved playing at the shop.

"Um."

"Datrina's just going to have to deal with it because he's my man, too."

"I heard that, Diamond," Datrina yelled from the other room.

"Like she don't know." Somolia looked from one client to the other and when seeing them smile, she went on. "Cake ain't shit without the ice cream, huh?"

"And strawberries ain't shit without a little chocolate," Diamond added. They all knew she was referring to the differences in their complexions and when seeing Diamond wink at Datrina, they all laughed in unison.

***

KP and Q were headed to the shop to see his wife and the rest of the women, when they recognized the pearl white Phantom glowing outside the Elegant Isles Detailing Shop. "Isn't that Chris right there?" Q asked while pointing.

"Yeah, that's him." KP swung his F-150 around and pulled in behind the Phantom. He had a few things to discuss with Chris and now that they were outside of the shop and out of the hearing of Somolia and the rest of the gossipers, he felt better about it. "Chris!"

Chris was talking among both the owner and a couple of workers when he heard his name being yelled and seeing KP and Q pulling around, he threw his hands up.

With all that was happening at and around the shop, he knew it was just a matter of time before questions were asked and lies were told. He didn't owe KP or Q any lies, but he owed them no loyalty either. "What's up?" he asked the two once they exited the truck.

"Chris, I need a word with you." KP led him away from the rest of the men and smiled at the youngster. "How's everything going with you, Chris?"

"I'm good man, what's up?"

"I just wanted to ask you a few things about Dell and Silvia."

"Like what?" Chris wasn't expecting this but since he was here, he might as well ease a weary heart.

"Has he been trying to get at her again?"

"Not that I know of. Not on that level at least." Chris shrugged as if it was nothing.

"The nigga gave her a huge check and I was just making sure it was business. She said it was for Antonio. You know anything about that?"

Instead of looking as if there was something to think about, Chris went into an improvised role. "Yeah, you know the nigga got them high-ass lawyers and he don't like Silvia paying all that money out on her own. That's all."

"Then there's the money you and Diamond brought into the shop a few days ago. Is she trying to get back in that game shit?"

"Who? Silvia?" Chris looked at him with enough question to raise doubt himself and told him, "Hell naw. I haven't heard about her doing anything, other than putting Diamond up on game about the way it should be played."

"What's in Miami then?"

"Just going to support some shit Diamond has going on."

"I've told Dell several times to leave her out of whatever he had going on and I don't think he's listening to me. If I paid you to get at him, would you?"

"Would I what?" Chris looked around then back to KP who was looking at him with a genuine concern.

"I know what you do for Diamond, Chris, and I knew what you did for her brother. I just don't want Silvia getting sucked back into that life, man."

"You don't have to worry about Silvia, KP, she's straight and if it's any consolation whatsoever, she's trying to keep Diamond from doing the same."

By the conversation they just had, Chris could tell that KP was trying his best to put things together concerning his wife and her dealings. And being that he didn't know that half, Chris couldn't give him the whole. Knowing that Diamond should be ready by now, he made his way to the Totally Awesome Hair Salon.

"What he talking about?" Q asked his friend as soon as they climbed back into the truck.

"Told me don't worry about shit."

"I'm talking about what he gonna do about Dell's punk ass?"

"Naw, he tells me that I'm tripping over nothing. Said let it go."

Q looked at his friend and asked, "Are you?"

"I might not have a choice. You know that nigga got a hit squad of his own and if I charge the nigga up the wrong way, I might be the one getting dealt with."

"What?" Scary-ass nigga, a nigga trying to fuck her again and you talking some shit like that." Q gave it to him the way he felt he should be hearing it, because there was no need in sugar coating anything.

"The check wasn't even for her?" KP added.

"Why in the hell he didn't just put it in the bank for Antonio like he's been doing?" And when seeing KP without an answer, he told him, "I thought so."

***

"You did what?" Camille asked, when hearing of King's latest outing.

"I went to Fort Worth and tried to find her." King poured himself a shot of vodka and began walking into the living area.

"So, now you're stalking hoes, King?"

"That can't be as bad as running them off or killing them, can it?" he asked without looking at her.

"Did you?"

"If I did, you'd know it and it wouldn't be something I hid from you either."

Camille turned on her heels and told Buddy, "Let's go."

Before she could disappear from view, King told her, "Don't worry. They couldn't tell me anything either." He was hoping the Fort Worth dealership could tell him something about the buyer of the sports cars, but when hearing they were purchased by the same owner, his thoughts took him to the players of the game he played. The salesman even gave him a description of the young woman and man that came into their establishment to make several high-dollar purchases, days apart.

Camille closed the quarter million into her Prada carry-on and had Buddy take it to her Porsche. This would be a trip she made alone for not wanting to expose her hand and the fact that she'd instructed Buddy to see exactly what Dell was doing outside of his meetings with her. In the game she played, a quarter of a million dollars definitely got the ball rolling and in some cases, heads too.

A Drug King and His Diamond

With Dell owning an investment firm, him being with large sums of money was nothing and if Camille played the cards right, she'd have more than some property investments.

**

Silvia had been doing most of the talking, while Raymond fumbled with the papers he continued to pull from his briefcase. The attorney visit they were having not only allowed them all contact visits, but offered them the comfort of knowing their conversations were private. Raymond just made them look like the representatives they were while there.

She'd informed her cousin of the happenings with both his sister and Dell and as attentive as he should have been to her, he was more focused on Raymond.

Antonio leaned back and nodded in Raymond's direction and asked, "What's the play, Raymond?"

"Um, we gotta play it by ear now, Antonio." Raymond failed to look Antonio in his eyes and it didn't go unnoticed.

"You want me to tell you what I think?" Antonio looked from him to Silvia.

"And what would that be?" Silvia said.

"I'm talking to Raymond, cousin. He's not comfortable right now."

"I'm good, I'm good." Raymond settled for a second, then went back to stuffing papers into his case.

"I'll tell you what, Raymond. We've been doing this shit too long to start lying to each other now and you know I know you better than anybody. So, what's up?"

Raymond sighed and told them, "Dell is planning on sending Diamond at King and Camille. He's already set up some kind of meeting with Camille about a possible investment of some kind."

"What?" Silvia looked at Raymond quizzically. They'd spent well over an hour together on the drive up, but this was the first time she was hearing the matter and it was making her look as if she didn't have the hold she was claiming to have on Diamond.

"I spoke against it but he started talking about your indictment and the fact that they could have possibly had something to do with the charge for wanting to get us out of the way."

"I told you I was going to handle that end." Antonio leaned forward and looked at Raymond. "And what the hell is Diamond supposed to be doing? She's not on that level of game and she damn sure isn't ready for no shit like that."

"I know and I voiced that much, but Dell has hair on his own ass about it. He says it's a win- win for us."

"Risking my sister's life sounds like a win-win to you, Raymond? What the fuck you thinking, man?

"You got me trying to watch the girl's every move for the sake of the Circle and you and Dell pulling some shit like this!" Silvia said, thinking back to the unexpected visit from Dell and told them, "That's why he brought me that big ass check, a pay off."

"A check?" Antonio asked her while watching Raymond.

"Yeah. A hundred and fifty thousand dollars."

"Dell insists on going after King, huh?"

"You could say so."

"And the teams ready to move when he say move, huh?" Antonio looked beyond them to the guards on the outside of the glass

"As always."

"Have you heard from Orlando yet?" he asked Silvia.

"Got a text from him earlier. Thumbs up."

"Well, make sure she knows what's at stake here and I don't think she's ready for stepping in a nigga's circle just to find out their role, if any, in the charges against me. What happens when they find out that's her plan, who's going to make sure my sister is alright?"

"Chris is with her and you know he's not going to let anything happen to her or anything that she deals with."

"So, Chris is in on it also?" Silvia was starting to understand that the moves being made around her was really out of her control. "I might as well stop asking questions and acting as if I'm in the know, 'cause it's apparent that I really don't know shit about what's going on around me."

"Make the transaction with Orlando and let her handle the rest and don't tell her I know anything. If she knows, I know her next moves, she's going to try to prove a point and that's when mistakes are made." Antonio looked at the wall clock behind them and added, "I'm going to talk with both her and Chris when they get here tomorrow."

"Good luck with that," Silvia sighed, before gathering the empty cans from the table.

"I heard that Dell has a new home. Have you seen it?" Antonio smiled at Silvia and continued, "I'm more than sure you have, though."

"As a matter of fact, I've still yet to see it, but maybe I need to."

"I'll go with you, just so it won't look as if other factors are in play," Raymond said, laughing as he helped Silvia stand and pushed the empty chair in.

"Matter of fact, I'll get KP to go with me. How does that sound?"

The ride back home was a one-sided conversation as well as a continual apology to Silvia for not informing her on the things they knew mattered. Diamond might have been a little hard to handle at times but it was still their duty to allow Silvia the insight she needed to understand the things she did and why. After it was understood that Raymond would report whatever findings to her and it not go past the two of them, Silvia told him." "Clean your shit up, Raymond, 'cause now's not the time for error."

***

Camille parked alongside the cobalt blue Bentley, popped her trunk and climbed out. She liked the way Dell awaited her. Once the carry-on was pulled out of the trunk of the Porsche, she followed Dell into the First Nations Bank. The money she brought would be the deposits used to get the ball rolling and with a need to invest in both the market and what Dell had going on, she came with her a-game.

Dell ushered her into the elevator and pressed the eight button. He'd gotten at one of his clients who managed the bank and reserved the conference room for the next two hours. He wanted this meeting with Camille to look as professional and as profitable as could be.

"Conference room, I suppose?" Camille typed an entry into her iPhone and looked back at him.

"Nothing but the best for you, Camille."

Once the elevator opened, Dell led her into yet another room and offered her a glass of sparkling water. "I want to show you my business portfolio."

Camille smiled over the rim of the glass and told him, "My pretty comes without the stupid, Dell, and I'm more than sure you know by now I'm not interested in some put-together portfolio. We have more pressing issues to discuss." She walked over to the window overlooking the bank's lot and immediately spotted Buddy across the street. "I want in, Dell."

"Excuse me?"

"I want in on the distributing you got going on." Camille watched him, saw his shift in posture and continued, "I must say, I do like the front, but now I need to see the face behind it."

Dell poured himself another fill of water and told her, "Distribution of what, Camille?"

"Cocaine and whatever else you got going on."

"Cocaine?"

"And since you just accepted my payment, you work for me now, or should I say work with me now?"

Dell laughed. This wasn't the way this meeting was supposed to go, but since they were here, he played the card he was given. "A quarter of a million wouldn't even get the trucks rolling, Camille. What would that get you, less than ten kilos, if that?"

"As I've said before, the quarter was just for the meeting and I'm more than sure this setting came with it," she told him while looking around the conference room.

"Where are you trying to distribute, Camille?"

"I want San Antonio."

Dell immediately thought about his promise to Diamond and the fact that she'd be able to expand into the very area Camille wanted. Being that his plan was to push King from both the area and the game, he didn't see the harm with it, but because it was Diamond, he at least needed a little time so she could plant her fences, if not build her home.

"I'll tell you what, let me get at a few associates I deal with and see if we can make that happen. Is this going to be a move you make alone or do you have a group of partners, because this price tag can get pretty interesting?"

"Oh, yeah, I do have a group coming with me and don't you worry about a price tag. I'm more than sure you'll make it to where we'll all profit from it."

Hearing those words created yet another possibility for Bell and when thinking about the numbers alone, it was downright irresistible. The way he saw it, Diamond would still be paying the fees she was obligated to and if he could get a percentage of the distribution from Camille and King before the takeover, he'd be set for life. "And the profit is what it's all about, right?"

Camille held her glass up in agreement. "Right you are."

Kengyon thought about all that was going on with him and his team and when looking at the things that mattered, it irked him that Camille would speak of wanting to invest in her own properties. He'd dealt with several regulators for the longest and for her to insist on dealing with a guy he knew nothing about, he could only think it was done in an attempt to distance herself from him. The fact that he'd accused her repeatedly when it came to sabotaging the relationships he formed, did factor in, but it was his insecurities of her freedom that carried the most weight. He'd asked her about the guy she only knew as Dell, but couldn't get anything more than, "You've met him before," out of her. In an effort to show his trust for her, he didn't pry and against his gut feeling, he wasn't even going to.

Nicole Goosby

Chapter Eight
The following morning

With so much being said inside of the Totally Awesome Hair Salon, Chris felt it would be a good idea to take Datrina along to the visit with Antonio McClendon. But, he failed to consider the fact that she was neither on his visitation list or that she'd have to wait in the car while they did visit. He really just wanted her to know she was welcomed.

"You two go ahead, I'll just hang out at the shop until you get back." Datrina stood, grabbed her keys and gathered her purse. She and Chris made the trip to the McClendon home earlier that morning, because Chris thought it would be a good idea and now that it wasn't, she saw herself as being the third wheel.

"I'll tell you what, Chris, why don't you just chill this time? I got it." Diamond stood also. Seeing Datrina languished in such a way didn't sit well with her. At the shop, it was a different story but seeing her mood dampen did something to her.

"Antonio's going to be expecting me, Diamond, and you know it."

"I can handle that nigga. Hell, you have a girl and other responsibilities of your own."

"And we also have business to conduct and you ain't good with business or conduct."

"Yeah, whatever, nigga. It might just be that I'm not good at kissing a nigga's ass."

"And I am." Chris grabbed his keys and instead of allowing her to answer, he asked, "Which car are you taking, so I can take a look at it?"

"I'll be pushing my 'Vette today. I want him to see it anyway."

Diamond held up her hand and said, "Here." She walked into the dining area and pulled out twenty-five thousand dollars from the safe her brother had installed behind the china cabinet.

"What's this for?" Datrina asked after stuffing the money into the William Jennings bag she carried.

"Do some shopping or something." Diamond then handed her the keys to her pearl white Bentley Coupe. "And put some miles on it for me."

Chris only watched her because he knew Diamond, and knew she felt that he was offended by the statements she made in front of his girl. The things she was sure to say always rolled off his shoulders, but being that Datrina was getting the treatment he would have gotten and normally did when Diamond felt she'd said the wrong things, he allowed it.

"You letting me keep your Bentley, Diamond?" Datrina asked, knowing the only other person able to drive it was Chris and at times, Silvia.

"And don't tear my shit up. And don't let Chris drive it either."

"I thought I was going with you?" Chris frowned.

"Stop thinking, nigga. I'll get at y'all when I get back."

Diamond climbed into the Corvette coupe and smiled at the both of them.

The low growl of the supercharged Calloway spoke its ability and promise. She could tell by the way Chris was looking that he didn't approve of the move, and instead of fighting with him over it, she put the car in gear and nodded.

"I got him, Chris. I got this."

"And drive like you got some sense, Diamond."

"You know I can hardly stop doing stunts when I drive."

"Anyway, don't get yourself killed behind the wheel."

"Okay."

Seeing the wrought iron gates open, she slowly pulled out of the cobblestone driveway and as soon as she turned onto the pavement of the street leading away from her house, she floored the sports car, its dual traction grip propelling her in a launch-like fashion.

"That girl is going to kill herself, Chris."

Chris looked after the car until it disappeared from view. "Naw, she's got it."

Diamond selected the distance mode on "her" detector, pressed play on her playlist and once the tunes of "XO Life" by Lil Uzi was blasting through the twelve-speaker stereo she had installed, she pointed the speedometer past the eighty-five mph limit, and thought about her next moves. Even with the world on her shoulders, she was going to win and this was the promise she made to herself.

Dell had been thinking of Camille and the things she proposed for most of the night, and once he'd run over the numbers with a few of the associates he dealt with, he was sure it would be something he should have done a long time ago. The difference between his now and then was that Antonio McClendon was both calling the shots and making the moves firsthand.

Not only was Antonio a real player, he was the one that started the Circle. He pulled together a few friends as well as family from their day to day, with the promise of making them as rich as they wanted to be.

Dell remembered that day like it happened seconds ago. He'd been working as a realtor for Century 21 for over five years, and had still yet to see his income increase. He'd sold several properties and was promised both advances and increases with the firm, but it wasn't until he closed a deal with Antonio McClendon that he realized he'd been working for the wrong people. Antonio began showing him how to move properties like the drugs he was used to moving.

Once Dell saw the profit in telling people one price but paying another, a much lesser one, his name became one sought after and his credentials soared also. The properties Antonio owned weren't only nice, but were paid for by the other people that made investments with Dell.

Now that he'd run his course with the boss, he felt a business venture with Camille would also have its own reward. With her wanting to distribute drugs of her liking and drugs he'd been connected to, ever since Antonio put Dell in position, his part would be both minimal and silent. He'd tax both Camille and King, collect a tax from Diamond and Chris, and continue to play both ends. In one year's time, he'd be richer than all of them combined.

Dell walked out onto his patio entrance and smiled to himself. He'd done pretty damn good for himself and he owed it all to the boss, Antonio McClendon. Hoping things would fall into place sooner than later, he dialed a series of numbers and when the speaker came online, he told him, "Pull the guys in. I will have some work for them shortly." He looked down at the quarter million Camille gave him just the day before. One thing he did like about the woman was that she was about her business, and she did have the money to conduct it with.

***

Silvia was in the middle of her debate with Somolia when Raymond walked through the doors of the salon. Women were under dryers, held over sinks and even modeling freshly done hairdos in the mirror until they smelled his fragrance. Raymond prided himself in wearing some of the most intriguing and expensive cologne out and when seeing the common reaction, he smiled. "Good morning, ladies."

"And a good morning to you also, Raymond." Somolia left her client standing at the sink, in order to get a close-up visual of the man all eyes were on. She'd liked Raymond for years now, but he never had the time for her. That was, until now and in her attempt to show the other women he was a promise of hers, she told him, "We need to talk, Raymond."

"Um, yeah, okay."

He looked around at the faces that watched him and continued smiling. He knew he was clean and was glad that he selected the peach linen pants, cream-colored linen shirt, brown gator belt and matching, square-toe hard soles. The gold big face on his left arm held twelve-and-a-half-carat diamonds around the rim and on his right wrist sat an eight-carat bracelet he had custom made. His six foot two frame allowed him to tower over all the women easily and as short as Somolia was to him, he had to damn near bend over to talk to her.

"Why don't we do dinner tonight? I have this nice place that recently opened I would like to try out."

Somolia knew what she was doing and letting a bunch of thirsty women know her card had been played was a must.

"Why don't we get together and do something tonight?" Raymond said to Somolia, still looking around the salon.

Silvia and KP had been in her office for the past hour, in a heated conversation that spilled over into this day from the night before. And when hearing Raymond's voice in the other room, she stood. "Let me see what Raymond wants now."

KP looked back at the doorway and told her, "I guess it's some things y'all did not get to discuss yesterday."

"Stop being so damn jealous, Kevin. If I wanted to be with another nigga, I would have done so by now." She walked past him and into the front room as if nothing had happened. "Raymond, what's up?"

"He's taking me out to eat tonight and you're invited," Somolia said.

Silvia slowed her stride and looked from Somolia to the other women and told her, "Oh, okay then. I see, you pissing on trees now, huh?"

"No." Somolia winked at Raymond and told Silvia, "I know what to piss on."

"I'll bet you do, Somolia, with your freaky ass. Don't pay that woman any mind, Raymond."

Somolia said to Raymond, "Not mind, honey, money. Pay me with money."

Raymond looked towards KP and told him, "I don't know how you do it, man."

"You got to know how to overlook shit around here," KP told him, while looking at his wife.

"Whatever," Somolia and Silvia said in unison.

"What's up, Raymond, do we need to step in my office for some privacy or what?" Silvia knew that was a blow for her husband and when seeing him walking out of the double doors, she knew it was felt.

"Naw, I was just stopping by to see what was going on and to see who was doing it." He looked over at Somolia and told her, "I might be trying to get pissed on tonight."

"Well, half a drink and twenty dollars will definitely get you that. Ain't that right, Somolia?" Silvia laughed, walked to the door to see KP leaning against his truck and added, "Let me go out here and rub this nigga's dick right quick."

"I wish I had me a dick to rub." Somolia winked at Raymond and offered him a seat at the station next to hers. "Come sit down, Raymond, so you can tell me what you're going to do to me tonight."

Diamond laughed when noticing she'd made the drive to the Three Rivers Federal Facility a full thirty minutes faster than she and Chris did in the Rolls Royce. After folding her signature Chanel shades and sliding them into her clutch, she made her way to the electronic doors. Today she wore a loose fitting silk blouse and a pair of flared trousers that accented her thin frame and long legs. She knew she was looking as good as the money she spent to do so.

"Excuse me, ma'am?"

Diamond turned to see a couple that looked to be in their late thirties and smiled. "What's up?"

"Do you model? 'Cause you are absolutely gorgeous," the woman asked her, while her husband looked on with admiration.

"Um, not anymore," she lied.

"I told you we'd seen her somewhere before," the guy told his wife as they made their way to the parking lot.

After waiting for her brother for every bit of ten minutes, she stood and was about to inquire about him until she saw him walk through the door at the opposite end of the room.

"I was just about to come and get you," she told him, before jumping into her brother's embrace.

"Your patience still messing with you, I see." He kissed his sister's forehead and held her at arm's length. "You looking real good, sis." He fixed a strand of hair that fell onto her face. "Your crazy ass is supposed to be on a billboard somewhere." He shook his head and allowed her to seat herself. That was something she'd want.

"Just give me a little more time, Bro. I'm making some moves and if everything moves like I want it, I'm going to paint my shit in the sky." Her smile spoke volumes as well as showed him her promise.

"I still don't like you getting caught up in this shit, Diamond, but you're looking like money."

"Nigga, don't start that shit. You sounding like a choir is supposed to pull up on us or something."

Antonio looked around the room towards the vending machines. "Where's Chris?"

Nigga had to spend some time with his girl, she's tripping on us being together twenty-four seven."

"Hell, you would too."

"You know I'm not the type to sweat no nigga." Antonio laughed at her.

"What?"

"That's because you haven't had one, Diamond."

"Whatever, niggas get at me every day," she lied.

"Yeah, right."

"I'm for real, nigga. A nigga pulled up on me the other day at the light, waving and shit."

"Waving?"

"Hell yeah, at first I thought the nigga wanted to lose some money, 'cause he was in one of those Audi RB's and I was in the Calloway, but the nigga just kept staring at a bitch like he knew me or something."

"Where you was at?"

"Dallas."

"Dallas? What the hell you doing in Dallas, Diamond?" Antonio got serious.

"Picking up some money. Chris was with me," she told him, knowing he'd find comfort in that if nothing else.

"So, what this nigga look like, Diamond?"

"I didn't really pay any attention like that, but he was a very attractive, clean-cut dude."

"When are you gonna get a nigga and sit your ass down some-where?"

"A nigga's numbers are going to have to double mines just to get some conversation, so let's say, never."

Antonio shook his head and told her, "Money ain't going to buy you love, Diamond. Matter of fact, you're going to be wanting to give it all just to keep it."

"Keep what?" Diamond asked.

Love, true love."

"There you go with that shit. I'm not looking for no love right now, nigga. I'm on my grind full-time and any time after that."

"Love finds you when you least expect it, Diamond. Don't say I didn't tell you."

Diamond just looked at her brother, because this was a topic they hadn't talked about in a while and now that they were, she was hoping like hell he hadn't heard anything negative from his appeal attorneys. "What's up, Bro? Why you getting all soft on me?"

"I'm not getting soft on you. I would love for you to find you a good man and settle down. One of us needs to."

She watched her brother speak of a life outside of the prison's confines and outside of the life they both lived. She watched the way he smiled when envisioning her perform the duties of a married woman living the good life, and as beautiful as he painted them himself, she had a picture of her own to paint.

"I'm going to run all this shit, Bro, and if a dollar is made out here, we gonna get a dime of it. A couple hundred million and I'm out, Bro. I'm out."

"A couple of hundred million? What the fuck you smoking out there? Shit, when we was coming up in the game, we told ourselves a million was the goal and you talking about a couple of hundred million. How long you think you got, Diamond, 'cause the players don't last that long."

"That's why you get motherfuckers to play it for you."

"The only way you're going to see numbers like that, is if you step outside the game and build on something elsewhere."

Diamond leaned forward and smiled. "That's why I'm thinking about going into property investments, hotels, vending and construction. I already got the players, Bro. All I got to do now is put the team together."

Antonio listened to his sister and the plans she had for herself and as much as he wanted to believe in it, he didn't want her to put too much belief into it. He himself had dreams and plans, but the game dealt a different hand. A hand he had no choice but to play.

"I'm telling you, Bro, I got this shit. Just ride with ya little sister. We gonna be alright. I promise you that."

When seeing his sister walk towards the doors of the visitation room, Antonio McClendon said a short and silent prayer for the woman that just walked out. He prayed this wouldn't be the last time he saw her and also prayed that instead of her finding her downfall, she'd find that true love. That love would pull her from the hate she was tangling herself in.

Nicole Goosby

Chapter Nine

KP walked around to the driver's side of his truck, climbed in and slammed the door. He'd secured several contracts throughout the city and was looking to make a nice return, but when looking at the twenty-nine thousand five hundred dollars check, he couldn't help but remember that one check given to his wife that dwarfed his better efforts. On top of all the things they were dealing with, she still expressed her need to go to Miami the following weekend. He'd personally asked her if there was something wrong with their marriage and instead of her giving him the answer he hoped for, she only told him, "If you think there's something wrong, then I guess there is." Thinking of the things he'd have to do to secure his marriage, he kept drawing blanks and this was the reason he was lost in the thoughts he was having.

Q climbed into the truck and immediately noticed the sour mood his friend was in and instead of offering words of both encouragement and comfort, he told him, "At least wipe your nose. You running around here crying about the shit, ain't doing nothing. You need to be checking that nigga Dell. The way you was looking at that little ass check, you could have fooled me."

KP replied, "That little ass check just means you got a little ass check coming. How about that, and guess what, I'm going to have to give that to you Friday."

"Friday?"

"Yeah, nigga, Friday." KP rolled his eyes and pulled out of the parking lot and headed for the bank.

"That's fucked up, nigga. I wished you would have told me that shit before I climbed out of my bed this morning. Your ass would have been working by your damn self today."

She said something about going to Miami this weekend," KP told him without thinking.

"What, what the hell you talking about?"

"Nothing."

"Nothing? Sound like something to me. Who's she going with, Dell?"

"The hell if I know. He might have something to do with it though."

Q shook his head and told him, "Now you know why the check came. He wants her to meet up with him, so they can fuck around and now she playing you like some random shit got her needing to go to Miami."

"That's what it looks like, huh?" KP agreed.

"Hell yeah, nigga. He's showing her the choice she should have made. Your broke ass ain't got it like he do and he showing you and her."

"You think so?" KP looked over at his friend and instead of defending his wife, he said, "I'm not going to keep going through this shit with her."

"I know I wouldn't. I would have canceled her ass."

"Here I am, breaking my fucking back, trying to bring something to the table and as soon as a nigga pull up with a big ass check, she's telling me she has to go to Miami for some shit for Diamond."

"For Diamond? What the hell she got to go for her for? They doing that cousin shit, homie. You know they're going to lie for each other."

KP thought about the words his friend spoke and knowing that was something they always did, he made a left at the nearest light and headed for the Totally Awesome Hair Salon.

Seeing them change course, Q frowned and asked, "Where we going, nigga?"

"We going to Miami too."

"Nigga, you'd better take your ass to the bank and get some more money first, 'cause that little ass shit you got ain't gonna do nothing but get a nigga lost, and besides, do you even know which parts of Miami they going?" Seeing his friend's mind spin, Q told him, "That's fucked up."

***

Camille was completing a call with one of the guys she dealt with, when she saw King's Cadillac C6 pull around to the back of the house. He'd called her earlier to make sure she'd be in pocket, because there were some things he wanted to discuss with her before her trusted bodyguard arrived for the day. She had more than a pretty good idea of the nature of the discussions he wanted to have and now that he was there, it was time to get it over and done with. As soon as she heard the beep of the security system, she walked into her den area, pulled a medium-sized rat from the box Buddy brought her the day before, and threw it in the aquarium where her five-and-a-half-foot ball python awaited his meal. She was watching the prey and predator dance when King walked in behind her.

"Feeding your alter ego, huh?" King told her after sitting the groceries he brought on the marble counter.

"Very funny, Kengyon. Very funny," she told him, before turning to tie the curtains of her floor to ceiling windows.

"You know what, Camille?"

"I don't think I've had the honor of meeting her yet. You should bring her by sometimes." Camille busied herself around the house hoping it would hurry the situation along. Well, I owe you an apology."

"For what this time, King?"

"I haven't exactly been showing you the trust I should have for you and I'm sorry, Camille."

"Isn't that sweet," she told him without a hint of emotion. "I never even noticed in the first place."

King walked up behind her and spun her to where she faced him. He looked down at her and smiled. "You are my superwoman, you know that, right?"

"Am I?"

"Always have been." King kissed her forehead, pulled her to him and smiled.

"What did you do, Kengyon Johnson?" Camille pushed herself from him and frowned.

"Why is it that I have to have done something, Camille? I'm just hugging my best friend. Is there a crime in that?"

"Snakes hug their prey before devouring them also, King."

"Oh, so now I'm the snake?"

"Are you?"

"Would a snake give you this?" King reached into his pocket and pulled out a Cartier box, held it before her and opened it.

Instead of reaching for the multi-carat diamond necklace, she looked up at him and said, "My loyalty for you is weighed in carats now?"

"Not at all, Camille, not at all." King took the necklace and clamped it behind her neck.

"It's cold."

"Ice usually is." He then walked her to the mirrors above the aquarium and looked into the mirror also. He smiled when seeing the colors dance around her neck, but when he looked into her eyes, his smile faded. His thoughts taking him back to the woman he pulled up alongside at the light, back to the day he thought he saw the love of his life.

"You hear me, King?"

"Huh, what you say?"

"I said, I like it, but I already have two similar to it."

"Oh, yeah, that's why I got this to go with it." He then pulled out another box and opened it, exposing the matching bracelet.

"How much did you spend on this, King?"

"A little of nothing," he lied. When selecting the set, he at first questioned the twenty-five thousand dollar price tag, but when thinking about who it was for, it didn't even matter. All he knew was that it would have to cost more than any piece of jewelry he'd ever brought a woman before.

"Still throwing your money away, I see."

King walked back towards the kitchen and told her, "I want you to look good in Miami. I need you to look like money."

"So, that's what this is all about." Camille shook the diamonds around her wrist and laughed. "I knew all that superwoman shit was a front for something."

"Is that what you think?"

"Hard to think of it any other way, King."

***

Raymond was awakened by a warm sucking sensation and the popping sounds she made, along with the gags and moans she managed, had gotten him harder and harder and before he knew it, he was thrusting his hips to the rhythm she held.

"Shit, Somolia."

"Ummm, umm." With one hand she squeezed and jerked at the base of his penis and with the other, she pinched and rubbed her clitoris as fast as she could. Instead of her being the drunkard last night, he found his way to the bottom of a couple of bottles of Cîroc and half dozen shots of cognac. As soon as they found the inside of Raymond's home, they wrestled out of their clothes and he chased her around the multi-roomed mansion. The positions he was able to put her in, both surprised and amazed him, and even after he came three times straight, she was still able to get him hard again.

Feeling himself about to come, he reached and pulled her up by the shoulders and pushed his tongue into her mouth. "Umm, girl, you trying to kill me or what?"

"Just trying to satisfy my man," Somolia told him before squatting over him and inserting his penis into her wet, meaty pussy. Her short fat fingers only gripped half of his girth, but her pussy was able, to take all eight-and-a-half inches of him.

"You like that, babe, you like when I do it like that?" she asked, while grinding into him.

Instead of responding verbally, Raymond grabbed each side of her thick waist and began pulling her down and thrusting upward faster and faster. The spanking sounds their flesh made, along with the moans and grunts filled the room and when feeling her tense up, Raymond flipped her onto her back and raised her left leg, his angled strokes causing her both pleasure and pain.

"I need this, Raymond. I need this, baby."

"Umm-hmm." Raymond bit his lip, wiped the sweat that threatened to fall onto her and continued his stroke, and when seeing the thick creamy cum streak his manhood, he bent down and began sucking her clitoris and swallowing her orgasm.

Knowing what men liked, Somolia screamed her pleasure, pushed at his head and tried to backpedal. "Okay, Raymond. Okay!"

"Pussy taste like some bubble gum or something." He stood, placed both his hands on his waist and said, "So you just going to leave me like this?" He looked down at his throbbing erection and made it jump.

"You stretching my pussy out, Raymond and my damn jaws hurting like hell." Somolia rolled her eyes as it there was nothing left for him. She knew how to play the game, but being that many of the guys she dated didn't do anal, she stopped initiating it. Seeing Raymond's mischievous grin, she told him, "Don't even think about it, Raymond. The answer is no."

Raymond climbed onto the bed and squeezed her hardened nipples. "Please, babe."

"I don't know about that, Raymond, I haven't—"

Before she was able to complete her lie, Raymond rolled her over, spread her legs and spit into her ass. "First time for everything, babe."

Chapter Ten

For most of the week, Silvia was on edge and KP could tell. He'd inquired of her role in the upcoming trip to Miami and as far as he could tell, it was nothing but a formal meet and greet for Diamond. He at first thought it would be a modeling venture of some kind, but when overhearing her speak of the money they'd be taking, he couldn't dismiss the idea of her involving herself in the very things she swore not to. On top of everything, despite of what was going through his mind, he couldn't put a finger on Dell himself. He'd called his contact several times, but received no answer and now that the day had finally come, it was as if they were trying to keep tabs on him instead of it being the other way around.

"Man, stop tripping and take us to the airport," Silvia told him while carrying her luggage to the Phantom.

"Yeah, KP, stop tripping with that bullshit, she ain't got time to be lying up with some nigga." Diamond stood on the porch making last-minute calls and after completing her last one she told the group, "Let's get this shit in the air."

Chris had driven Datrina, Diamond, and himself to Silvia's, under the impression that it was already understood that KP would deliver them to the airport, but when hearing his protest, he couldn't help but think of it as a sign that things wouldn't go well at all. He'd personally told KP not to worry about the things he was assuming, but that was now a mountain for him to climb alone.

"We need to be on our way, y'all," Chris reminded them. He climbed in the back of the car and sat next to Datrina. He liked the fact that she agreed to partake in something that seemed to be important to him. He also promised her she'd be able to do a little shopping while the business end of the trip was being conducted. He refused to leave her at the salon, where he was sure there would be talks about all the things he was doing and the reasons he didn't take her along.

Silvia loaded the last of her luggage while KP trailed her and after she'd placed the last duffle bag info the spacious truck, she held out the foreign key for him. "Here."

"You know how I feel about this, Silvia. I'm trying to make this work for us, but—"

Diamond cut him off before climbing into her sports car. "You can talk about all that shit on the way, man. We got somewhere to be, KP, like right now."

He looked over at Diamond and when he turned back to face his wife, she was closing the passenger's door of the Rolls Royce.

"So, I'm not talking about shit, huh?"

"Not right now, you ain't," Chris told him just before closing the rear door himself.

Seeing all the players against him, KP reluctantly walked around and climbed into the driver's seat of the car. He looked from Silvia—who was typing something into her phone to Chris and Datrina, who were having a hushed conversation of their own. He sighed, turned the ignition and shook his head. He tried to dismiss the idea of him taking his wife to some meet-up spot with a possible lover and when thinking of who he might be, he couldn't help but think of Dell. "Y'all think I'm a damn fool, huh?"

"I do believe you think that of yourself," Silvia told him while checking herself in the compartment mirror.

"And I'm supposed to believe this bullshit y'all feeding me about the trip being about Diamond." He looked around for the black coupe and frowned.

Diamond pulled out of the driveway and headed for the air-port herself. She'd been looking forward to this moment for two weeks now and with her first purchase and over a million dollars at stake, she knew her moves had to be calculated as best as they could be. Even before the purchase was made, she had several contacts waiting for her and at the prices she was talking, she knew they'd wait until her return.

Silvia hadn't been in possession of this much money in years and now that they were on their way, she knew there was no backing out. The calls had been made and the deals had been done. It was now that she began thinking about the possibilities of their trip. Since she hadn't spoken with Orlando in a while, there was a chance that he could be making a play for gains of his own. Then too, she knew better. Then, there was the possibility that whoever he was putting in play could have some underlying motive neither of them knew about. If nothing else, it could be the feds were just waiting for them to on board their flight to make a bust. When feeling her stomach turn and bubble, she looked over at her husband and lied, "I'm glad Diamond is finally deciding to do something with herself."

"Yeah, whatever."

Seeing her husband with an attitude, she wasn't about to deal with it at the moment. Silvia pressed the mute button on the radio and turned in her seat.

"Chris, they did a very nice job detailing the car."

"Silvia, do you mind if I talk to my girl for a while?" he told her, knowing she was trying to avoid conversations with KP.

"Y'all got plenty of time for that, besides, I'm nervous as hell."

"I don't know why, it ain't like you got to do anything," KP told her, knowing she had more than a supporting role in the ordeal.

"Just drive, Kevin." Not wanting to add to her nervousness, Silvia pulled out her phone and called the salon. She'd left Somolia in charge, as always, and knew she had some picture to paint that could, definitely take her mind off her situation.

Somolia was sitting in her chair, writing dates and times in her ledger when the phone rang. The rest of the women were going about their day with the clients they had and the chores they kept up, but she was waiting on a call that hadn't come yet. Hoping like hell it was the caller she expected, she seductively answered, "Totally Awesome Hair Salon, how may I direct your call?

"Somolia?"

"Yeah, what's up?"

"Girl, you sound like some mistress or something. What y'all doing up there?"

Somolia sighed, rolled her eyes and said, "Didn't I just finish talking to you less than an hour ago?"

Well, I'm just calling to see what's up. Has he called you yet?"

Somolia spun around so she could see herself in the mirror, licked her lips and told her, "Hell naw, but I just feel he ought to have called me."

"Mm."

"I'm not tripping though, his loss, not mine." Somolia checked her messaging to see if she'd missed a text and when seeing none, she told Silvia, "Girl, he's texting me right now, let me see what this nigga want. I'll call you back later."

"A lie ain't shit to tell, Somolia. You know?"

"Tell me about it," KP butted in.

"Girl, I've got shit to do, Silvia. Call me when y'all get there. Bye!"

Datrina caught the small talk between Silvia and Somolia, and when seeing Silvia wearing a wide smile while lowering her phone, she asked, "What's she talking about, Silvia?"

"Nothing, lying like she always do."

"It runs in that shop," KP told them.

"Girl, don't pay him no mind. He's dealing with wild thoughts." Silvia looked at her husband and smiled. "You can get real silly at times, you know that?"

***

King at first thought he'd be elated to finally be headed to Miami in search of his lost love, but when seeing his carry-on being loaded into the back of his Escalade, his thoughts took him to a place he hadn't been in a while. It took him back to the day when he saw his ex, do the same thing. The argument they had and the things said. It was then that King learned of the power in words. And it was then he learned that when a woman's fed up, there was nothing you could do to change it.

He watched Camille walk from room to room with her cell phone to her ear. And by her sudden laughter and attempts at muting her responses, he couldn't help but think whoever was on the other end of the call must have been saying and doing all the right things. The one thing that he did notice about her was that she was way too relaxed to have done something as foul as his thoughts painted for him.

Once Camille's bag was placed in the rear of the truck, Buddy opened the rear door and stood there.

"I really hope you have things in order, Kengyon, because I'd hate to have to make changes on your behalf." Camille climbed into the truck, adjusted her shades and reclined

"Everything is taken care of, Camille. First class all the way." King climbed in himself while Buddy jumped behind the wheel. He sighed and continued, "I really hope I find this woman, Camille, I really do."

"Well, it seems as if you're looking forward to it." Camille scrolled through her phone, until she was looking through the photo files she had. She deleted several pictures and videos, to make room for the few she promised to take of herself on the beach. Being that this trip was to be looked at as a vacation of sorts, she was going to make the best of it.

King glanced at the photos on her phone and when seeing her delete a couple of him and her at various places he looked at her. They'd been best friends for as long as he could remember and he was hoping they'd remain. Ever since he'd started inquiring and accusing her of sabotaging his relationships, she'd been putting space between them and this was something he was seeing daily. The subtle hints she shot at Buddy and the way she spoke above his head caused him to think that things were changing between them and this was not his intention in the least. He did trust Camille, he valued her opinion and respected the decisions she made with their business, but one thing he couldn't let go of was the fact that she didn't want to see him with another woman.

"Camille, can I ask you something?"

"The question should be, would I answer the questions you asked me." She told him before lowering her phone and looking straight at him.

"I'm serious."

Camille exhaled and told him, "I am also."

What's good enough for you?" King turned slightly in the huge chair of the vehicle and reached hand.

"What do you mean?"

"I'm talking about when it comes to the women I choose, what's good enough for you?"

She looked past him then out of the window she was closest to, her thoughts of the matter spinning. "I mean, I'd at least want you with a woman that's right, King. I don't want to see you taken advantage of or seen as some kind of trick, although you play the part all too well at times."

"A trick?"

"A trick. Have you forgotten about those?"

"I doubt very seriously that any woman would consider me a trick, Camille."

"Then your doubt is as shallow as a sidewalk puddle."

"Because I want to see a person do and be better, makes me a trick? Is that what you're telling me?"

"When you continue to pursue the expense of it, it does." Camille shook her head and pulled her hand from his grasp. King reached for it again. "So, you thought I was a trick at first?"

"Maybe."

"Nava did care for me, Camille. She really did and I know it. She—"

Camille cut him off, not caring to entertain thoughts of her or her name. "Let me tell you something, King. If and I did say if, she was at all committed to the relationship you claimed was there, it would have been nothing to keep her from it. Love don't allow it."

"How could she do anything else, when you threaten her with looks and words, Camille?"

"When has threats kept me from doing anything, Kengyon? When has words defined the person I am without my actions?"

"You and Nava come from different places, Camille. She has a totally different outlook on life and the ways it should be lived."

"Well then maybe that's the problem. The two of you look at life through totally different lenses."

"That, or she was made to look at her situation differently."

"That might have been something you asked her, Kengyon. I've no interest in the question or the answer."

"I loved her, Camille. I still love her."

"Well, then go find her and if she loves you back the way you think she does, then there you have it."

"And what if I can't find her?" King massaged the back of Camille's hand, played with the multi-carat ring she wore and added, "What if she can't be found?"

"Then your trip was all for nothing."

"So, tell me now, is this trip all for nothing?"

Camille smiled and removed her shades before saying, "We'll soon find out, I'm sure."

Buddy pulled into the parking garage and parked in the reserved spot that read, "Supervisor". He'd been instructed to use the space when they arrived. Once Camille's carry-on was unloaded and King's small bag was also, Buddy locked up the truck and followed them into the terminal doors. After tickets were checked and bags were identified, Buddy saw Camille to her seat and made sure she was straight, and found his several chairs back. If there was ever a problem, it would be one he handled and when thinking about the possibility of actually seeing the woman his boss despised, he was sure he'd be able to handle that as well. Either way, Nava was not allowed to return with King. Not now, not ever.

KP pulled around to the rear of the Red Bird Airport, spotted Diamond's 'Vette by the hanger and looked towards his wife. Him being instructed to take them to the airport was one thing, but when learning he had to drive to Dallas, it was apparent he really didn't know the half of what was going on with his wife.

He pulled the Phantom alongside Diamond's car and parked. Silvia had decided to take a quick nap and instead of waking her, he climbed out with a few questions of his own. "What are we doing here, Diamond?"

"What it look like, nigga? Silvia! Silvia!"

"You are taking a jet?" KP looked around them, then back to Chris, who was smiling from ear to ear.

"Talk to Diamond. It was her idea." Datrina grabbed her bag and was the first to board the eight-passenger Lear jet. This was a first for her and she was dying to capture the moment.

"Is Dell behind this?" KP watched his wife as she climbed out of the car and looked over the hanger.

"Where's the pilot?" she asked them.

"He's over there talking to Diamond," Chris told her before following Datrina up the stairs.

"Dell making sure you get the best, huh?"

Instead of answering him, Silvia rolled her eyes and walked towards Diamond and the guy she was talking to. There was no need to entertain figments of her husband's imagination.

After seeing to it that the luggage and the cases containing the money was onboard, Silvia and Diamond walked towards the jet.

"Here." Diamond handed KP the keys to her coupe and told him, "Drive whichever you want and they'll lock the other up in the hanger."

"I'm going to keep the Rolls then."

"Don't fuck my car up, nigga!" Diamond waved and disappeared up the stairs also.

Once he and Silvia were standing at the bottom of the stairs, he grabbed her by the waist and pulled her to him. "You know I love you, right?"

"Yeah, you just have a hell of a way of showing it, at times." Silvia reached up and kissed his lips.

"I'm not losing you, am I?" KP looked into his wife's eyes, hoping there was some way he could convince her to stay. Hoping like hell she wasn't about to leave him to see another man.

"This trip isn't about me, KP, and I've told you that repeatedly but this is something I have to do for my family and I need you to respect that."

"I do and I'm sorry if I-"

Diamond stood at the top of the stairs and clapped. "That's some sand shit, y'all. If I didn't know any better, I would have sworn you was trying to get her to stay but nigga we got some shit to do. We'll be back in a week."

KP looked down at his wife and when feeling her pull away from him he told her, "Just come back to me, Silvia, please."

Silvia smiled. She loved seeing her man's sincerity and concern. "And if I don't?"

"I'll die without you, babe."

Silvia cleared the last step, just as they were raised and quiet as it's kept, she prayed like hell that everything went well. The last thing she needed was to get caught up in a deal this big and this far away from home. As soon as she took her seat, the ground began moving under them. "Let's get this shit in motion," she told them.

"And let the games begin," Diamond agreed.

Somolia was finishing the French braid on her client when the courier walked into the salon. Her not hearing from Raymond was breaking her heart, because they'd told each other some promising things and now it had been days since she'd heard anything from him. Her mood had soured and all the women at the shop knew it and as much as she likened herself to "Superhead", it was yet to be established.

She walked around her station to meet the thin guy. "Can I help you?"

"Yes, I'm looking for a Somolia Rhodes," he told her when looking over the package.

"That's me."

"Um, I have several packages for you in the truck. Can you please sign here?" He turned the board for her to sign and walked out.

"What's all that about, Somolia?" one of the women asked her.

"You know how niggas are, girl. Them and their surprises."

When seeing the huge boxes being wheeled inside, Somolia smiled. She unwrapped each of the boxes as fast as she could and when seeing the expensive gifts, the designer bags, perfumes and thousand-dollar gift cards she knew she'd done her job and that Raymond was now hers. And instead of texting him with complaints of his whereabouts as she'd been doing, she only typed, "Thanks."

Raymond was in a conference with several associates when the iPhone on his hip began vibrating. He was hoping it wasn't Somolia with some nagging text or call, because she'd been crowding him ever since their encounter and the last thing he needed was for her to be this clingy woman that didn't realize the role she was to play. When seeing the short text, he smiled. It amazed him how women settled for gifts and presents, instead of honesty and loyalty. And, if that's all it took for him to get what he wanted from her, then that's what he'd give.

Chapter Eleven

That following morning, KP decided to clear his schedule and chill for the day. He'd called Q earlier that morning, told him he had a surprise for him and that he'd be by shortly. Hoping it wasn't some drama uncovered about Silvia and the guy she swore not to have been more than business associates with, he told KP, "Don't put me in the middle of no shit, nigga."

KP pulled the Phantom into Q's driveway and hit the horn. And, when seeing the curtain in the dining area move, he smiled. "Bring your gummy worm built ass on, nigga!" he yelled from the cabin of the Rolls Royce.

Q opened his front door and shook his head. After grabbing his phone, he slowly made his way to the passenger's side of the imported luxury. He could not believe this was happening at all, and to see the wide smile on his friend's face only set his spiel in motion.

"Throw them ugly ass shoes in the trunk, nigga, and reach in that compartment right there and spray some of that fresh scent around them gray ass feet you got," KP told him, before pressing the button that closed the passenger's door without assistance.

"You happy now, ain't you?"

"What?"

"Yeah, you happy as hell now. Ya girl and them throw you the keys to a Rolls Royce, and you forget all about her fucking with that nigga that's got her flying across the way, just so they can do what you ain't doing to her."

"Shut up, clown. We got the car for a week, we gonna do our own thang. How about that?" KP backed out of the drive and looked at his friend. "Where you want to go, nigga?"

"Take me by this hoe's house right quick. I might as well get you some pussy, since you ain't getting none from your own wife."

KP smiled and said, "I'm not tripping on that shit anymore. I'm going to do my own thang."

"If I was you, I would have kicked her ass, man. You know damn well they fucking around." Q looked around the Rolls and said, "I would have put my foot right in her ass before she left. That nigga would have been like, 'Damn, KP gotta big ass dick."

"Shut your dumb ass up, Q."

"I would have had that nigga tasting shoe every time he licked her," Q continued.

KP thought about some of the things Q said and instead of entertaining some of the things he felt his friend was spot-on about, he thought of a few places they'd stop by. If Silvia could have her cake and eat it too, then he was about to do the same.

"That nigga would have bent her over and been like, 'Did you know Jordan was on your ass?"

As they rode, Q painted the very picture he'd been trying to get his friend to see for the longest. He'd been seeing the signs for a while now and he was more than sure Silvia was stepping out on him. He liked Silvia, but he didn't like the things she was putting his closest friend through.

Somolia opened the shop a little earlier than usual, because she was really hoping Raymond would come through before hours. She'd been thinking of a surprise she could give him herself and when thinking of something cheap and spontaneous, she decided on having him come to the shop so she could take him in the back and show him just how much she missed him. She texted him as soon as she finished showering and told him when to meet her, but that was hours ago. Patrons and clients had come and gone and every time the bell announced a person entering, she looked for Raymond.

All Somolia wanted was a man of her own, a man she could spoil, take care of, and blow his mind sexually. She knew she wasn't as desired as most of the women that frequented their place of employment, but she knew how to keep a man and that's what she felt mattered.

"Girl, why you over there peeping out of that window like that?" one of the women asked, when seeing Somolia routinely check the parking lot.

"Girl, I'm just making sure them bank people ain't trying to repo a bitch's shit. I got a notice in the mail, talking about I'm delinquent and some more shit."

126

"Yeah, they always be fucking up like that," said another woman, who was getting her mani/pedi done in a metallic orange color.

Hearing the vibrating phone, she flipped it over and was about to smile until she saw the number belonging to Silvia's husband. Knowing he was about to hit her with more Q than A, she sighed and answered, "What do you want, KP?"

"Damn, it's like that? I was just calling to make sure every-thing was straight."

"We good on this end, where you at?" Somolia asked, hearing loud music in the background.

"Rolling."

Hearing a voice in the background also, Somolia asked him, "Who was that?"

"That's Q's crazy ass."

Somolia frowned, looked up at the wall clock and asked him, "Aren't you supposed to be working, KP?"

"Took a day off so I could get my 'freak' on."

"You what?" Somolia asked, not sure she heard him right.

"Yeah, you heard me. Me and Q trying to see what we can get into."

Somolia knew KP wasn't talking about anything and instead of wasting her time with him, she told him, "Put Q on the phone, right quick."

KP handed Q his phone and shrugged. It was always that So-molia tried to get at him, but Q swore on everything that the women he messed around with were nothing less than dimes.

"What's up?" Q asked when seeing KP hand him the phone.

"Somolia wants to talk to you."

"About what?"

KP threw the phone to him and said, "Find out, with your ugly ass, nose so wide it look like two baby fists bumping."

Q looked at the phone before saying, "What's up, Somolia?"

"That's what I'm trying to find out. What's up?"

"What you want to be up, Somolia? I don't have time to be playing with you."

"Come over my house tonight and I'll show you, see what you do when this ass up in the air."

KP choked when hearing the words Somolia spoke. He knew she'd say some of everything, but he never once heard her say things of that nature to a person she wasn't intimate with. And, when seeing his friend act as if it was a first for him, he couldn't help but laugh.

"Lying ass nigga. You been fucking Somolia?"

Q placed his finger over the speaker and told KP, "Shut your fat ass up, she's gonna suck both of our dicks, nigga."

"I'm not about to let that woman suck my dick, are you cra-zy?"

"Shh." Q could tell that Somolia was feeling herself, but he wanted a promise for the both of them. "If I come through there, I'm bringing KP with me. You're going to have to suck both of our dicks, babe. I told him you was a fool with it, but he's scared you're going to tell Silvia."

KP swerved two lanes trying to get the phone from Q and after hearing him include him in such an act, he swung at him. "Punk ass, nigga!"

"Hell, Silvia told me to suck his dick anyway."

"She what?" Q asked, not really hearing what was said.

"Yeah, she told me I can suck his dick just the other day and she was serious too."

Q only looked at his friend. The picture he'd been painting him was now coming to life in the worse way. She'd been neglecting him sexually and now that she was off for a fix of her own, she commissioned Somolia to take care of the very thing she didn't want to do.

KP fell silent when hearing Somolia's confession. There was no way he would have believed the words that fell from her mouth, but because of the most recent events and talks between he and Silvia, he couldn't help but believe her.

"Tell her we'll be through there after she closes the shop. You cool with that?"

"I guess so." Somolia acted as if she didn't care, but the truth was she'd been wanting to suck KP's dick even before he married

128

her friend, Silvia, and now that she had that chance, she was going to and she wasn't going to tell anyone.

"Who was that?" one of the women asked when hearing Somolia talk about sucking some dick.

"Q's lying ass. I know he ain't going to do nothing," she lied. She knew Q would be there, but she was also hoping KP would be too. And since Raymond wasn't returning any of her calls or texts, she was going to go on about her day, and night for that matter.

Miami, Florida.

Diamond smiled to herself when hearing the alarm clock sound next to the queen-sized bed she'd been sleeping on. Instead of them sharing rooms as Silvia suggested, Diamond had Dell set them up in different suites at the Raleigh Hotel, which sat on the beach. She'd been to Miami several times, but this was the first time she was there to conduct a business deal worth over one million dollars. It was usually her brother doing his thing, but now that she was in the driver's seat, she was enjoying it in the worst way. Silvia already told her a car would be sent for them later that night and for her to just chill out and relax a bit. Datrina had hoped to go shopping, but Chris talked her out of it, not wanting to be seen before they were able to see. This was why Diamond picked up her room phone and paged them.

Datrina answered on the third ring. She and Chris had made love most of the night and as happy as she was, she still wanted to get out and see the sights.

"Hello?" she answered.

"Y'all finished sucking on each other yet, or what?"

"Diamond? Girl, why aren't you asleep?"

"Asleep? Shit, I'm starving, what's up?" Diamond stood, walked over to the wall-length mirror and looked over her figure. Even though she wasn't modeling for anyone, she still felt keeping her model-like figure was imperative. Even in her Victoria's Secret bra and panties, she still knew she was a prize worth winning and thinking of just that, she told Datrina, "Let's go down by the pool and do breakfast, and wear that lime green two-piece too."

After hanging up the phone with Datrina, she called Silvia to make sure the day's events were still on.

"Good morning, Diamond, what's up?" Silvia asked, knowing full well who the caller was. Patience wasn't one of Diamond's strongest suits, and if anyone was ready to get the day over and done with, it was her.

"I'm starving, cuz, let's go down by the pool and get some-thing to eat."

"They do have room service, Diamond, try that."

"Well, you stay cooped up in the suite if you want, me and Datrina are about to clown by the pool."

"You're supposed to be laying low until after the deal is done, Diamond."

"We're just going to sit by a damn pool, Silvia, you acting like we about to buy out the bar or something."

"Well, go ahead and stay out of trouble. The last thing we need is an altercation that involves the authorities, Diamond."

"Well, you go back to sleep. Me and Datrina will be by there later."

Diamond showered, lotioned and chose a yellow and peach two-piece bikini, that showed all the reasons she should have been a model. After touching up her hair and powdering her face, she grabbed the see-through wrap, tied it around her waist and headed down the hallway to Chris and Datrina's suite.

It was now she hoped there would be a few men around to gawk at her and if they had some balls, they might just approach her. She'd love to be able to tell her brother that happened.

Chris was standing in the window of the eleventh-floor suite overlooking the beach when Datrina finished her call with Dia-mond. He'd been thinking about their next move ever since they touched down and after hearing Silvia's concerns, he felt where she was coming from. There were components to think about when dealing with people you didn't know, as well as people you hadn't dealt with in a while. On top of all there was to think about, was the fact that he knew Diamond wasn't consider-ing the downward pos-sibilities of what was about to take place. Not only was this trip about a purchase bigger than any she'd done, this was the beginning or the end of something much bigger. There would be both strings and ties if need be. Diamond didn't only have to think about the team she was putting on the field, she had to think about the teams that already were.

Datrina, seeing Chris in deep thought, walked up behind him and wrapped her arms around his waist. "What's bothering you?" she asked him, before kissing his shoulder.

"This is where we make or break, babe, and to be honest with you, I pray like hell Diamond is ready for this."

"Why wouldn't she be? How hard can—"

Chris cut her off and turned to face her and told her, "Like I tell Diamond all the time, a hundred dollars will get you killed, half a gram will get you murdered and we playing with over a million. We out of towners and as fair as the game is, we are just that, fair game."

"Well, don't underestimate her, Chris. She's been seeing this kind of thing and who knows what Antonio has taught her."

"Yeah, well I'm still going to be there with her and if she burn, I'm burning too."

Datrina turned when hearing the knock on the door. "Let her do her thing, Chris, but as of right now, we're about to go down to the pool and do the diva bitch thing." She went to open the door.

"Is that all you're going to wear?" he asked, but when seeing Diamond walk in their suite with pretty much the same things miss-ing as his girl, he didn't expect a response.

Diamond walked in and immediately frowned at Datrina's two-piece. "Damn, girl, if I was a nigga, I'd have you in a tub of marsh-mallows, with your chocolate ass."

"Whatever, Diamond." Datrina closed the door and smiled at Chris.

"You make a bitch want to be gay, Datrina." Diamond couldn't help but compare their shapes and looks. She envied Datrina's build, thick and toned thighs, forty-inch hips, her chocolate com-plexion and her small waist and thirty-eight-inch breasts. To her,

Datrina had nothing to be worried about when it came to men desiring or approaching her.

"See, that's what I be talking about, Diamond. You're trying to poison my babe's mind."

"What?" Diamond looked at Chris, then back to Datrina as she walked away. She shook her head when seeing that the bikini Datrina wore barely covered the crack of her behind. "Girl, you're gonna have to let me squeeze your shit."

"Yeah, we need to find you a man, Diamond, you turning on a nigga." Chris laughed and headed for the adjoining room. It was about time he got his day started. "You get at Silvia yet or what?" he yelled from the other room.

"Yeah, she's doing her. I told her that me and Datrina about to go down by the pool and order us some breakfast and she started talking all that—"

"Well, just be careful, 'cause we don't need no unnecessary heat," he told her, before she could finish.

"Yeah, that's what she was saying."

"Well, you ready or what?" Datrina asked, with her floppy hat and shades in hand.

Diamond looked over herself and unwrapped the sheer wraparound. "I am now."

Don't forget we in Miami," Chris told the two of them.

"Yeah, and what happens in Miami, stays in Miami," Diamond told him while looking at Datrina.

"I'm not talking about no shit like that, Diamond. I'm talking about the way niggas approach women around here. We all know what disrespect is, right?"

Nigga, ain't nobody got time for that Madea shit. If and when I feel disrespected, a nigga gonna know it. Plain and simple." Diamond grabbed Datrina's hand and led her out of the suite.

As soon as the Town car pulled under the canopy of the five-star hotel with the beach front view, King tipped the driver two hundred dollars and climbed out. While he stood and spoke with a few of the youngsters hustling at the entrance of the hotel, Buddy was making sure Camille was straight. He gathered her belongings and was standing, awaiting further orders. With a smile on his face that said he at least heard what he wanted to hear. King paid the youngsters fifty dollars apiece, and headed for the hotel's entrance. Once information was exchanged and keys were handed out, he gave Buddy both his and Camille's and told him, "Take her on up, Buddy. I have to make sure the luxury liner sends a car for us later."

King prided himself in the fact that he was able to make Camille worthy arrangements and when seeing she had no complaints of the things he'd put together, he felt even better. While at the registration desk, he conducted a couple of calls and once it was understood they'd need a car and driver on hand for as long as they were in Miami, he smiled, agreed and thanked the guy on the other end of the phone.

The next thing he needed to know was what clubs were jumping at night and if there were any new spots to be and women to see. He saw a few hip-looking guys that looked to have been hustling the area and walked towards them. He knew he wasn't a familiar face, but neither was he giving off some undercover cop vibe. "How's it going, fellas?" He greeted them. "I'm just trying to find out what's good around here and what the night life looking like?"

"I got Champagne Kush and Mango Haze that run twenty dollars per gram," one of the guys told him. "And I've got some xo's, handlebars, roofies, blue dolphins and some fentanyl for when you really want to do some posting."

King smiled. He wasn't a drug user, but knew it wasn't a good look to ask a million questions and not pay for the answers he received and instead of being that person that did, he pulled out a hundred dollars and said, "Give me some of that Champagne Kush." He looked around them to see who was watching them and asked, "Where all the bad bitches be at, which clubs be on fire?"

Hearing that, they all began speaking at once until the older of the bunch told him, "Everything is pretty much the same as it has been for a while, ROB is still where all the bad bitches be, but it be some that escort only and they don't do the club shit anymore. Who you trying to find?"

King didn't want to look or sound as if he was stalking, but it could be they knew exactly who he was looking for. And being that Nava was one of the baddest strippers on the scene at the time, he was hoping they'd at least heard of her.

"Chick named Nava, Lave, Neva. Have you heard of her?"

One of the guys frowned and told him, "Light-skinned broad with hazel eyes, used to dance at Dreams? Man, that bitch strung out now. Some niggas got at her and gave her a bad batch of white and I heard one of them niggas put her up on some heroin and they ran through her and the money she had."

King found himself walking away in both rage and confusion. To hear that she was still alive came with a bittersweet feeling, because she hadn't gotten at him in anyway. He'd been worried sick about her whereabouts and health and here she was, back doing the same things she did when he first met her, and fell for her. To hear that Nava Munez was now some everyday whore broke his heart a million times.

He stopped, looked up at the lights indicating the next arriving elevator and stepped over. He was going to tell Camille what he'd learned, cancel everything else and they'd be back in Dallas before nightfall. Now that he knew Nava was back in the world he unsuccessfully tried to pull her from, there was nothing there for him. Just as the elevator bell dinged and the doors opened, he looked up and saw her.

Diamond was just about to step off the elevator when she looked up to see a familiar face. She wasn't able to place him, but she swore she'd seen him somewhere before and instead of just staring, as he was doing her, she politely said, "Excuse me."

"Oh, um, you. It's you," said the guy.

"Do I know you?" she asked, now realizing he knew her also.

"Yes. Yes, well, we didn't actually get a chance to meet, but I remember you from the intersection of Illinois and Westmoreland. You were driving a metallic black Corvette. I never forgot you from that day." King stepped backward, allowed the elevator to close and told her, "I haven't been able to stop thinking about you since."

Diamond smiled. This was the guy that pulled up and waved at her. This was the same guy she told her brother about, the same one that Chris joked about. She did believe in coincidences, but this one was more than that. "It's cyber black and it's a Calloway Corvette," she laughed.

Datrina, seeing things about to unfold, told her, "Let me go and get us a spot by the pool, Diamond."

"Is that supposed to be flattery?" Diamond asked, when taking his hand and shaking it.

"That's honesty, Diamond. Do you mind if I call you that?" King held her hand a little too long and when feeling her pull away, he said, "Oh, please forgive that. It's just that you've been a picture with no name and now that I'm actually meeting you, I'm tripping for real."

Diamond knew game, but when looking at the guy in front of her, she saw something else. She looked around them, then back to the guy in front of her she saw something else. She looked around them, then back to the guy. "What are you doing in Miami?"

"Um, vacation. Me and a couple of friends of mine are here on a quick vacation, and you?"

Even though she was the one that asked the question, it being asked of her caught her off guard and when remembering the reason she was there, she lied, "Modeling gig got me and my team here." She looked back at the direction Datrina went and said, "That's my sister and stylist there."

King looked deep into Diamond's eyes and told her, "You are absolutely beautiful. That day I saw you, I even looked for you. I went as far as calling the dealership to see where the Corvette was purchased."

Diamond frowned at him, but something in her told her he was serious and to see if he was all game or not, she asked, "And?"

"And, I found out that there were two of the cars bought at a Fort Worth branch."

"Really, they told you all that?"

"Everything except your name and where you lived. If they would have done that, we would have most likely been having this conversation on your porch."

Diamond laughed. "I doubt that very seriously, but what is it you're wanting with me?"

King looked toward the direction her friend went and told her, "Can I please join you for your breakfast, if it's not too much of a problem? This is something I feel I have to tell you."

Diamond thought of the possibilities both Chris and Silvia spoke of and if he knew something she needed to know, then she was about to find out. "I guess I have a few minutes, come on."

Kengyon could not in a million years believe his luck. He'd come all the way to Miami in search of the woman he grew to love, but found the very woman that consumed his every thought. He told himself the next time he ever ran across her again, he was going to tell her just how he felt and now that he was about to have breakfast with her, he was about to do just that.

"Everything is on me, Diamond. And, by the way, my name is Kengyon."

Having heard the name before, Diamond wasn't sure what to do or say and to be sure this was really happening, she asked him, "Kengyon?"

"Yes, but my friends call me King for short."

Chapter Twelve

By the time Somolia opened the shop, two people were awaiting her. She had a blast the night before and was really hoping it could be done again soon or at least again. She at first looked for a text complimenting her on the night they shared, but when seeing no one had texted her, she shrugged and told herself, "I'll hear something later." Once the lights were turned on and the blinds opened, she welcomed a pair of angry clients.

"Girl, we've been waiting on your ass for twenty minutes," said a heavyset woman with worn braids.

"Who was it this time, Somolia?" the other woman asked, before following them inside.

"Oh, just this guy that's been sweating me, I finally let him fuck."

"Who, girl?" asked the woman with the braids.

"You'll never believe me, so I'm not even going to say nothing."

Somolia walked across the salon floor and plugged up the curling irons and turned on the flat screens around the shop. She'd lie as long as they entertained her and with so much to lie about, it would be closing before she actually tired of it.

"Bitch, stop lying all the damn time, shit."

"Have I ever lied to y'all about a nigga sweating me?" Somolia stood between them with both her hands on her hips and when seeing them laugh, she added, "I bet you I'm not, and I can prove it."

KP climbed out of his bed, walked to their bathroom and ran some steaming shower water. He stopped in front of the wall-to-wall mirror and just looked at himself. He shook his head in disbelief. He'd made some mistakes in life but for the life of him, he still couldn't believe he let Q talk him into something as stupid as the stunt they pulled last night. There would definitely be repercussions for mistakes of that magnitude and even though he didn't partake in any sexual acts with his wife's friends, it was the thought that convicted him and would be used against him one day.

He and Q had made it to Somolia's home a little past midnight and once they were invited in, he began having second and third thoughts about his reasons for being there. It was the way he and Somolia looked at each other that wouldn't allow him to as much as speak to her in other fashion than the way he'd been doing. Even after the drinks she made for them and the things promised, he still couldn't make himself violate the vows he'd given his wife.

His thoughts continued to paint pictures of his wife and even when visualizing her with another man, he still couldn't do it. They'd been there all of twenty minutes, when Somolia began taking her clothes off and talking about all the things she was going to do to them. And when seeing Q's excitement about the whole ordeal, he politely stood and excused himself.

"I can't do this shit," he told them before fishing out the keys Diamond had given him. Even if Silvia was stepping out on him that would be something she did alone. As much as he wanted her to feel what he was feeling when it came to the men she befriended, he couldn't do it. Silvia was the love of his life and wasn't going to be the reason that changed.

KP walked over to his dresser, picked up his phone and dialed his wife's number. It would be an hour ahead where she was and he was hoping she was not only awake, but without guests. If nothing else, he was going to tell his wife that he both loved and trusted her.

Silvia and Chris had been talking numbers ever since he arrived and having received a wake-up from Orlando, it was about to go down. The butterflies she had at first were replaced by fear, then anxiety. The sooner they got things done, the sooner they'd be back in the air and Silvia couldn't wait. She walked to the huge patio window and was about to open the blinds for a better view, when her vibrating phone startled her. Silvia looked back at Chris, who was still busying himself with the chore of making certain the money was right. She saw KP's pic and smiled. She answered, "My shop isn't on fire, is it?"

"Hey, babe, what's up?"

"Nothing important, just waiting."

"Well you know I had to call to make sure you were alright and to—"

"And to make sure I wasn't with some imaginary man," she added.

"Yeah, I deserve that one, huh?"

Silvia walked towards the breakfast nook, realized how hungry she was and said to Chris, "You hungry?"

"Who you talking to, Silvia?

Seeing this as her chance to play the game he'd been accusing her of, she lied, "Oh, um, nobody?"

"Silvia, don't play with me. Who's there with you?"

She looked towards Chris, got his attention and snapped her fingers, signaling for him to play along.

Chris shook his head, trying to disagree, but went along with her anyway.

"Should I order room service?" Chris asked, loud enough to be heard.

"Silvia! Who the fuck is that?" KP yelled into the phone, causing her to hold it away from her. She suppressed a laugh and told him, "That was the television, babe."

"That was a man's voice, Silvia, I heard him."

Knowing her next move would push him over the edge, she told him, "Let me call you back," and hung up. There was two things Silvia knew and one of them was what KP was dealing with. He continually accused her of the things she'd done before but promised to never do again. It was something she was tired of and as soon as he called back, she was going to allow Chris to answer the phone himself. Just to show her husband that he worried about the wrong things.

KP saw the red screen glow on his phone, ending the call and instead of accepting what he'd just heard, he pressed redial. He knew for sure there was a man in his wife's presence and he was going to find out who he was. "I know this bitch didn't," he told himself while waiting for her to answer.

Chris hated being the one in the middle of the drama women were sure to surround him with, but he never had a choice in the matter. He knew what Silvia was trying to prove and he also knew what KP was going through, but the side had been chosen already. Seeing Silvia give him the ringing phone, he disguised his voice and answered. He didn't normally play the games, but because Silvia was insisting, he went along with it.

"Hello?"

"Who the fuck is this and what are you doing answering my wife's phone?"

"What you mean your wife? Silvia and I have been dating for over a year now," Chris lied.

"Dating! A year? Who the fuck is this?"

He hated doing KP that way and when trying to hand her the phone, she only pushed it back and gave him the thumbs-up. "My name is Marlon, and you are?"

"Marlon! The fuck you mean. I'm KP. Kevin Pierson, the same as hers."

"The same as her what?"

"Her name, roach-eating ass nigga. Where's my wife?"

"Um, she just stepped out. Call her when I leave, KP, I'm—"

"Put that bitch on the phone, Marlon. Put that bitch on the phone, Marlon. Put that bitch on the phone now!"

Hearing the man curse his wife, Chris wanted nothing more than to ease a broken heart, but by the way Silvia was now looking herself, neither of them was about to be appeased. "KP, this Chris, man, what the fuck you tripping on, nigga?"

"Chris?"

"Man, you tripping with that bullshit. You know this woman ain't fucking off on you." Chris went off and when seeing Silvia walk out onto the patio, he continued, "Silvia heard you, man, and now she's fucked up with me."

"Tell her I'm sorry, Chris. Tell her."

"I'll tell you what, KP, I'm going to tell her to call you herself, man. I'm not getting in the middle of that shit." Chris hung up and walked out onto the patio with her. "You alright?"

"Boy, I'm not paying that nigga no attention. Now he sees how it feels to find out his stupid ass was wrong. Let him sweat for a minute." Silvia smiled at him and said, "By the time we get back, I'll be queen all over again."

"You wrong for that, Silvia. You're going to have that man tripping for real now."

"Sometimes you have to leave a person with the guilt their thoughts punish them with."

When hearing the ping of her burner phone, Silvia held up a finger and said, "Yeah?"

"The car will be there at eight."

Silvia sighed and told him, "We'll be ready."

"Diamond only, Silvia. He wants Diamond to come alone."

"What?" Silvia asked, knowing she'd been the one to negotiate-ate so far.

"I'm only the courier, Silvia. The man himself wants to speak with the young McClendon."

Silvia sat her phone down, looked back at Chris and shook her head disbelievingly. There was no way this was happening.

"What's up, Silvia? What he talking about?" Chris walked towards the window and looked towards the entrance of the hotel. He'd been sure of his surroundings and hadn't seen any cars of luxury arrive.

"They're expressly demanding that Diamond be the negotiator in this deal."

"You serious?"

"I'm afraid so."

"Okay, okay, we got this." Chris rubbed his hands together and looked behind him, then towards Silvia. "Yeah, she got it, Silvia."

"Diamond isn't ready for no shit like this, Chris. She get there and say the wrong thing or do the wrong thing, she might not be coming back."

Silvia fell onto the day chair and closed her eyes. She said, "She's not ready for this, Chris."

"Well, ready or not, we're here now and besides, what could possibly go wrong?" Chris smiled, walked up behind Silvia and began massaging her shoulders. "We're here now."

***

King knocked on the door to Camille's suite, looked back towards the elevators and placed his eye to the peephole. He knew Buddy was most likely watching him that very moment. Before the door could open all the way, he pushed past Buddy and began searching for Camille. "Camille! Where you at, Camille?"

"What is it, Kengyon?" she called back from the terrace she was standing. He walked out, stood beside her and smiled. "She's here. She's at this exact hotel."

Camille sighed, turned to face him and asked, "Who, King, who's here?"

King laughed, he could see the anxiety she was trying to conceal and as much as he enjoyed reading the telltale signs she was trying not to display, he told her, "Her name is Diamond."

"She changed her name to Diamond, King?" Camille rolled her eyes and shook her head. These was the things she discussed with him and the reasons she disliked his collection of women.

"No, I'm talking about the woman I tried to track down in Fort Worth."

"Fort Worth?" Camille frowned, pushed past him and walked into the spacious kitchen area. "Is she stripping also?"

"Hell, no. She's here for some kind of modeling gig," he told her.

"And you believed her?"

"Yeah, why not? What reason does she have to lie to me?" King raised his palms, looked towards Buddy then back to Camille.

"You'd be surprised, Kengyon."

King told her about the conversations he had with the group of guys that were hustling outside of the hotel and to prove he did, he pulled out the sack of Champagne Kush and threw it on the marbled counter. He then went on to tell her he found out that the reason they were there was because he refused to believe in the truths she'd been trying to get him to see for the longest. When telling her that Nava was now strung out and washed up, he could see the relief in her countenance. He again apologized for bringing her all the way to

Miami in an attempt to shame her for an act he thought she was sure to have had something to do with.

After telling her of what he'd learned about Nava, he then smiled warmly and told her about the model he only knew as Diamond. He told her about the breakfast he paid for as well as the promise of seeing her again once she'd settled her affairs in Miami.

"I need to go out and get her a gift, Camille. Any suggestions?"

Camille couldn't believe what she was hearing or seeing. Here it was he'd just spoke about meeting a woman he only knew by some moniker and he was already talking about buying her a gift of some kind. As bad as she hated admitting it, her best friend was a trick in every sense of the word. "Yeah, give her everything you got."

"I'm serious, Camille. I want her to know I'm interested."

"I am also. She'll really know how into her you are if you do that." Camille just watched her friend. They'd come to Miami in the hopes of finding a woman he claimed to love more than any, but here he was talking about giving gifts to a woman he just mer. To her, King was one of the savviest businessmen she knew, but when it came to his heart and what he thought were real emotions, he didn't know his up from his down, and it was about time for him to learn. "You bring us all the way down here for this, King. Are you serious?"

"This can't be just a coincidence, Camille. I mean, what are the possibilities of this? I ran into her at an intersection clean across states and here she is in the hotel in Miami! Come on, Camille."

For one of the few times in the course of their conversations, Camille really didn't have the words for him. She knew coincidence, but this was something entirely different. She then thought about the fact that the woman could possibly be some kind of stalker herself, that went through extra measures to do what she wanted to, but couldn't wrap her mind abound it fully. Either way, she was going to find out more about this woman called Diamond. "Maybe you're right, King, she might be the one. Let's just see where this thing goes. She might be some broke bitch that saw a win."

"Really? I doubt that very seriously, Camille. The woman was driving a Corvette, a one hundred thousand dollar Corvette if I might add, and now she's in Miami doing some kind of modeling."

"Well, just promise me you won't be talking about some rushed engagement in the next month, King, and please don't buy the woman anything other than a single rose. Anything other than that, you will be looked at as the trick you are. Believe me."

King smiled at his friend. This was a first and when thinking about the things Camille agreed to and promised in the past, but seemed to have forgotten or reneged on, he told her, "I'll see you at home in a couple of days."

"You'll what?"

"The two of you can go home. I'm going to hang around for a minute."

"Can you believe this shit, Buddy?" she asked, referring to the giant for the first time since King's arrival.

"Love does that, Boss Lady." Buddy shrugged as if it was something he understood with simplicity.

"That's not love, Buddy, that's disparity and stupidity and I despise both."

Datrina and Diamond had stopped by their rooms to change and talk and after confirming the fact that the guy she just met was the same, Kengyon Johnson that Raymond spoke of, Diamond told her, "I've got to keep this snitching ass nigga close."

"Doesn't worry you that he just so happened to be here at the exact time you're to take care of business, the same business that Antonio was conducting before he got jammed up?" Datrina was careful not to say anything incriminating and after walking through their suite, looking under several lamps and behind a few of the pictures that adorned the walls, she looked at Diamond and laughed.

"Yeah, you feel real stupid right now, huh?" Diamond remarked.

"Never can be too sure, Diamond."

"Well, he said he was just here on vacation, so I'm going to take him at his word until I find out otherwise, and if he is here trying to build a case on me—" Diamond stopped herself when thinking about her brother and the things he continued to school her with.

How long you think you got, Diamond?" these were the words she questioned her with when it came to the plans she had for herself.

Diamond looked up at Datrina and said, "Let's go see what Chris and Silvia talking about."

"Are you going to tell them that you ran into him?"

Diamond stopped, mulled over the idea and said, "Not right now. Silvia's already on edge and if she heard something like that, we'd probably be leaving money and everything."

After locking up her suite, she and Datrina headed for Silvia's. She thought about the man she just met and couldn't help but feel that something was off. He was so soft spoken and polite, but then too, Chris was also and he was as ruthless as they came. Knowing the position she'd have to play to get inside of King's ring, she told herself, "That tomboy shit ain't going to work."

"Not at all Diamond. Not at all."

Silvia walked Diamond through things until she was comfortable enough with the fact that neither she nor Chris would be present doing the ordeal. She made sure she knew the importance of this meeting and the fact that business was to be looked at as short-term, and if there was promise to continue such actions, then she'd need to consult with her team first. The last thing she wanted Diamond to do was walk into this situation with them under the impression that she was alone.

"Come on, Silvia. You're acting like I'm new to this shit. I got this."

Once Diamond's hair was touched up and she was actually dressed like she wanted to be taken seriously, instead of some common street thug, Chris nodded. She would definitely do as far as looks were concerned. "That's the Diamond I'd like to get to know if I was single."

"Shut up, nigga." Diamond stepped into a pair of platform shoes that elevated her will above her five foot ten height. The black linen pantsuit she wore with the low front, showed the silk and lace

Nicole Goosby

bra she wore and the blue diamond necklace. She looked in Chris' direction and nodded towards the two duffle bags containing the money. "Is it all there?"

"Not a penny short."

When hearing the ping of her burner and seeing the short text reading, "I'm here," she exhaled. "Let's go." Silvia, Chris and Datrina agreed to have dinner at the restaurant until things were finished.

With over a million in cash, Chris led the way, Datrina followed close behind and Silvia and Diamond brought up the rear.

Camille had actually gotten tired of hearing King and the plans he seemed to devise on such short notice. She tried to get him to talk about other things several times, to no avail, and instead of faking the smiles that began hurting her face and head, she told him, "Well, while you're planning your next escapade, me and Buddy are about to go have us a quiet dinner downstairs and prepare for our departure in the morning."

"Keep her out of trouble, Buddy. You know how she is." King laughed before walking out of her suite and into his own.

Camille and Buddy exited the elevator, walked towards the hotel's five-star restaurant. She was being handed a placement ticket when she saw the all-black Rolls Royce Wraith pull under the hotel's canopy, with the two all-black Escalade EXT escorts surrounding it.

She watched as the driver walked around to stand at the rear door of the luxury car and when seeing him appear to be looking for someone, she subtly looked around also. That's when she saw a guy with two duffle bags exit the building and hand them to one of the guys traveling in the truck that was following the luxury car. It wasn't until the tall, beautiful woman wearing the black linen pantsuit walked out and was greeted by the driver that she thought of Nava Munez. She and the woman could pass for sisters easily, but the one thing Camille immediately noticed that told her the woman she was seeing wasn't Nava, was that she was definitely much taller. "I'm willing to bet that's this Diamond, King's talking about. The

146

only thing that's intriguing me is why would a model need an armed escort?"

"There's definitely something about her, Buddy. She might not be some broke gold digger or even a stripper, but whatever it is, I'm more than sure King ain't looking for it."

King thought about ways to make an impression on Diamond and the only thing he could think of were the words Camille told him about being looked at as some trick. He wasn't about to mess this one up and if he could help it, the last thing Diamond would know is that he was a lot richer than he claimed. He'd greet her with a colored rose and see where things went from there. Something he did recognize was that as beautiful as she was, she wasn't a model and she wasn't there for some modeling gig, as she claimed.

He smiled to himself when thinking of the fact that she was probably in Miami, in an attempt to get away from some controlling or abusive husband or boyfriend. During their conversations, she was quick to wave off the comments he gave her and instead of them talking about her and her endeavors, she wanted to know more about him. And when hearing that she wanted to keep some things private, he knew she was looking for a way out of whatever situation she was in.

Besides, she knew very little about the modeling world, but so much about life and after learning she was only twenty-five years old, she had this feeling time wouldn't wait for her.

Nicole Goosby

Chapter Thirteen

While sitting in the back of the luxury car, Diamond enjoyed the passing scenes of South Miami. She liked the way her supplier rolled and even made a mental note to at least upgrade her brother's fleet. She was offered her drug of choice as well as entertainment and instead of doing a drug or watching one of the many movies the driver offered, she dialed in on the playlist and selected the tunes of Sade's, "No Ordinary Love."

With her thoughts taking her from the deal she was about to do to the meeting she had with Kengyon Johnson himself, she remembered all the things her brother told her about life and the decisions you had to make in order to live it. The fact that she was about to do this transaction alone boosted her confidence. Also, it created a sense of anxiety. Upon noticing the headlights of the escort behind them turn off, she looked into the rearview at the driver, who was now smiling and nodding his approval.

He drove her past six-foot hedges, rounded yard fountains, entryways and homes that told her she was in a very upscale neighborhood. Once they pulled up to a tall black gate that displayed the letter "M" in its center, it opened slowly. Even with the headlights of the luxury car off, she could see the glowing home. Yard lights aligned the driveway and the front of the house and when seeing the palatial pillars draw near, she was also able to see several huge dogs roam freely. Once the car pulled to a stop, she readied herself and when the back door opened, she was politely pulled out by another guy that stood at the bottom of the stairs.

The entire front of the home was nothing but tinted glass, and she was sure they were being watched by someone other than a security detail of some kind. Just before entering the home, she was able to see around a couple of the pillars towards the back of the mansion and saw a couple of guys unload the duffle bags Chris gave them earlier. She then remembered something her brother told her years ago. "Don't forget what you allow people to remember you by, 'cause the reasons you give for it, just may be the reasons they come for it."

"Ms. McClendon, this way please," said a woman that looked to have been in her late thirties. Diamond immediately noticed that the woman was elegantly dressed and at the same time, lacking the confidence she felt she should have had.

Diamond followed her through a long foyer of black marble floors and huge ivory and marble statues, until they entered a living area that took her breath away. "This motherfucker got money for real," she told herself when walking past three tiger cubs.

"Make yourself comfortable, Ms. McClendon. Your host will be with you soon."

The older woman smiled at Diamond and walked out of the living area, leaving her to admire the art, antique furnishings and the cubs that continued to frolic around the room. This being her first time ever seeing a tiger cub in person, she bent down and picked it up.

"A bitch need a couple of these at the house." She set the cub down and watched it run to join its siblings. This was the life she wanted to live and it was now that she promised herself that she would.

"In about seven months, they'll be sent to some zoo and adopted by thousands of people that'll never get to touch them."

Diamond turned to face the voice and saw a short, plump guy that looked to have been every bit of forty-five years of age. He wore a pair of loose fitting slacks, a floral shirt that was opened enough for her to see the thin gold chain and the huge nugget bracelet on his right arm and the gold watch on his left. His hair was balding slightly at the top, but his facial hair was neatly trimmed. To Diamond, he was a guy you never looked at twice and wouldn't have ever believed was as rich as he was.

She smiled, looked back at the cubs and said, "You can't help but outgrow some situations but unlike them, we have the ability to choose what's next."

"And I agree, Ms. McClendon." He walked towards the wet bar, held up a bottle of cognac and once she declined, he asked her, "The question now is have you decided what's next for yourself?"

"I'm afraid so," she told him while following him to the bar and accepting a seat across from where sat.

Diamond leaned forward, crossed her legs at the ankle and watched him. He was nothing like she imagined, but everything she understood.

"Well, yes, that's something we should all remember daily, Ms. McClendon 'cause that day will come."

"Call me Diamond," she told him.

"And call me, Sergio."

"So, you're the one I'm spending money with?"

Straight down to business, is it?" he asked her with a smile of his own.

"I prefer it that way."

"Speaking of money and business, I was told that I shouldn't discuss either with you, being that your brother was recently arrested and charged under a federal indictment. Am I to worry about that?"

"My brother's situation has nothing to do with you, or myself for that matter, and I would rather we keep it that way."

Sergio watched Diamond over the rim of the glass he was drinking and told her, "So, you wish to keep the money coming?"

"If that's what it takes for me to live like this, then yes."

"This lifestyle's not for everybody. It's only for them that can separate the business from the pleasure—"

"And money from power," Diamond said, continuing the quote he was sure to say. She'd been told the same thing when Antonio called himself teaching her about the game and the way it changed a person.

"You're an old soul, Diamond. At first, I thought I would be meeting some young woman whose face was only used to attract, but you are more than a beautiful face. You remind me so much of my—" Sergio's voice trailed off as his thoughts consumed him.

"Of your what?" Diamond knew he was stalling with the conversation, but when seeing him trail off in thought, she knew that part of the night and this meeting was real.

"Pay me no mind, Diamond. My old age, I guess."

"For a second there, I thought you were going to say, your wife, if not one of them."

"Oh, no, young Diamond. Those were not my thoughts at all and um, I'd rather not talk about her, my daughter, that is."

"Well, one day in the future, you're going to have to tell me about her."

Sergio laughed. "So, there will be another meeting between us?"

"Why wouldn't there be?"

"There are no guarantees in life, Diamond and when it comes to people like us, the less we guarantee, the less we obligate ourselves."

As if on cue, a guy walked into the living area and told him, "There's a slight problem with the money, boss."

Sergio looked towards Diamond and asked the guy, "What kind of problem?"

"It's only one and a half million, sir."

"Yes, there is a problem there."

Diamond looked from Sergio to the guy standing in the doorway. What was the number she was told to bring? "Where is the problem with that?"

"My apologies, Young Diamond, I forgot to inform Orlando that it was all or nothing and being that it was a mistake on my end, you have the option of concluding this meeting now and taking your money with you." He raised his brows, awaiting an answer.

"I didn't bring my people to Miami for nothing."

"Well, there you have it," he told the guy and dismissed him with the wave of his hand.

"What was the problem?"

"It's nothing, Diamond. You now owe me two hundred thousand dollars is all."

Instead of questioning him about what he felt she owed, she only smiled and told him, "It will be sent at my earliest convenience."

"Do you even want to know what you owe me for, Young Diamond?"

"Not really, probably for your time or something."

He then led her down a set of stairs and through another walkway until they were at the rear of the mansion. Once there, he pulled open a set of doors and instructed another guy to open the doors of the EXT. "There's a rule I live by, young Diamond. Always check your work. That goes for me as well. I once gave a person fifty kilos free because I failed to check what I was giving them." He pointed into the back of the EXT and told her, "There's two hundred kilos here and at eighty-five hundred a kilo, that's one point seven and that's why you now owe me two hundred thousand dollars. I only deal with two and better, Diamond."

The ride back to the hotel was the quietest ride she ever had in her life. The toughest decision she had to make was sending the product ahead of her to the airport to be loaded on the Lear jet. This was the first time she realized she had no one to pick up the shipment and instead of insuring herself, she'd become that liability for not doing so. "Never travel with your product in the same automobile," he told her before closing her door. Diamond then thought about how her brother got jammed up with product and money in the car he was in.

That wasn't a mistake she'd make ever again. After hearing a heartfelt story about Sergio's daughter and the life she now lived and the reasons he disowned her, she felt for the man. He'd introduced her to a lifestyle she couldn't understand, and when being told that she reminded him so much of her, Diamond knew he was looking forward to seeing her again. While being driven down the winding driveway and past the yard fountains and high hedges, she thought about King. It was something about him that wouldn't leave her thoughts and she knew it wouldn't leave, at least not until she'd gotten him out of the way and took all he was worth

King sat and thought about his next moves, once he got back to Dallas. He'd personally told Terry to pause everything until then. Thinking about the grievances he had against him concerning the prices he was charging, he knew once they found a new supplier with a better price, he'd more than likely have to meet the demand. As good as he and his team was doing, the expansion Camille talked about in the San Antonio region was now something to consider. As long as he was able to deliver the product they wanted, it would be something they did and if a threat ever presented itself, he'd have to deal with it as best he could. When hearing the door to his suite open, he stood and faced them. "How was your meal?"

"Rewarding, I should say." Camille stepped out of her heels and walked into the walk-in rest area.

"Rewarding in what way, Camille?" He knew how she was when she called herself looking into a matter and when seeing the way she walked past him without as much as a smile, he knew she was up to something.

"I'm certain I saw your Diamond leaving the hotel tonight."

He walked to the door and stopped. "Leaving?" That had to have been someone else, because he and Diamond had agreed to do breakfast as well as dinner, before parting ways.

"Yes, Kengyon, leaving. She climbed into a luxury car and was followed by armed detail. You know anything about that?"

"Armed detail? Are you sure?" King walked towards the patio and looked at Buddy, who was nodding his agreement to Camille's assessment.

"She did say something about having to take care of some business, but why would she need an armed detail?" he asked himself more than anyone else.

Camille walked out of the rest area wearing a dark pink gown and slippers.

"You mind if I sleep in your suite tonight, 'cause I already checked out of mine."

"Um, yeah, but are you sure it was her?"

Camille sighed and told him, "King, I have other things to do than tell you about a woman you should know more about than myself. Me and Buddy have a flight to catch in the morning and I would love to get me some sleep before doing so."

With a need to see her again and hoping it was nothing to the picture his best friend was trying to paint, he told Buddy, "Let's give Boss Lady some time to herself."

Chris and Silvia had been looking at their phones, hoping Diamond would at least text them to let them know that everything was cool. It had been over an hour and Silvia had begun worrying and thinking the worst.

"It don't take this long, Chris, something's wrong. I can feel it."

"Nothing is wrong, Silvia, just chill. We'll hear something in a little while. You know how that woman is." Chris walked to the window and looked down at the street. He was hoping like hell he was right.

"I'm telling you, Chris, I—"

"Silvia, please stop worrying about Diamond. She knows how important this shit is."

Before Silvia could respond, her phone began vibrating and when seeing the hope Diamond displayed across it screen she exhaled. "Thank God." She pressed a button and asked, "Where you at, Diamond? What happened?"

"I'm on my way back now. We all good, I got to go. Bye."

"Diamond! Diamond!" Silvia looked over at Chris and told him, "That tramp hung up."

"I told you she was alright, didn't I?"

Instead of answering him, she grabbed her shawl and headed for the door. She was going to be there when Diamond did show. "Let's go downstairs and wait for her, Chris."

Chris looked at Datrina, closed his eyes and shook his head. He knew how Diamond was and sitting up waiting on her was something he didn't do. "Next time, you need to stay at the house, Silvia."

"Oh, don't worry about that at all. If she fucked things up for herself, then that's on her, but I'm not ever doing this shit again. Ever."

King and Buddy were standing at the corner of the hotel's gift shop when the black Rolls Royce pulled under the canopy of the hotel alone. He smiled when seeing her being treated like the jewel she was and was about to make his presence known, until he saw a guy and a mixed breed-looking woman greet her instead. And from

155

the way the driver nodded and hurried to leave, it gave him the impression that wherever she went and whoever she went to see, must have been important. He looked up at Buddy and told him, "That's my Diamond right there, Buddy. I've got to have her."

"A King's Diamond, huh?"

"That she is," he agreed. "That she is."

Chapter Fourteen
Three Rivers Federal Facility

Antonio walked into the visitation room and smiled at the pair awaiting him. He took in each man's attire and nodded. His associates were looking like success and as long as they were, he'd be also.

"You want anything to eat?" Raymond asked, before either of them sat.

"Yeah, just grab a few things of your liking." He told him before pulling out his chair and watching Dell do the same.

"How's it going in there, Antonio?" Dell looked over his boss and seeing the diamond-encrusted medallion around his neck, he asked him, "You finding religion now or what?"

Seeing Dell notice the medallion, Antonio told him, "My way of finding the truth, is all."

"And which truth would that be?" Dell adjusted himself, straightened his gold cufflinks and placed both arms on the table, subtly exposing the big faced Rolex he recently bought.

Not the one to miss Dell's gestures, Antonio laughed, crossed one leg over the other and said, "You'd be surprised."

You need me to do anything, other than make sure them lawyers are taken care of?"

"Silvia has all that taken care of." When seeing Raymond walking towards them, he got serious. There were some things the three of them needed to discuss and he didn't want one to hear and the other not to hear. Once Raymond was seated, he told them, "I made sure nothing said or done implicated the Circle and I expect for my wishes to be respected and carried out. I told the both of you before I left, that I wanted Diamond to do other things besides getting sucked in shit and look where she is now."

"That's your sister, Antonio, and you know her better than either of us. You know once she has her mind made up, that's a wrap." Dell told him of the things conveying the fact that there was no danger in it. He looked to Raymond for confirmation. The thing Dell prided himself in was keeping things both together and in motion.

When it came to the Circle, he'd always do what he felt was best and getting them to see it was something he continued to do. "She's making her own way, Antonio and before long, she'll be at the top of the chain."

"Or under the ground," Antonio added.

"As long as we keep her under wraps, everything will be just fine, Antonio," Raymond opened one of the bottled waters and took a long swig. The need to make both his presence and his words weighed.

"So, what's the plan now, where are we with our investments?" Antonio changed the subject to less challenging matters. Despite them telling him that things were as they should be and Diamond was right where they wanted and needed her, he knew differently. Not only did he know Silvia had her hands full, he knew discomfort when it came to his sister. He changed the subject.

"Yeah, well, the market is good right now and I was thinking about opening a door in the social media arena. There's this start-up that I've been looking into and Raymond as well."

"I was also thinking about a few franchise salons. I'm more than sure we're ready to put Totally Awesome Hair Salons in at least two other locations. A half a mill would more than accom-modate it and I—"

Dell cut Raymond off and said, "Salons are so outdated and the competition isn't something I'd be enthused about investing in."

"We'll let Silvia run them. I'm more than sure she can handle that. Her, Datrina and Somolia can have their own. We're already looking for ways to clean our dollars and I think it'll be a good source to do so."

Antonio listened to both of them and their pitches. He liked the fact that they were both doing what he paid them to do, instead of trying to follow in the steps he'd set out for the longest. One thing he always told both of them was that they had their own lanes, and it would be best if they both stayed outside the box.

This was also the way he was able to keep thing together when the feds did come for him. Their investigation was so sudden and had only gained momentum for three months. They didn't have any conversations, not one confidential informant willing to be exposed and no records of any criminal activity in his past, nothing besides a couple possession charges and unlawful carrying of a concealed weapon. The fact that it was said he attempted to commit murder was something he was sure would be overturned on his appeal, because there was no victim. There was only a bunch of hearsay, a couple of written affidavits and a few pictures of him with other known drug dealers and cartel members.

With the McClendon estates, properties and cars being under the investment firm's umbrella as props, properties for rent and part of an inheritance from people with the McClendon name, the feds couldn't seize or confiscate anything. And being that the car he was in at the time of his arrest was a rental car, and the drugs and money were in a compartment that seemed to have been untouched for longer than he'd had the car, those were the only things taken and used as evidence against him.

Knowing it was just a matter of time before he was back on the streets, he needed them to go in a different direction. One that would walk them out of the game and the lifestyle they were used to.

"Why don't we do both? We have the funds, the team and the knowledge. It's a win-win all the way around." Before either of them could respond, he told them, "I also need for the two of you to scale back on spending. I'm hearing about all these big purchases being made."

"Why is that?' Dell asked, knowing the comment was made in reference to him and his new home.

"At least until we get from under this shit. I don't need them coming back trying to dig up our shit, because we started getting careless."

"Well, what do you want us to do about our next shipment?"

"Chris and Diamond still gets sixty, send the rest to Austin. We can afford to shut down shop for a minute until things die over. That sixty should hold her for a while."

"Anything else?" Raymond asked before gathering the empty wrappers from the table.

"I have a couple of guys about to walk and I'm thinking about putting them in play."

"Putting them back in the drug game?" Dell asked.

"Not exactly, I'm thinking about something totally different." Antonio looked towards the guards and began standing. This visit showed him more than any motion picture could.

"Well, let us know when you want to move and how," Dell told him, before extending his hand for the shake.

That next morning, Silvia was at Diamond's room door before the service people. She hadn't slept and hadn't heard the entirety of the meeting with the drug lord. All Silvia knew was that they had two hundred kilos of cocaine waiting at the airport for transport.

"Diamond, open this door," Silvia called from the hallway.

Hearing the morning greeting, Diamond looked at the automatic clock sitting atop the mahogany dresser and sighed. She'd been asleep for only four hours and here Silvia was, beginning her day before she wanted to. After throwing her legs over the end of the mattress, she groggily walked into the living area and unlatched the door. "Damn, Silvia, I just laid down."

"Well just get your ass up then. You sleep when you die, Diamond."

Diamond followed Silvia into the suite and offered her something to drink. "You thirsty?"

"Fuck all that shit, Diamond. We need to be getting to the airport so we can get this shit back. Ain't no telling what's happening to that shipment."

"Chill, Silvia, damn. We already took care of that." Diamond took a couple of sips of the juice she poured and sat the glass on the counter.

"We, who the hell is 'we', Diamond?"

"Chris is already there," she told her while showing her the text he sent, along with the huge smiley faces. Silvia saw they were on top of their business. The thing that was worrying the hell out of Silvia was the fact that they'd have to fly back in the same jet as the product, and she was dying to get that over and done with.

"When did all this happen, Diamond, and why didn't anyone tell me about the change of plans?"

"Well, I know you and Chris told me last night you were tripping on the fact that you hadn't thought about us having to travel back with all the things that could have each of us behind bars, so I solved that problem."

"So, now Chris and Datrina taking the risk?"

"Nope, just Chris. Me, you, and Datrina got to do some shopping."

"Shopping? Are you serious, Diamond? We have more pressing issues to attend to and you're talking about going shopping?" Silvia pulled out her phone and dialed Chris' number.

"Everything is taken care of, Silvia. A boss has to be able to organize at any given minute." Diamond crossed the room and sat on the sofa facing the huge glass windows and continued, "You've done what you were paid to do, Silvia, let me handle the rest."

"There you go with that boss bitch shit, Diamond. Have you ever considered the fact that all some people do is sit and plot? Have you even thought about the fact that we're the ones out of bounds and that the hustlers around here know that? Don't even get me started about the fact that people play this game without rules, without principles, and without regret. Jacking or having another party jack you for all that shit, is a part of it also, Diamond."

"Well, one thing I've learned is that when they do come, they're coming. I've made the proper provisions for such actions and I'm confident enough to tell you to chill, I got it."

"Well, I'm about to head to the airport, so I can leave with Chris. I know he doesn't want to make the trip by himself."

"You'd better hurry up then, because he's scheduled to leave within the hour!"

Diamond watched as Silvia made the call for the car and after hearing her speak with Chris about the flight they were to catch together, she smiled. Her plans were coming together sooner and better than she thought.

Chris lowered his phone and laughed. He at first owned the idea that Silvia would at least want to schedule a separate flight, because of the risk she'd be taking when boarding the jet. Then, he voiced his concerns to Diamond about her wanting to stay in Miami, knowing there were more important things to do at home. He and Diamond went over her plans for King until the wee hours of the morning. And after it was agreed that he'd return home, along with Silvia and that she and Datrina would entertain King for a bit, he grabbed all he owned and headed to the hangar.

Not only was Chris there with the shipment, but Diamond had Sergio's men guard them both until the jet was in air and afterwards, there was even a car sent to take both her and Datrina shopping.

King had been watching the entrance of the hotel ever since they'd left his suite. He was looking for signs of both the car that was to take Camille and Buddy to the airport, as well as Diamond at whatever early morning ritual she had. They'd both texted and talked most of the night and he was more than looking forward to the brunch, the drinking and the possible dinner later that night. He told Camille about most of their conversations, but failed to inform her that he'd be with her for much of the day.

While waiting for the car's arrival, he prayed Diamond hadn't ventured to the reservations he made for both of them. He'd thought all night about how that would leave an impression with the woman he only knew as Diamond and after hearing that she and her stylist wanted to do a little shopping, he insisted on being their escort.

"You're acting as if you've somewhere else to be, Kengyon." Camille noticed how he continued to look back at the entrance of the hotel and the strip under the canopy. By the way King called himself rushing her off so he could do go knows what and seeing his actions now, she saw the obvious.

"I'm just trying to make sure you get to the airport on time," King lied.

"Really? The flight doesn't leave until another hour." Camille looked at the time on her Rolex, then to Buddy and said, "I guess we're no longer welcomed, Buddy."

"Looks that way, Boss Lady."

"Well, whatever and if you must know, I have a breakfast date with Diamond and I'm hungry as hell."

Camille looked over at King, rolled her eyes and before she could tell him some of the words that were dancing around in her mind, she couldn't help but notice the redbone chick with the green eyes and the blowout hairdo. Camille recognized her from a date and time in the past, but couldn't put a finger on it and before she could point the fact out to King, who was still looking in the opposite direction, the woman climbed into the back of a Town car and was sped away. It was nothing to see familiar faces wherever she went, but with things happening at this rate, it caused her to re-evaluate the coincidences.

"I know that woman from somewhere, Buddy and if I'm correct, she ain't from Miami." After her bags were placed in the trunk of the limo, she climbed in and looked at King. "Please don't bring any fleas home, Kengyon."

King leaned in, kissed her forehead and smiled. "I'll be home in a couple of days. Hold it down for me." Before Buddy was able to fully close the door, King told her, "Thanks. I'm sorry you have to make this trip without reward, but thanks."

He watched the back of the limo disappear and after checking the time on his watch, he pulled out his phone and texted Diamond. "I'm downstairs."

Diamond looked at her phone and smiled. Now that Silvia was out of the way with her worrying and such, it was time for the game to continue. "He's downstairs," she told Datrina.

"Okay, I'll be down there shortly."

"The way this nigga be talking, I'll know everything about him before I eat." Diamond slipped into a Dior cutout blouse and wore it as a dress, slid on a pair of strappy sandals and grabbed her signature Chanel shades. Datrina applied a coat of ginger gloss to Diamond's lips and powdered her face. And to throw the visual he had of her, Datrina folded Diamond's naturally long hair under a shoulder-length, blonde Chinese bob. This morning was to show King the model he thought she was.

"By the way you looking, he ain't going to want to talk." Datrina walked around Diamond to make sure not a string or strand was out of place and once she was satisfied with what she was seeing, she told her, "You're crazy as hell, Diamond, you really are."

"This nigga the reason my bro locked up, Datrina. He got this coming in the worst way."

"Just be careful, Diamond. You hear me?"

"Careful ain't even the word we're going to use right now. Datrina, 'cause ya girl about to get real careless, 'ya feel me?"

By the time Silvia arrived at the private hangar, Chris was already ready to roll. She watched the security detail pull out and exit the lot and smiled when seeing the so-familiar face. As soon as the car stopped and the door opened, she stepped out to a smiling Orlando. She hadn't seen him in a while and was now hating it.

Instead of greeting him with a hug or kiss, she slapped him across his face.

"What was that for?"

"That was something I should have done years ago." She smiled, reached up and kissed his lips. "I've missed you."

"My world hasn't been the same without you, Silvia. You know that, right?"

"That'll be something I'll never know then, Orlando, but I'm glad you're here now." Silvia walked past him to where Chris was.

"I wouldn't have missed this for the world and you know that."

"We straight or what?" she asked Chris, instead of answering Orlando. That was neither here nor there and she knew the only reasons he was there now, was because of the business Diamond and Sergio conducted.

"I'm serious, Silvia." Orlando reached for her hand and turned her. "I'm serious."

"Yeah, okay, we good."

"Let me make it up to you."

"Make it up to me, how in the hell are you supposed to do that?" Silvia faced Orlando and frowned. He'd left her to fend for herself years ago and she'd done well in his absence

"Just name it and it's yours. Anything."

Silvia thought of a couple of ways to make him pay for leav-ing her and the one thing did come to mind was the debt she didn't want

Diamond leaving with. "I owe Sergio two hundred thousand dollars and I need you to take care of that before I board this jet."

"I got you." Orlando pulled out his phone, dialed a series of numbers and when reaching the person he wanted to speak to, he told them, "Send the old man two hundred thousand dollars, courtesy of the Young Diamond."

"I have other things to attend to at the moment, Orlando, but I will be back."

Silvia climbed the stairs and took a seat across from Chris and smiled. Once things were taken care of, she would definitely return and that was something she promised herself.

Chapter Fifteen

King sat and watched Diamond while she ate. She was absolutely beautiful to him and he even admitted that beauty was a weakness for him. The way she was able to transform her appearance and still look as beautiful as she naturally was, made him look at her in a totally different light. He looked for Nava at first when seeing her, but they were total opposites. Where Nava prided herself with the game she knew and how she felt it should be conducted, Diamond spoke of being a student of life and gladly admitted she still had a lot of things to learn. He like the fact that Diamond neither did any drugs or drank, unlike Nava, who couldn't seem to go a day without either. He also liked the idea of Diamond trying to do something with her life, instead of complaining about how unfair it was.

He forked his potatoes and veggies and asked her, "How long have you been married?"

"Excuse me?"

"I was looking at the ring on your finger and couldn't help but notice the discoloration on your wedding band finger."

Diamond looked at her finger and laughed. She hadn't even notice that. "No, sweetheart, I'm not married, haven't been married and I'm not even looking to be."

"It would just seem to me that men would be killing themselves to tie you down. You're as beautiful as they come."

For the first time during their breakfast, Diamond slipped. "Beauty is deception in more areas than some would hope and at times, it will do more harm than good."

"Yeah, tell me about it." King's voice trailed off along with his thoughts. Nava was exactly that.

"You speaking from experience or what?"

"See, that's what I'm talking about, Diamond. You speak wisdom and you stimulate the mind. I've been thinking about some of the things you said all night and as young as you are, I can't help but think you've been through more than you're telling me. And I like your reserve."

"Well, I doubt you'd find interest in something you know all about and I very seriously doubt it would hold your attention."

"With you, I'm pretty sure there's more to you than profound quotes and a pretty face. You might even be dangerous, a heart-breaker."

Diamond watched him smile and that caused her to smile also, "What?" she asked, now unable to control herself.

"I've been looking for you forever, Diamond."

She dipped a cucumber in vinegar and told him, "I doubt that very seriously, Kengyon Johnson."

"Do you believe in love at first sight, Diamond?"

"Do you?" Diamond eyed him seriously.

"At this moment in time I can truly say, yes."

Diamond wiped her mouth and told him, "There are plenty of things to see and love, so I guess it goes a little deeper than you loving something at first sight."

"I guess I'm a lover of beauty, because I'm definitely seeing what I love right now."

Diamond held up her juice and proposed a toast. "To beautiful things and the reasons we love them."

"To beautiful things and the reasons we love them," he repeated after her.

Diamond frowned when seeing Datrina walk their way. She hadn't realized she and King had been there for as long as they were. Most of the time was spent looking into the other's eyes and that wasn't a part of the plan at all.

"Good morning, you two." Datrina walked up and smiled at both of them.

King stood, offered his available chair and took another from a vacant table. "Here, sit down."

"Thank you, Kengyon." Datrina acted as if she hadn't heard his name pronounced before.

"It's Kengyon, but call me King," he told her when seating himself a little closer to Diamond this time.

"Um, how was your night?" Diamond asked, hoping that Datrina would catch on, instead of speaking as if they'd been up plotting most of the morning.

"Oh, I slept like a champion. And you?"

Diamond smiled, looked at King as if there was some unwritten script to be spoken and told her, "I really didn't get any sleep last night, or this morning for that matter."

"Well, that sounds better than some of the stories I've heard."

Datrina looked at King and winked, making it seem as if he was the reason for Diamond's unrestful reasoning.

"I guess that's the day and life of a model," he told the two of them.

"I guess it is," Diamond agreed.

"Well, are you ladies ready to do some shopping?" King asked and stretched his arms to where one would briefly be around Diamond's shoulder.

"Those would normally be magical words, but my agents only gave us our business allowance and nothing for our leisure." Diamond lied. Everything now would be played to see exactly where King was, financially as well as emotionally. He'd offered to pay for their meal and now she was about to see just how tricky he was.

"I damn near forgot about that, Diamond. That's why I'm glad I brought a little something-something just in case." Datrina pulled out four hundred-dollar bills and waved them as if they were stacks.

Seeing her friend play a low-faced card, Diamond held her winner and dished out a much smaller number. "Well, I have about two-fifty on me. We'll be able to get something to take home at least."

King watched the two as they searched through their clutches to scrape up something and anything. The idea of her being a high-priced call girl or even an escort flew from his mind and after thinking of what Camille said she saw the night before, there had to have been some other explanation for that. Instead of asking a bout of irrelevant questions, he clasped his hands together and told them, "I'll tell you guys what. I'll front the both of you some cash and you can just pay me back later. You know, a little at a time."

"What do you mean by, front us some cash?"

King smiled. "That just means I'll give it to you now and you pay it back later, is all."

Diamond leaned away from him and asked, "How much money are you talking?"

"However much you need."

"Really?" Diamond twisted her lips at him, then looked towards Datrina. "And what do we have to do for this 'front' you talking about?"

King laughed at the two of them, grabbed Diamond's hand and told her, "You already did it, Diamond. Let's go do some shopping."

By the time Somolia made it to the salon this morning, KP was sitting in the parking lot. Waiting for her. He could have easily opened the shop, heated the curlers and did some of the easier chores, but his mind was on one thing and one thing only. He knew Silvia would be back later in the week and he wanted to get a few things straightened out with her, and he wanted to do this before the day got underway and things kept him from doing so.

Somolia climbed out of her Lexus 1S and smiled. She hadn't seen KP in a couple of days and had a pretty good idea of what his unexpected visit was about now. "Hey, KP, what's up?"

"Somolia, we need to talk right quick."

"About what?" Somolia unlocked the door, walked in and entered her security code and headed towards the back.

KP followed.

"What's on your mind, Kevin?"

He looked to the front of the shop to make sure they were alone and before he could turn, she stopped, causing him to damn near run over her. "Oh, um, my bad," he told her when grabbing her waist and keeping her from falling.

In an attempt to balance herself, Somolia clamped into his arms and pulled him to her and that caused their bodies to touch at places that shouldn't have.

Somolia smiled, stood back and straightened her blouse.

"Um, about the other night," KP looked down at the flooring and said, "I wasn't really going to, um—"

"KP, you tripping over nothing, nigga. I knew you wasn't going to let me suck your dick. I know what's up, man." Somolia grabbed her clothing shield and slipped it on.

"So, you straight, you ain't tripping?"

"Do you want me to trip, KP? I mean, you acting like I ain't never sucked your dick before."

"Naw, I'm not tripping like that, I just don't want to start no shit when Silvia gets back."

Somolia looked up at him and saw the dismayed expression he bore and decided to play with him a little bit. It wasn't every day that she got a good laugh at KP's expense and this was an opportune time for her.

"I'll tell you what. You let me suck your dick right now, I won't tell shit." When seeing him stare at her with his mouth agape, she added, "You don't have to fuck, just let me suck that dick?"

"Are you for real, Somolia?"

"It's up to you, KP."

She then acted as if it was nothing and began to walk past him.

KP grabbed her by the arm. "Somolia, okay-okay, I'll let you suck it. Come on."

Somolia stopped, turned and was about to laugh and tell him she was just joking, until she saw his dark, thick dick and its pink head. She swallowed hard. One thing Somolia loved was sucking dick and when seeing KP's inches away, she knelt, looked up at him with her slanted gray eyes and licked her full lips. This would not only be their little secret, it would be one of the biggest secrets they shared.

Silvia was lost in the thoughts she was having and hadn't heard a word Chris spoke to her. When they were in the air, she overheard the ATC operator telling the pilot that all was clear. She looked over at the four duffle bags that sat towards the rear of the Lear and smiled. It had been years since she'd partaken in such negotiations and to know that she not only still had friends with major benefits, but was able to dial in favors without favors, boosted her confidence. She thought about the job she'd done for her younger cousin and remembered the words she spoke about having done her job and to leave the rest to them.

"Yeah, well, the two of you are on your way now. Dell or not, she has access to the same people her brother dealt with."

She sat back and closed her eyes. She hadn't stressed that long in a while and decided it was time for her to get back all the way. Her business was booming, and Raymond had continually been talking about other Totally Awesome Hair Salons in different cities as well. The investment firm he and Dell headed was doing exceptionally well and showed no signs of slowing. Everything was good with Silvia Pierson. Everything.

"You hear me, Silvia?"

"What, what did you say, Chris?"

"I said, I'm going to have to take the work to the shop for a couple of days."

"For what?" Silvia questioned him with a look that told him she didn't think so.

"Diamond wants to play it safe until we get ready to distribute it."

"What the hell she got that big ass house and all them other properties for? I'm not about to have this shit sitting up in my salon." Silvia looked out of the window at the clouds below them and said, "Hell, naw!"

Chris laughed. Them holding the work over at her salon was never something talked about, but when seeing her lost in whatever thoughts she was having, he just felt it would get more than a response. "I'm just fucking with you, girl."

"Matter of fact, where are you going to keep it?"

"If I tell ya, I'll have to charge ya," he told her playfully.

Instead of allowing him to answer that, Silvia held up her hand and said, "Never mind. I don't even want to know."

"All I know is that they'll be gone in a couple of weeks. Diamond's been making promises as well as looking forward to them."

"Chris, why aren't you trying to get that woman to settle down? Get her to doing something other than this shit?"

"You know how Diamond is, Silvia. If she sees it and wants it, then it's just a matter of time before she gets it, or does whatever things to do so."

"She's stubborn, Chris. She's reckless and she's brash and for some reason, she feels as if love is over two moons, past the sun and right up under heaven."

"She'll find it, Silvia, don't worry, she'll find it." Chris spoke just to ease Silvia's mind. Diamond wasn't looking for love and if you were to ask him, he was sure she didn't even know what it looked like.

When thinking of just that, his thoughts took him to the picture he saw of Datrina and Diamond that morning, not too long ago. The way they were looking at each other and what he was sure would have happened if he had not announced his presence. He looked at his phone hoping to find a signal and when seeing none, he sighed, looked at Silvia and told her, "She might even be looking in the wrong place."

With her head back and her eyes closed, Silvia told him, "Hope not."

By the time they arrived back to the hotel, both Datrina and Diamond had bags from Fendi, Gucci, Macy's, Louise Vuitton and Victoria's Secret. They had items from top designers such as Valentine, McQueen, Couture, Dior, Chanel and Christian Louboutin. And, even with over sixteen thousand dollars spent, King never flinched, never complained or even asked the price. Diamond knew it was all done in his attempt to impress her, along with the fact that he knew she could pay him back as soon as they did get home. But to hear him say, "I only ask that I get to see you in these outfits, Diamond," it put a huge smile on her face.

"And out of them, I imagine." She faced him before the door swung open and before he had a chance to step out.

"That's totally up to you," he told her, before pulling her out behind him.

Seeing a bigger wheel begin to spin, Datrina frowned at Diamond and told them, "If you two don't mind, I need to get up to my room and make a few calls for us both. I know they're probably worried like hell that we haven't at least checked in."

"I'm not trying to keep you two from business and—"

Diamond cut him off. There was some more things she wanted to know about the infamous King and he wasn't about to get away that easy. "We're going to hang out for a bit longer, then I'll be up."

King waved over a couple of the guys that worked there and after giving them instructions to assist Datrina to her suite with both her and Diamond's purchases, he held out his arm. "Shall we?"

"How is it you're able to make such a purchase, King?" Diamond asked, knowing there was about to be some lie that followed.

"I've invested my money wisely."

"In what?"

"A number of things, why, you planning to invest also?"

Diamond led him out onto the hotel's patio and signaled for the waiter to bring them two waters. "Maybe, if it's something worth investing in."

"Um, well there are millions of things to put your money behind, Diamond. You just have to study the market you're trying to field, and be sure it's something you want to do."

Diamond watched him for the familiar signs of discomfort. She told him, "You've got to know the market and the players, so to speak."

"Yeah, you could say that," King agreed.

"And where there's competition, you do what you have to," she advised.

"Well, there's always going to be competition in whatever, Diamond, so the smart thing to do would be to just make sure your investments are those you can live with."

"Well," Diamond began, and when finding the words to say, she told him, "If I ever decide to invest in something, I'm going to make sure there's a way to rid myself of the threat."

King held his head to one side as if he wanted to agree, but couldn't. "Put it like this, Diamond, if and when you become scared of a little competition, that's when you need to pull stakes and appreciate your wins or loses."

"So, you'd head for the hills?" Diamond asked.

"Yeah, you might as well, because there's always going to be another investor and better investments, why trip on one or two?"

He shrugged as if the understanding was common logistics.

"How much would I need to begin something like you did?"

"Um, wow, Diamond. I started years ago and just now started really seeing my money, but um, you'd do good to at least have a hundred-K for any real investment."

"What would you have me invest in, if I came up with that money?"

King frowned, looked around them and then back to Dia-mond. "Are you serious?"

"Hell yeah, I'm serious. You think we're here just to make small talk? I could have done that with anyone." Diamond watched his posture adjust and continued, "I know you're doing more than what you're telling me and I'd like to do what you do."

King nearly choked on the water he drank. This wasn't ex-pec-ted in the least and when seeing her sincerity, he decided to see just how far she was willing to go. "You absolutely sure about this?"

"Find out."

"I'll tell you what, we'll discuss this over dinner." King fin-ished the drink and pushed his chair backward.

"I have a better idea. How about we discuss it at your home? If I see a good enough reason to invest, there will be nothing to talk about and what better way for me to decide than to see how you live."

King stood, walked behind her and pulled her chair for her. He liked the idea of having her at his home and very much loved the possibility of keeping her there.

"I would love that, Diamond. I really would."

After it was agreed that they'd keep in touch, he saw her to her suite. In King's mind, this was just the beginning and if he had a say in the matter, it would not be the end. Once he was on the elevator, he smiled to himself. He looked at the signs before him and realized the blessing he'd just received. "A King's Diamond," he told himself before stepping out and heading for the room he'd been staying in.

Diamond closed her suite's door and called out to Datrina. She had definitely done what she set out to do. "Datrina?"

"Yeah, Diamond, I'm out here."

Diamond walked out on the terrace and stood beside her friend with a smile plastered across her face, one that spoke without being spoken to.

"You like him, don't you?"

"What, girl, are you crazy?" Diamond looked out over the beach and thought of just that.

"I saw the way you were looking at him, Diamond, and you weren't faking that." Datrina shook her head and added, "I hate to say this, but you two make a good couple."

"It's supposed to look like that, Datrina. Deception is a very beautiful creature."

"Well, just don't deceive yourself, Diamond."

Those were the words that made her turn, look at Datrina with question and think of some of the things Antonio told her. This was something she continually did when around King and it was now something she noticed.

"Let's go home tomorrow, Datrina. Something tells me I'm going to have to become this wig-wearing bitch for a while."

"I was thinking that also. It just might be time you moved into something a little smaller than that mansion you're staying in."

"Now that you said that, I'm moving into your loft." Diamond pulled the blonde wig off and laughed.

"You know you're welcomed, Diamond."

"You and Chris can stay at the mansion until I get this shit over with." Diamond thought about the person she was about to become when Silvia's words found her. "You've got to become that person, Diamond. You knew the consequences, yet you still chose to play the game, so embrace it."

Once it was decided that they'd do the first-class travel and swap the lives they lived, Diamond's thoughts played scenes of her and King, the time they spent together, the talks they had and of course the promises she made. She even caught herself smiling when he referred to her as a "King's Diamond". And when painting the picture of the way it all ends, she added, "And a dope man's demise."

Nicole Goosby

Chapter Sixteen

It had been two days since they'd returned from Miami and Silvia was starting to think of the reasons she should have stayed. Not only was KP acting strangely, but Somolia wasn't as nosey as she normally was. The vibe around the shop was still cordial and active but something was missing, something she knew she had to place her finger on.

"Somolia, come in here for a second," Silvia yelled from her office. Seconds later, Somolia peeked her head into the doors entrance and smiled.

"What's up, Silvia?"

"I mean, that's what I'm trying to find out." Silvia frowned, and when seeing her friend peek around the door instead of coming in, she asked her, "Is there something I need to know?"

"Why you ask that?" Somolia's brows raised. She sat across from Silvia and began looking at every and anything but her, something she'd done in the past when it was something she wanted to keep secret.

Knowing the last things they spoke of were the things that happened between her and Raymond, Silvia leaned back in her chair and said, "What did he do, Somolia?"

"Who?" Somolia shifted in her seat and looked back at the door.

"You know who, play stupid if you want to, Somolia." Silvia gave her a stern look. It was always Somolia that wanted to know what was going on with her and for her to start keeping things from her now wasn't about to happen, at all.

Somolia sighed, looked her friend straight in the eyes and told her, "He made me suck his dick, Silvia, and told me not to tell you."

Silvia chuckled, shook her head and before she could respond, her office phone rang. When hearing that the caller was a building contractor, she placed a hand over the phone's mic and told her, "We'll talk about this later, Somolia, with your nasty ass." When seeing Somolia exit her office, Silvia half-laughed. Here Somolia was talking as if she had the man on lock, but complained about him not returning her calls, receiving a few gifts and now she's shamed because the man got what he wanted and obligated her not to tell. That was definitely the Raymond she knew.

Somolia walked back to her station and exhaled. To have that off her chest was one thing, but when seeing and hearing Silvia's response, it surprised her to no end. All she had to do now was make sure it was never a topic again.

King and Diamond had been spending countless hours on the phone ever since they returned, and as many times as he offered to drive out to Fort Worth to see her and even have a car sent for her, she continually declined. She continued to tell him of certain business obligations she had and the fact that her contracts had her to where she'd have to up and leave at any given notice. All he wanted to do was see her and regardless of the ways he came up with, there was always something keeping her from it.

"We can at least video chat, Diamond. I need to see you," he told her in a pouty voice.

Diamond smiled, looked around at the many things that made a mess and told him, "I have rollers in my hair and I'm still in my PJ's. I'm not about to let you see me like this."

"I don't care about all that, Diamond. I want to see you like that. You are beautiful and I doubt it'll tarnish that in any way."

"Yeah, well, just let me get things in order and we'll have plenty of time for that." Diamond snapped her fingers at some of the movers and hushed them as best she could with sign language. She didn't need King asking her a million questions about voices in the background. With a few things to do before leaving the loft, she'd moved in and she told him, "I'm going to text you later, 'cause I have some things to do."

Diamond hung up and stepped over a couple of the boxes she had the movers bring her. Being that Chris and Datrina's place was already nicely furnished, the only things she brought were clothes and accessories and of course, her Corvette.

This would be the way she lived for a little while and she was going to make the best of it.

Datrina had seen to the McClendon estate plenty of times, but never really explored it the way she did now. The vaulted ceilings, the big arched hallways, and the closets and dressing room of the guest home alone had her walking and staring in awe. Not to mention, the huge indoor garage that housed cars she hadn't even seen. Not only did Diamond bless her with an experience Chris could have easily provided her himself, she allowed her to see exactly the way things would be. One of the few things Datrina disliked about living here was the size of the house when alone. Even though there were security measures in place, she still couldn't see how Diamond did it.

Datrina walked into the theater room, stood in front of the wall unit and projector. "You've got to be kidding me. She's walking away from all this, just to prove a point?

Chris, knowing the way things were set up, grabbed the remote, pushed a series of buttons and watched the room transform before them. The lights that aligned the ceiling dimmed to where she could barely see him and the huge wall unit seemed to come alive. "Which movie you want to watch while they finish unpacking our shit?"

"I'll check something out later, I have to make sure they don't mess up my things."

Once they were in the living area of the house, Datrina faced Chris and told him, "Yeah, we definitely have to step our game up, 'cause after walking through something like this, there's no way you can settle for too much less."

"I thought you wanted to take it slow?"

"Yeah, that's before I realized we weren't moving at all." She laughed. These were definitely living conditions she could get used to.

"Well, I have to make a few runs and bend a few corners. With Diamond on the other end of the game for a while, I'm going to have to make it happen." Chris leaned forward to kiss Datrina's lips and squeezed her ass. "You know what it is when I get back."

"Well, then you need to hurry up and do what you got to do," she told him, before walking off to check on the movers

Chris entered a security code once in the storage garage and after hearing the low hum on the small vault opening, he pulled out twenty-five kilos from the work they purchased in Miami and loaded them into the two duffle bags he carried. The deal he was about to conduct was one he'd done many of times and as much as he trusted his people, he still wouldn't allow himself to get too comfortable in any event. Diamond had called him several times to let him know she would handle it herself, but he insisted on keeping her away from the things that could possibly expose the plans they had.

He at first didn't like the idea of her being so close to King, and that she'd eventually have unassisted moments and dates with the guy, but this was a game she wanted to play and it was also something she wanted to do alone.

He snatched the keys to his Dodge Durango and loaded up, knowing it would take at least an hour and a half to drop off and pick up. Right before he pulled out of the cobblestone driveway, his phone chimed and when seeing the huge diamond displayed, he sighed and answered, "Yeah."

KP and Q and the rest of the crew continued to busy them-selves with the renovating and cleaning of the Palm Tree Apartment Complex and were looking forward to the nice payoff it was sure to reward them. Being that this project was a spur-of-the-moment thing for KP, he selected seven dudes from the labor yard that he knew did good work. He and Q talked about the situation with both Silvia and Somolia for the past couple of days, and as bad as KP wanted to come clean to his wife, Q had plenty of reasons he shouldn't.

They were loading old plywood and sheet rock into one of the dumpsters they rented when Q stopped, sat his end of the load down and told him, "Your stupid ass do some shit like that, it's going to be something she use to justify the reasons she fucking off on you."

"But what if—"

"Fuck a what if, nigga!" Q cut him off, before wiping his forehead with the back of his gloved hand. "You don't pay shit, hell, I'd get my dick sucked from now on if I was you. What if you did that?"

"I'm not like her, man. The shit just don't feel right to me."

Q laughed, picked up his end and carried it to the truck.

"The way that bitch suck dick, I—"

"I'm not talking about Somolia, witch-broom built ass nigga. I'm talking about this 'behind the back ass' shit with my wife." KP turned and walked back to where the other guys were finishing up and told him, "She said nothing happened in Miami that I should be worried about and Chris did too. I'm just glad she's not upset still."

Q followed behind him and frowned. "Upset for what?"

"I called her a bitch when I was talking to Chris and she heard me."

"And?"

"And nothing. I got mad and jumped the gun and—"

"Fuck that shit, nigga, she just acting as if she was, so you'd forget about the reasons you called her one in the first place. Can't you see how they play the game, nigga?"

KP sat next to the truck and grabbed a bottled water from the cooler and threw it to Q. "You really think they playing a game with a nigga?"

"You're damn right. She all of a sudden takes off to Miami, and that's after receiving a shit load of money, and tells you don't trip because she's doing something for Diamond's crazy ass. You fucked around and let her hear you call her a bitch and now you ain't feeling right. Nigga, you'd better play or get played." Q gave him a self-explaining expression and took a long swig of the water he was drinking. To him it was as simple as that.

"If some more shit come up that points to some foul shit on her part, I'm leaving her ass, man. I'm going to pack up my shit and I'm gone."

Q choked on the water he drank and looked at him with contempt. "And what the fuck is that going to do, besides usher in one of them rich niggas she already fucking? You got to hurt a bitch, nigga. Tear her shit up and shit like that."

"I'm not about to tear up no shit. What I look like, clown, running around the house snatching clothes and shoes and shit?"

"Better than you looking right now. Ya face longer than a football right now."

"Yeah, well, the next time I see some suspect shit, I'm out."

"You ought to walk up in that gossip shop and tell all them hoes that Somolia made you let her suck your dick."

KP stood. "And how you think some shit like that going to look? Her little fat ass making me pull my dick out and sticking it in her juicy ass mouth. Huh?"

"That motherfucker is juicy, ain't it? That little motherfucker can suck the felt off a tennis ball, with them big pretty ass lips." Q was staring at the ground, but was thinking about Somolia and the things he knew her to do. As many times as he'd experienced it for himself, it was still something he looked forward to and still lied about. The things he and Somolia did would remain between them.

"The day you get married, you'll understand where I'm coming from."

"Nigga, I know exactly where a nigga's coming from and if I was you, I'd still be coming in Somolia's mouth, 'cause ain't no telling who coming in Sil—"

"Don't say it, nigga! Don't say no shit like that about my wife."

KP threw his unfinished water bottle across the way and headed for his truck. He'd heard enough from his friend.

Silvia hung up with the contractor and was about to dial KP's number to see if he'd be interested in some work, when Dell surprised her with his presence. He knocked on her door before entering and finding a seat adjacent to her desk.

"Hey, Dell, what's up?"

"I'm just bringing a couple of dollars by for Diamond. I called her earlier and she told me she was going to be here."

"Well, she hasn't been here yet, so if you want, you could just leave it with me."

Dell looked back towards the door to make sure they were alone and when seeing no one around, he asked her. "What's up with you, Silvia?"

"I'm good, Dell, I'm good."

"I mean, you need anything or what?" Dell licked his lips and winked at her.

"Anything like what, Dell?" she asked him in an exasperating tone. She knew Dell's antics and wasn't new to the games he played.

"You know I miss you, right? You haven't even been out to the house yet. What's up with that?"

"Nothing." Silvia shrugged nonchalantly. "I thought about dropping by but just haven't got around to it."

"Yeah, well, you know you're always welcomed."

"I'll bet I am, Dell. I'll bet I am."

"So," Dell shifted in his seat and asked her, "How was Miami?"

"Oh, it was really nice. We shopped, saw some sights, took care of a little business and came back. Why?"

"Well, it wasn't until afterwards that Diamond spoke of needing some money to cover an expense while you all were there. Is she gambling now or what?"

Silvia watched Dell, saw through him with experienced eyes and knew he was really fishing for information she wasn't about to give him. "It was really nothing. You know how it is when you really feel as if the odds are in your favor."

"Well, as long as she's not forming any kind of losing habit."

"I doubt she'd be the one to do such a thing."

"Well, I'll let you get back to it. I see you're in your element, but I still want you to know that the invitation is extended. Come check me out sometime."

To break the silence between them and to distract herself from the thoughts she was now having, Silvia told him, "Yeah, I just might do that, Dell."

Five minutes later, Dell returned with a huge duffle bag and dropped it on the floor of her office and winked. "See ya soon, beautiful."

Silvia smiled, watched him leave again and sighed. She'd told KP that there was nothing going on between her and Dell, but she knew it was only a matter of time before that changed again. The only thing she hated was the fact that Dell didn't know how to keep his emotions out of it and instead of playing the position he was given, he wanted KP to know the one he couldn't play.

King was finishing up a call with the florist when Camille and Buddy walked through the living area of his home. He knew she had conducted a little business with some of her contacts and she was bringing a lump sum of cash, so he had the counters at "ready" just in case.

"Thought you wasn't coming for a minute there," he told her.

"I'm sure you did."

"King, who were you just on the phone with? The way you were smiling, I could have sworn you just found out you were the winner of the Powerball or something."

"Powerball, no, winner, yes. That was the florist and I was just getting a few estimates of a few things, is all."

"Hmmph, that sounds like you." Camille walked over to where King sat and stood before him, blocking his view and making him look up at her. "I'm not going through this shit with you again, Kengyon. If this bitch take you fast, fuck over you in any way or break that little fragile heart you swinging around, I'm not going to say shit." She pointed her finger at him and continued, "You know I love you, right?"

"Bore me with another topic, Kengyon, 'cause I'm serious."

King sat her across his lap, wrapped his arms around her waist and looked up at her. "She might be the one, Camille." He smiled.

"That's exactly what I want you to understand, King."

"Woman, you're tripping. She's nothing like Nava at all. She's in a totally different game than she was." King's smile told her that he was in thought even while speaking to her and seeing him in this state, she felt it was her responsibility to make sure it lasted, and he knew this. "I'm going to see where it leads us."

"Like I said, you're on your own with this one, King." Ca-mille stood, straightened her mini-dress and pushed his head and said, "And don't accuse me of shit." She walked towards Buddy and stopped. "And the next time you want to globetrot, hoping to find some strung-out gold digger, you're going alone."

King looked through his contacts, saw Diamond's number and thought about sending her a nice text, along with a few emoji's. He'd already got with the florist and was looking toward to the arrangements they promised would have her feeling some type of way and to top it off, he was going to get at a few people he knew himself. One way or the other, Diamond was going to become that woman. She was going to become Mrs. Johnson.

Nicole Goosby

Chapter Seventeen

Early that Saturday morning, Diamond stopped by the mansion so she could inform Chris and Datrina of her day's event before they got busy, and to get her Bentley Coupe for the day. She'd told Antonio that she'd be there a little earlier because she had a few things to do with King and wanted to be back by the time he began inquiring of her whereabouts. They'd been spending more and more time on the phone via Snapchat and Imo and today she knew he was looking forward to her arrival. He also hinted a surprise he'd been having for her and to make it seem as if she was also, she put emphasis on how much she was.

She entered the grounds and was walking from the drive to the garage when Chris met her by the doorway. He smiled when seeing her dress and hairdo and said, "That's the new Diamond or what?"

"At least for a while. A bitch got to look the part, nigga."

"Could have fooled me. For a minute there, I thought you was really feeling this nigga."

"Yeah, I'm feeling like breaking this nigga off."

"Well, you know to be careful and you know where I'm at if you need me."

"Yeah, so, where we at on that issue?" she asked, wanting to discuss anything other than King.

"I'm going to Houston today and after that we'll be right at ninety."

"Oh. I would have been off all that shit by now." Diamond continued to the garage, hit the button on the keys remote and climbed in.

"Yeah, I didn't want to front too much before we actually looked at, at least two. We right on the mark though. Don't worry about this end, you just be careful."

"Well, let me go see what's up with Antonio. I promised I'd be there early."

"You coming back to get the 'Vette or what?"

"Yeah." Diamond pulled out, hit her horn and was on her way. One of the things she couldn't shake was the possibility that King wasn't the one to set her brother up, then too, she knew it wasn't something a person would just up and admit, especially to a person you just met. He'd told her about his upbringing and the reasons he felt the streets offered more promise than any job or career and that was a view of hers also. But, when hearing it from a person that had so much going for themselves, she slightly frowned at the reasons he gave, although they were her own.

She knew of three properties he owned and the fact that his best friend, a woman named Camille, often stayed at either and it was nothing to see her at whatever hour of the day or night. The only thing King hadn't disclosed yet was if he ever had a personal issue with Antonio, or the fact that he had him removed from the equation.

For the first time since she'd been plotting against Kengyon, she actually agreed to the fact that they played a game where all could win.

KP awoke to the smell of cinnamon waffles, scrambled cheese eggs, pork chops, and potatoes. He threw his legs over the edge of the bed, slipped on his socks and made his way to the kitchen of their Forest Hills home. The night before, they talked about their marriage and he was once again promised that nothing was to concern him as for their marriage was concerned.

KP walked into the kitchen, walked up behind Silvia and kissed her neck. "I love you, babe."

"Um-hmm," she responded with a mouth filled with egg

"Are you going in today, or do I get to spend the day with my wife?"

"I would love to, but I have some things to do inside and outside of the salon today."

"Well, let's do something tonight."

"Yeah, let's."

After a hearty breakfast and the promise to make time for the other that night, he watched Silvia tidy the kitchen and go about her morning. He'd been thinking of something to do for his wife all night and now that he saw the small window he needed, he quietly scooped the keys to her Boxster and hurried to take the brown envelope outside. He'd cashed his checks, paid his workers and was looking to bless her with the five thousand dollars in cash and the card with a poem. He entered their garage, walked over to her car and with his truck parked as close as it was, he had to go around to the passenger side before he could gain entry. He was just about to place the envelope and card in the passenger's seat and saw the duffle bag and the card that sat atop it. With a curiosity unquenched and a pretty good idea what it contained, he unzipped it partly, saw the cash and zipped it back. He then read the card.

I came by the salon to see you
and would like for you to come
back out to the house.
Dell

KP backed away from the duffle, the card and the car. He could not believe what his eyes were showing him or what his heart was telling him. Seeing Dell's writing and signature, along with a huge sum of cash, he pushed the brown envelope inside of his robed pocket, closed the passenger's door and walked back into his home, back to the lies and back to the woman he loved. "Bitch."

With it being a minute since hearing from Camille and promising her he'd consult with some associates of his, he smiled when seeing her number on his phone. He'd been thinking of more things he could do with her, as well as to her and now that Diamond was making progress with King and the things he had going on, he felt it was time to wrap Camille in a little of game himself. He'd already used some of the money she gave him to meet Diamond's demand of needing some cash as well as bought himself a few pieces of furniture for his home. He answered, "Hello, beautiful. How are you?"

"Wanting to know where we are with that investment we spoke about."

"Always, straight to the point, huh?"

"Why should there be any other way, Dell?"

Dell walked over to his bay window, pulled one of the heavy curtains aside and looked over his neatly manicured lawn. He'd come a long way from where he started and wanted it to be known.

"As a matter of fact, I really want you to come check out this property I just bought and let me know if this is something you'd be interested in."

"Where is it located?"

"Outskirts of Fort Worth, secluded area, few neighbors and a hell of a luxury." Dell turned and began walking back through his home. He'd show her the property and make sure it was something she could see herself living in and if she was game, he'd sell it a few mill more that the price he paid.

"When is open house?"

"Whenever you want it to be," he told her as seductive as he could

"Well, give me until later, because I do have things to do and I'm sure you'd want my undivided attention when I do arrive."

"I have a lot to show you." Dell concluded his call and smiled. If things went as planned, he'd have both cake and ice cream.

Camille lowered her phone and shook her head. She could tell from the tone of Dell's voice that he wasn't thinking clearly and had other things in mind, but what she wanted was to check Dell out for future plans herself. She knew he'd most likely expose the fact that he was on and as boastful as he was then and was now, it would be something he did before anything else.

She made sure her count was as it should be and told Buddy, "We're going to Fort Worth to see what kind of layout this clown's got."

"As you know, I'm always packed and ready to go, Boss Lady." He patted the fully automatic pistol under his left arm and smiled.

"There are more ways to play the game, Buddy and when niggas think with their dicks," she paused and looked back at King then said, "they end up getting fucked."

Once again, Diamond smiled when seeing that she made the four-hour drive in a little over three and a half hours. She parked the Bentley as close to the outdoor visiting area as she possibly could.

Her brother spoke of wanting an outdoor visit and she wanted his friends to see the way the young McClendon's rolled. Before she was even able to kill the ignition and step out of the coupe, she could see guys peeking over the top of the short wall that separated the visiting area from the lot

Today, she wore an off the shoulder blouse, a pair of bell-bottom slacks, and heels. Her appearance was slightly altered because of the aqua blue contacts and the shoulder-length, black and blonde wig she paid over six thousand dollars for. To her surprise, Antonio was brought out faster than he'd ever been and when seeing her brother, she stood, ran and jumped into his arms.

"Girl, I didn't know who the hell you was, jumping on me like that." He swung her around, and told her, "Damn you looking good."

"Got some shit to do later on, Bro. You know a bitch gotta play the part."

"Shit like what?" he asked her before pushing her seat under her.

"You know, a couple of business deals and shit like that."

"Oh yeah?"

"Even got a couple of photo shoots lined up," she told him, loud enough for the people visiting besides them to hear.

"Well, you be careful with that, because you know how shady them guys can be. Have you thinking you're going to be shooting for one thing and you end up posing nude for some X-rated website or something."

"I wish a nigga would try to play me with some shit like that, I'll have his ass under some grass somewhere."

Antonio looked at the woman sitting before him and closed his eyes. He tried his best to envision her in other ways, but that wasn't working out the way he planned at all. Here was a very beautiful woman that just couldn't see the potential she had in herself. Instead of doing something as promising as modeling, she chose to play the streets and the games that had no rules.

"Still ain't got a boyfriend yet?"

"Yeah, I got a lot of them, why?" Diamond lied and smiled a smile that made even him smile also.

"You serious, Diamond?"

"Nigga, you tripping."

"Am I? You pulled up on me looking like this, smiling when I ask about a boyfriend, and you claim I'm tripping. You're up to something."

"Well, a bitch a boss now, so I have to look like this." Diamond leaned forward and fingered his identification card. She liked the ring those words left in the air. "You want something from the machines or what?"

"Yeah, matter of fact I do."

Diamond stood, strolled off with a walk that told the room, she was the bitch they either wanted or wanted to be. It was the same walk she'd been practicing for moments just like this and when looking back and seeing her brother smile his approval, she smiled also. As of now, she was going to be that bitch.

Antonio thought about all the things he'd been told regarding his sister and all that she showed him. He knew the plan and the play and it was now that he was glad she was portraying the woman he knew she'd become. As bad as he wanted her to do other things with her life, he liked the idea of her being exactly what she wanted to be at that moment. He just didn't want her doing what it took to become it.

King walked Camille and Buddy to the rear of the house and after closing the door to her Porsche, he told her, "Be careful."

"I need to be saying the same to you, Kengyon."

"She's finally coming by." He smiled.

"I'll be back later to make sure you're still alive at least."

King stood back when hearing the turbocharged exhaust belch from the rear of the sports car and told her, "Yeah, you do that."

Once they were gone, King called the florist and made sure everything was still scheduled. He ordered a couple dozen arrangements, two huge bears he was more than sure she'd like, and even got her a box of Turtle candies. He smiled when thinking of her response and couldn't help but think of the response he got when doing something similar with Nava. Earlier, he made reservations for dinner at The Cheesecake Factory off Northwest Highway and I-75. Tonight he was going to win at all costs, and his prize would definitely be Diamond.

KP was sitting at the kitchen table when Silvia walked out from the rear of the house dressed for the day. He watched her act as if all was well and when seeing her smile and wink at him, he couldn't help it. He asked her, "So, what's up for the day?"

"We already talked about this, didn't we?" she asked in return.

"You know, you really should take care of your business a little better than you have been."

"What the hell you talking about now, Kevin?"

He watched her put in her earrings, apply a coat of lip gloss and smack her lips.

"You sure are looking good just to be going to the salon."

"I told you I had to take care of some business outside of the salon, Kevin. Where is all this coming from?"

KP stood, walked towards her and pulled out the brown envelope he had in his robe pocket. He tossed it on the table beside them. "I called myself surprising you with a card, a poem and a couple of dollars. But, when I got to your car, I found that someone had already beaten me to it with much more than I could ever give, and he even said something about you coming back out to his house, Silvia. What was all the shit you was telling me last night and this morning, huh?' KP looked at her with teary eyes and when seeing her smile, he backed away. "You're not going to change, Silvia."

"I take it you're talking about the large sum of money sitting in my car that I didn't want to leave in the salon for obvious reasons and I'm more than certain now that you didn't read who the card and the money was addressed to. Your insecure ass can see a pair of panties in the wash and swear a bitch cheating. If I wanted someone other than you, he'd be here. I—"

"You really think I'm stupid, Silvia? You think I don't know what the fuck is going on around here, huh?"

"First of all, you need to watch both your tone and your language, 'cause I haven't cursed you in any way."

"You keep putting me through this shit and I'm trying to be here for you, I really am, but you making it hard as hell."

"Um, I have other things to do than stand here and tongue wrestle with you."

"And while you was in Miami doing your thang, I was getting my thang done too."

"Well, I hope like hell you enjoyed it, because I enjoyed myself so much, I'm about to go back—"

Before he knew it, KP slapped his wife across her face and grabbed her by the neck. "Bitch, I knew you was still fucking that nigga, that's why I let Somolia suck my dick!"

Silvia brought her left arm around over his hands and twisted her body, a move she'd learned in self-defense years ago, which caused him to stumble slightly. And, after grabbing his wrist and pulling him to her, she used her weight and his momentum to deliver a cartilage crunching blow that staggered her husband and caused him to fall back on the tinted glass table where the brown envelope sat. She caught her breath and pointed. "Get out of my house, Kevin. Get out of my house now!"

"This my house too," he told her, while holding his nose to make sure he wasn't bleeding.

"You don't pay shit here and I'm the one that makes sure of that, but you know what, you stay here. I'll leave." She pushed past him and headed for their garage. "And you tell that bitch, Somolia, she can have your sour dick ass!"

KP could only watch his wife speed away. He'd never put his hands on his wife and never would have, had she not said some of the things she did and when thinking of Antonio and what he'd do once he found out, his world began closing in on him. "Dammit!"

Diamond's plan was to stop by the house to park the Bentley and retrieve her 'Vette, but after seeing that she'd sped past the I-20 turn off, she decided to go ahead and make the Dallas stop. King had been texting her ever since she pulled out of the facility's parking area and when seeing his emoji's and several diamonds, she smiled. "Nigga must think he about to get some pussy or some-thing," she told herself, before hitting him back with a couple of dog-faced emoji's.

Once she was in the city, she pulled up his address on her GPS pop-up screen and dialed his number.

King answered on the first ring. "Yeah, beautiful?"

"Good news, bad news, which do you want first?" Diamond asked, thinking of a lie to tell.

"Good."

"I'm in the city now."

"Bad."

"I'm not familiar with the GPS in this car they loaned me."

"What happened to your Corvette?"

"Nothing. They just wanted me to take the Bentley for a spin, I guess."

"Bentley?"

"Yep."

"Damn, I don't even have a Bentley," King told her.

"Well, you know how it is when motherfuckers want some-thing. They go that extra mile, hoping like hell you'll obligate your-self to doing the same."

"That modeling shit seems to be working for you, Diamond."

"You already know what I'd rather be doing, so save that mod-eling spiel for someone else." Diamond acted as if she was laugh-ing.

"There is no one else, Diamond. It's only you."

"Yeah, whatever, Kengyon."

"Guess I'm going to have to show you, huh?"

"We'll discuss this later, because I'm turning onto your street now." Diamond lowered her phone and as she drove past one stylish home after the next, she knew King was sitting on a nice piece of change, and when seeing the black gate with the huge lion centered in it, she nodded. His style was definitely like her brother's. Before she was able to press either button on the intercom system, the gates swung inward.

Diamond pulled past a couple of luxury trucks and a gray C6. She looked around for the Audi R8 she saw him in that first day but instead saw the very handsome Kengyon Johnson, standing at the bottom of the stairs. Off the top, she noticed he was dressed nice but what made her smile was the fact that the man had on the exact same colors as she. His cream-colored linen slacks went with her cream-colored pants, and his beige shirt that opened two buttons from the collar, matched the off the shoulder blouse she was wearing. She laughed, threw the Bentley in park and before she could grab the door handle, he opened it for her. She subtly rolled her eyes at the gesture and smiled her usual captivating feature and stepped out.

"You are breathtaking, Diamond. You really are," he told her, grabbing her hand and pulling her out of the foreign luxury.

"You're not so bad yourself."

"I try."

"Good job."

He looked over the Bentley and said, "A beautiful car for a very beautiful woman."

"So, this is the famous kingdom you speak so much about?" Diamond considered the fact that this was only one of his many properties and it might not have been as lavish as the McClendon Estate, but it would definitely do.

"This is the home I enjoy more than any. That's why all of my cars are here at this location."

"Where's the Audi?"

"Oh, that's Camille's car. I was just out and about."

"Really?"

King placed his hand on the small of her back and told her, "Come on. I want to show you the inside."

"I'm liking the pool already." As surprising as it was, Diamond neither objected, nor placed his hand elsewhere. This was a first for her, but it was the exact way her brother always told her a man should treat a woman. And when thinking of the reason she was there, she nodded. "Yeah, let's see what you really living like."

Chapter Eighteen

Silvia walked into her salon, looked around at the women and clients that were there and said, "Somolia, can I speak to you in my office for a minute, please?"

By the time Somolia walked in, Silvia was standing by the window, looking out at the parking lot at the passersby. She'd been contemplating ways she'd approach Somolia when it came to what KP alleged, but was coming up with blanks. This was something they'd been through years ago while she and KP was still dating, back before marriage was even thought of.

"What's up, Silvia?"

"What's up with you and KP? He said something about you sucking his dick while I was in Miami." Silvia watched her friend for the telltale signs she was known for giving.

"That's what I was telling you about when you first came back, Silvia. I told you about this already."

Silvia just watched her, saw the sincerity in her expression as well as regret in her tone.

"I was just joking with him at first, when I told him that if he let me suck his dick I wouldn't tell. But then, he actually pulled it out and..." Somolia looked downward and shook her head. "And, you know how I get when a dick is in my face, Silvia. I couldn't help it." Somolia cried.

Silvia wanted to put both her feet in Somolia's short fat ass, and as angry as she was about the whole ordeal, all she could do was laugh. Instead of telling Somolia what she could do and what she was about to do, Silvia looked at her and laughed, bent at the waist and laughed harder.

Seeing her friend finding hysteria in her confession, Somolia smiled and asked, "What?"

"You a nasty bitch, Somolia. You sucked that sour ass dick. He didn't tell you he had some kind of infection down there?"

When seeing Somolia frown and look off in thought, Silvia laughed even harder. "That's what your nasty ass get. I haven't sucked that nigga's dick in months and you pull up and wrap your lips around his shit." Silvia laughed until Somolia was out of her office. She knew Somolia was known for doing some foul shit, but this one of them times that topped all others. "Yo nasty ass!" Silvia yelled in between laughs.

Somolia walked to her station and thought about the putrid smell between KP's legs. She thought at first he just hadn't showered yet, but when remembering he was at the salon before it even opened, she realized that he hadn't come from work.

Somolia shook her head, looked up at the client that was now looking at her as if she knew of the things she'd done, and went back to her daily routine. She knew it wouldn't be long before everyone that came through found out what she'd done, and she also knew it would be years before she lived it down.

***

Camille pulled around to the back of the mansion and parked. She smiled when seeing the layout, because it reminded her of King's Ravinia home, only better. She climbed out of her Porsche and saw Dell standing on the second floor terrace, looking down at her.

"What you think so far, Camille?"

Camille nodded, closed the door of her sports car and began walking towards the glass doors. "It has its appeal, but it's nothing to call the bank about."

Dell met her at the entrance to the black marbled foyer and handed her a flute of champagne. "Welcome."

"Thank you," she told him while accepting the chiller.

"The asking price is six point two, but I'm more than sure we can move a mountain with around five point seven or five point eight. No one likes to just sit on the properties these days."

Camille followed him up the spiral staircase and into the pitted den area, where he entertained his guests. Instead of seating herself, Camille walked over to the second story terrace and looked to see just how much of a view it offered. Something she noticed off the top, was that Dell had no security system in place or monitors. She also noticed the grand piano sitting across the room didn't have any pedals. Camille prided herself on being able to play piano and when seeing a grand the size of the one Dell owned, there were certain things that stood out about it. She smiled when thinking of the disguised safe he had sitting in plain view. It could hold a couple mill easily and if she was right, that's exactly where he'd have it now.

"For five point seven mill, I'd expect to have a fleet of fine automobiles to go along with it." She turned, faced him and smiled. "But, I'm also sure we can make something happen in the near future."

"You drive a harder bargain than I thought, but sure, we could do something like that in the future."

"So…" Camille went over and sat at the wet bar. "And what of San Antonio?"

"Um, I um, need a little more time on that endeavor," Dell stammered.

"I'll be expecting to hear something from you soon, because I do have things to attend to and would like to at the earliest convenience."

"I agree."

Camille swung herself around until she was facing the piano again and to confirm her suspicions, she told him, "How often do you play?"

"Excuse me?"

"Piano. How often do you play piano? You have such a nice one."

"Um, it's been a while with that one. It needs some minor work, and as of now, it's just décor."

Camille smiled to herself and told him, "Such nice décor."

"You should see the bedrooms and other living areas."

"In due time, Dell, in due time." Camille sipped the drink she was given. Despite the words Dell spoke, and the subtle nods she made in agreement, her mind was elsewhere. Her mind was on King and the woman he continually spoke of like no other.

***

KP had been sitting in Q's driveway for ten minutes before he even made his presence known. There were things swimming around in his mind he really couldn't find resolve for. He'd put his hands on his wife and was now regretting it in the worst way. And, by the way she spoke to him afterwards, he didn't know if she was going to come home or not, tell Antonio or not, call the cops or not. What he did know was that he fucked up way past repair.

Q had been peeking out of his window ever since his friend called to let him know that he was on his way. He could tell something was off by the way KP avoided certain questions, mumbled at his statements and continued to sniff in attempt to clear his nose. He walked past his kitchen window, saw KP's Ford and went to grab his utility belt and phone. He headed outside.

"What's up, weeny head ass nigga?" he greeted him while climbing into the truck.

"I fucked up, Q," KP said flatly.

"You what?" Seeing the expression of his friend, he turned to face him and asked, "What you do now?"

"I hit her, man."

"You did what?" Q asked with a dubious expression.

"I hit my wife, Q. I did what you told me to do and now she's gone."

"Don't be blaming me for that shit, nigga. I just said what I would have done. I didn't say shit about you doing it." Q shook his head, closed the door and told him, "You did that 'cause that's what you wanted to do. Don't be talking about I told you to do no shit like that."

"You the one talking about hurt her and all that shit."

Q hit the dashboard and told him, "Motherfucker, I said get her clothes and shit. I—"

"Stanky ass nigga, you talked all that shit and now you acting like you ain't said shit."

"No, you didn't call nobody stanky, all that triple antibiotic ointment you got on." You ought to be—"

"Man, just shut the hell up! Can you do that for a minute?" KP tried to sort out the things piling up before him. He thought Q would have some more advice about the situation, but now he saw the man talked just to be doing so.

"KP?"

"What, what is it, Q? What the fuck you want, nigga?" KP faced his friend, rolled his eyes and looked back out the driver's side window.

"You know he's going to send somebody to kick your ass, right? They gonna find your dumb ass in a trunk somewhere. You're gonna—"

"You're gonna be with me too, big booty ass nigga, and you'd better hope ain't none of them just got out of prison for doing hard time either." KP started the ignition and chuckled, Q's words finding him in a place he couldn't hide. The last time he threatened to put his hands on Silvia, he and his friends were surrounded and given the promise that if the other allowed such an action, they would all be burned and buried alive.

"You're stupid, KP. You stupid as hell."

KP pulled out of his friend's drive and nodded. "Yeah, you right, stupid for listening to your ass."

"You think she's going to tell it? She might even add some shit like you tried to kill her or something."

KP gave Q a sideward glance and said, "Umph, would you?"

"You better be trying to find her and apologize or something. Climb on top of the salon and threaten to jump off if she don't forgive you."

"Shut up before I pull over and pour your yellow ass out and I'm serious, Q. I really am."

For the rest of the ride, they each dealt with the thought of being sought out, tortured or worse. Silvia might have been his wife, his pride and joy, but she was still Antonio McClendon's best friend, cousin and business partner and in the world KP now lived, there were and would definitely be repercussions for his misdeeds.

"You hear me, nigga?"

Instead of playing the game with his friend, KP lied. "Yeah, I heard you. I can't help but hear the stupid ass shit you be talking about."

***

After being given a full tour of the house, King led Diamond out onto the rear deck and leaned up against the wooden pillar.

"This is a nice house, Diamond, but I want to make it a home. I want to be able to come home, to provide for home and be there, be here." he told her while looking into her eyes.

Diamond looked away, placed elbows on the wooden support railing and looked out across the driveway at the selection of cars out. This was one of those conversations she didn't care for and as much as she liked the things he'd shown her and the things he spoke of, this was something she wasn't about to discuss with him now, or ever for that matter.

"Looks like a dealership. Don't it?"

"It definitely has the making of an exotic car lot at times. Especially when Camille's cars are here."

"Camille, you speak of her often, what's up with that?" Diamond put her back to the railing and looked over at him. Watched him smile at the mention of the name.

"Camille's damn near like a mother bear at times. She looks out for me when I fail to do it myself. She's very protective and has no problems letting a person know it either."

"Kind of like Chris is to me?"

"Yes, just the way you describe Chris, that how Camille is with me."

"Will she kill for you or should the question be, has she ever killed for you?"

King looked down at her, got serious and said, "I've never really given her a reason to. That's not something you do to people you claim to love."

"And the story goes like?"

"There is no story to it. When you love someone, you put them before you. Their happiness is your happiness and you don't wait for them to give their life or take a life for you, you give and take for them. That's what you do for people you love. But, if love is just a word you're able to attach to people and detach from people at any given minute, then yes, that would be your mindset."

"Sounds as if you have it all figured out, huh?" Diamond looked from him back out into a cloud of thoughts that swam towards her. Antonio had not only told her the same many times, he continued to show her. At every turn, he showed her just that.

She glanced over at King and frowned. There was more to him than she at first thought.

"As a matter of fact, I don't but I am willing to learn and that's the steps you must be willing to take when trying.

"Well, I feel that a person should show that loyalty first, then I'll consider putting them in a place other than one I can easily separate myself from."

"That's shallow, Diamond. No offense, but there are more ways for a person to show loyalty, besides putting themselves in compromising positions, just so you can detach when they fail to meet an expectation you place before them."

"I thought that's how you played the game. You use others to play the positions you need played and reward them for doing so."

King shook his head, swallowed and told her, "There are no rules when playing this game and as soon as you start thinking there are, they'll be too close to you and what better way to get close to a person than to show that expected loyalty? Yeah, you have those that play it also."

Hearing those words, Diamond couldn't help but think about the person she had to become. She thought about the words spoken as well as the actions displayed, and even though she knew he was right, she couldn't allow him to alter her vision. King would pay for what he did and if she had to be that shallow bitch to do so, then that's what it was going to be.

Chris pulled into the parking spot next to Silvia's Boxster, texted Diamond, left a thumbs-up emoji and climbed out. He'd already had over half a mill for the delivery he did earlier that day and after hearing that Silvia needed to speak with him as well as have him pick up some more money for Diamond, he made the stop before heading back out to the mansion. As soon as he walked inside the salon he could tell something was wrong. It seemed all got quiet the moment he entered and hoping he wasn't the topic of some wayward talk, looked towards his girlfriend and asked, "What's up?" He then looked to Somolia, who normally had something to say at all times to everyone that entered the salon.

"Nothing, just busy," she told him before looking towards Silvia's office.

"What's up, Somolia? You sure are quiet today."

"Ain't nothing, Chris. Just working."

To hear Somolia speak without asking of Diamond's whereabouts, confirmed something wasn't right and since no one was talking, he headed to the one person that would tell him all. He walked past them and headed to Silvia's office.

Silvia was taking a call when he stepped in her office door. He was about to turn and leave until he saw the bruise on the left side of her face. He watched her until she looked up and smiled.

"What happened to your face, Silvia?"

"Nothing, don't even worry about it. I handled it," she told him knowing he was going to trip. "The money is in my car."

"Silvia, what did you have to handle?"

She sighed, closed her eyes and told him, "Me and Kevin got into it this morning and I—"

Before she could finish her explanation, Chris was out of her office and walking towards the door.

"Chris!" Silvia stood, hurried around her desk and called out to him again. "Chris!" Chris stopped without facing her. "I said I took care of it, now come back in here so we can talk."

Chapter Nineteen

Camille followed Dell from one room to the next, from living area to living area and as elegant and polished as the property was, she still couldn't help but think of King and the things he might he doing. He'd been telling her so much about this woman named Diamond, it was as if she knew her personally. Then too, Camille felt she knew the type all too well. She'd promised she'd stay out of his relationships and that's what she was going to do, but that didn't mean she wouldn't get to know this woman for herself.

"You hear me, Camille?" Dell smiled, held the champagne bottle up and asked, "Refill?"

"I don't mind if I do," she told him and looked over at the wall clock. She had told Buddy she'd be just a little while and when seeing half an hour had passed, she pulled out her phone and sent the short text, letting him know she'd be a while longer.

"About San Antonio, are you even familiar with the area? I'd hate for us to step in that region without the promise of it being worthwhile."

Camille held up her champagne flute and told him, "You let me worry about that. You just get me the product and me and my people will handle the rest."

Dell thought about the shipment they had coming and thought about making a heavier purchase. Antonio had told both Raymond and himself what he wanted done with the next drop, but now he was seeing a nice profit in doing otherwise. The Circle was already making over five mil a month, but with this move, anything over the mark would definitely be profitable as well.

"I'll tell you what, Camille, how about I give you the hundred kilos at eighteen five and you, let's say, move them for twenty-three- to twenty-four-k each? You make around six hundred-k that way." Dell's brows raised while awaiting her answer.

"And you make damn near two mill, while me and my team do all the work and take whatever loss. Is that what you're asking me?"

"What if I can guarantee you six months of profits?" Dell asked.

"I'll tell you what, Dell. I'm more than sure that if I spend a cool mill, I could easily get a hundred and set my own profit margin. I'm also sure that you're the one with the product, but making it seem as if you're some middle man. You know the numbers and you know what I propose has a long-term to it. You scratch my back, I do the same. But, if you rub me the wrong way, I will burn your ass."

Dell watched her eyes look into his thoughts and partway through his soul. He then remembered the woman that stood before him. He remembered all the stories he'd heard of her personally, as well as the tales that came with those said to have dealt with her and got dealt with by her. At that moment, Camille was not only as beautiful as they came, she was also as deadly as they were.

"Is that some kind of threat, Camille?"

"You would have felt my threat by now, Dell, but if you can't understand what's real, then it will definitely make way for fear.

Dell walked past her to the wet bar. "It's just business, Camille. Nothing personal, you know that, right?"

"Well then, let's make it personal. I'll pay twelve thousand five hundred for each kilo and—"

Dell cut her off. "And I'll be taking the loss."

"The way I see it, Dell, if this was some short-term ordeal, then yes, I could see your dismay, but being that we're looking at the long-term of it, we both know there's promise in it."

Camille, checked her phone, looked up at Dell and said, "I'll be sending the money soon, so make the calls. We have work to do."

Dell followed her out to her sports car, opened her door and looked down at her and smiled. "So, when do I get to come to Fort Worth and see how you living?"

Camille smiled up at him and said, "I'm more than sure you'd love to make your money first, Dell." She backed out, pulled around the outdoor fountain and hit her horn. She waved with her fingers and yelled out, "I love the house, Dell."

Dell laughed, placed his hands behind his head and laughed some more. He'd climbed in bed with the sexiest snake he'd ever seen and her name was Camille. He looked back at the house and began shaking his head. He'd shown her exactly where he laid his head and all he knew of her was that she drove a damn Convertible Porsche and lived somewhere in Fort Worth, if that's where she lived.

Camille pulled out of the estate and as soon as she rounded the corner, she pulled alongside Buddy's Dually. "You get an angle on him or what?"

Buddy leaned forward and with his deep voice, he told her, "Just say the word, Boss Lady, just say the word."

"Not yet, babe. Let me see what all we can get out of this one. He definitely has something up his sleeves. I'm sure of it."

***

King loved the fact that he was able to empress Diamond with both his home and his living arrangements. To see her marvel at the many flowers he ordered for her brought a smile to his face and a feeling he hadn't felt in a long time. He walked up behind her and asked, "Can I hug you?"

Diamond frowned, was about to tell him that they were only flowers and meant nothing to her but instead, she smiled and nodded.

"I guess so, King, but don't start thinking flowers make me itch at all."

King grabbed her by the waist and pulled her to him. "The flowers were for the smile, the candy was for the treat and as for the itch, I haven't even thought about it." He pulled her to him and squeezed. Told her how beautiful she was and how much he appreciated her coming into his life when she did. He thanked her just for being her.

Diamond couldn't help but hug him back. She at first thought she'd feel him press his manhood into her, but she was feeling something totally different. She could feel his heartbeat, smell his fragrance and see his actions were genuine and for a few seconds she closed her eyes. And, for those few seconds, she was in her brother's arms.

Feeling herself squeeze him the way he was, she pushed herself away from him, avoided his gaze and told him, "I think we need to slow down, King."

"You might be right, because I can fall for that. Just to be in your arms, just for that feeling alone, I'd..." King stopped himself when hearing the familiar words run across his mind. Those were the same words he spoke to Nava and were the words she used against him. She knew he'd do any and everything for her, yet she still chose to revert back to the life he tried so desperately to pull her from.

Hoping to change the subject and the atmosphere, Diamond ate one of the caramel turtles and told him, "So, tell me about this woman you're steady comparing me to."

"No, no, I'm not comparing you to her. I was just saying how you reminded me of her, that's all."

"So, where is she now?"

"I really don't know Diamond. I mean, I,-" King thought about what he'd discovered in Miami and said, "I let her go. She wanted to live a life I'm far removed from now. The drugs, the alcohol, the partying, the people and the drama. I'm way past that now and I wanted that for her but—"

"But that's what she wanted for the both of you?" Diamond said, finishing the thoughts he was having.

"Something like that."

"Where did you meet her, King? I mean, what drew you to her?"

"Initially, I saw a very beautiful woman doing something I didn't think she wanted to be doing and—"

"What was she doing?"

"Dancing."

"Dancing?"

"Yeah, she was stripping, Diamond."

"Oh, so you trying to turn a whore into a housewife?" Diamond smiled, shook her head and looked at him.

"Not at first, I wasn't. I just wanted to see her do something other than what she was doing. I felt she had so much potential. I mean, she was sharp, Diamond. She knew things the average woman her age shouldn't know." He looked at Diamond and said, "Like you. The way you talk was the way she'd talk to me at times. I began looking forward to our talks, to the times we spent together and the things we did."

"She was a damsel in distress and you felt you was that knight in shining armor." Diamond asked, "She saw you as a trick, huh?"

"Why does everyone keep saying that? Camille, now you."

"I'm starting to like her already."

"Who? Nava?"

"Hell no, I'm talking about Camille."

"Oh, yeah, she's one of a kind also."

"If Nava meant so much to you, why didn't you try harder, King?"

"Believe me, I tried, Diamond, I really did, but there's only so much a person can do and when you've done all that, hey."

"So, what did Camille say about all of this? I know she had something to say. I know Chris would have."

King walked towards the hundred-thousand-dollar entertainment system and grabbed its remote, his thoughts taking him to the very name mentioned. "Um, to be honest with you, Diamond, when she left I just knew Camille had something to do with it because she didn't like her in the first place, thought she was playing me for the sympathy I had for her."

"And?"

"And ends up, Nava needed a reason to leave and Camille gave her just that. Now here I am, starting over."

"Or looking for a rebound."

"I don't think so, Diamond. I'm actually looking for some-thing better and I think I've found just that." He locked his eyes with her and smiled.

"And you thinking this better is me?"

Instead of answering, King only smiled at her. "Can I touch you, Diamond?"

Diamond dropped her head, sighed and asked him, "Where are you trying to touch me now, King?"

Again, instead of answering her, he reached for her chin, pulled her face upward and kissed her lips, looked down and saw her eyes closed and kissed her again. "I want you to be my Diamond. I want to be your King," he told her.

Diamond realized her mouth had fell open and caught herself. She looked away from him and said, "Don't ever do that a..."

Before she could finish her demand, King leaned down, turned her face and kissed her again, this time more deeply. When feeling her lips part he sucked her tongue, pulled it and began sucking her bottom lip.

Diamond found herself stepping into his embrace. This time, she could feel both his heart beating and the bulge in his linen slacks, a bulge he wasn't even trying to hide. She massaged him with both hands.

"I think we need to slow down," he told her. Diamond laughed. "Ain't that what you told me?" King smiled, wrapped both his arms around her and kissed her forehead.

"And I meant it too."

Diamond grabbed the remote from his hand and thumbed through a list of titles, until she found the one she liked. Once Sade's "No Ordinary Love" came through the surround sound from the bevy of speakers he had placed throughout the living area, she faced him and said, "This how you do all the women you bring here?"

"There's only three women in the world that's ever been to this house and you are the third."

"Yeah, whatever. You don't even know me, yet you invite me into your home and—"

"I'm inviting you into my life, Diamond."

"But you don't even know me, Kengyon. I just might be that bitch, Nava, all over again."

"That's a risk I'm willing to take, but I believe with all my heart you are that one, Diamond. I know there's such a thing as coincidences, but with you, there's so much more." He looked into her eyes and repeated, "So much more, Diamond."

Diamond did everything in her power to look away, to keep him from looking into her soul, from looking into the eyes of the very person that promised his demise elsewhere. She saw something when looking at King, wondered if he really knew of the reasons she was there, wondered if he really knew what he was inviting into his life, wondered if this was a risk he was really willing to take.

Nicole Goosby

Chapter Twenty

KP walked through the site for the third time, making sure everything was as it should be as well as cleared of any and all debris. The trucks he'd rented had been filled and sent to either the dump or the re-cycling plants where he'd sell the aluminum; resell the copper, the rubber, the foams and the plastics. He'd learned how to make the best of the work he and his crew gained contracts for.

He made sure the assignment was completed, but for most of his day, he couldn't stop thinking about his wife and the ways they parted earlier. He thought about the words that said to each other and more than anything, his actions. Not only did he violate the vows he swore to her, but he violated the promises he'd made to Antonio McClendon.

"KP!" Q yelled from across the now vacant plaza.

"Yeah, what's up?"

"We're ready to roll, baby. We all loaded up and ready to roll."

"So, what, y'all calling it a day or what?" KP liked the way his guys worked together and the way they were able to get things done either on time or hours before. With him agreeing to an hourly rate, KP's crew got paid anyway and being that many of them just wanted their money for the work they did, KP was able to pocket that much more. And now that Silvia was trying to put him out, he knew he'd need every penny.

"Let's go cash this shit in so I can get my cut," Q told him, before throwing his gear into the bed of KP's F-150.

"You act as if you have something to do today?"

"Yeah, I do." Q walked around the side of the truck and opened the passenger's side door.

"What you got to do?"

"Bills, nigga. Got to pay my bills. You ever heard of them or does your wife be the one paying all of them?"

"Nigga, I pay the bills. I give her the money and she do what she needs to do."

"Yeah, like I said, she pays the bills."

KP walked on the other side of the truck, waved over a couple of the guys and told them, "Good job today, guys." He paid them their cash and added, "I'll be calling you guys in a couple of days for another job."

"You sure?" one of the guys asked.

"Yeah, why would you ask that?" KP frowned.

"'Cause, Q said something about some niggas might be looking for you because of some shit you did."

KP looked across the truck at Q and rolled his eyes. "You know you can't pay that clown no attention." He thought about just that and smiled to himself. It was definitely a possibility.

"Well, if it's true or not, we appreciate you putting us on like you have been." They shook KP's hand as if it was their last time. One of the guys even patted his shoulder.

Reading the gesture couldn't be avoided and when seeing Q on the other side of the truck shaking his head, he told them, "Fuck all, y'all. Ain't nobody looking for me."

Q pointed across the street and said, "Them niggas in the truck over there been watching us all day."

Seeing him spin, look across the way and ask, "Who, where?" They all laughed, looked at Q and laughed some more.

"Fuck y'all."

KP climbed into his truck and slammed the door. They always played with each other that way, but this time was different. It was something he worried about. With a few minutes to play with, he dialed Silvia's number.

Chris had been listening to Silvia and her plans for every bit of an hour and was more than sure he could take care of something so small. He knew she was just wanted to change the matter, because he insisted on addressing the situation with KP. He felt it was an obligation of his to do just that and if Antonio ever caught wind that he didn't, there would be a hefty price to pay. He promised Antonio that he would step up in his absence and that's what he was expected to do. He was sitting in Silvia's office, looking over some numbers when her phone lit up. He started to page her on the salon's intercom at first, but decided against it when noticing KP's picture on its screen. He hurried to peek out of her office to make sure she was nowhere around, held up her phone and pressed a button.

"Yeah, what's up, KP?"

"Hey, who is this?"

"What do you need, homie, 'cause Silvia's busy and I'm not really in the mood for you right now."

"Chris?"

"Yeah, who else?"

"Say, man, I swear I didn't mean to. It just happ—"

Chris cut him off and told him, "What if some more shit was just to happen because you allowed something to 'just happen', huh?"

"Look, Chris, I really need to speak with my wife."

"What you really need to be doing is disappearing for a mi-nute, or until I get this shit situated."

"What, what do you mean, situated?"

"What you think, KP, better yet what were you thinking?"

"She already told Antonio?"

"And Antonio's really tripping about this shit," Chris lied. He just wanted KP to know there were things in play because of his actions.

"Please Chris, let him know that shit was an accident, man.

"I didn't mean it."

"Yeah, well, that's not the theory that's going around at all. So just chill out and stay out of the way, until I get this shit figured out. Silvia's trying to find out where you at now and if you're going to be home later, so I advise you to find somewhere else to sleep for a while."

"Are you serious, Chris? It wasn't nothing but one slap."

"You really think Antonio's worrying about it being one slap, KP? You really think that?"

After sitting Silvia's phone back on her desk, he watched her, Somolia, and Datrina enter the office and look at him as if the day's events happened because of him.

"Well, just make yourself comfortable then," Silvia told him and took a seat on her desk.

KP lowered his phone and looked at it. Chris not only told him what he feared was confirmed, but to hear what was planned for him if he was captured shook him to the core. "Shit!" he yelled and threw his phone in the console beside him.

Q climbed in, noticed the languished expression his friend wore and asked, "What the hell you looking like that for?"

They already looking for us, man. Antonio already put the hit out on us."

"Us?" The fuck you mean us, nigga?"

"You was the one that told—"

"And I'm the one telling you right now to give me my money and take me home. What the fuck you mean, they looking for us?"

"We in this shit together, nigga."

"The only thing we about to be in together is a fight, if you don't drop me off at the house. You ain't about to get me killed 'cause you running around hitting on that woman."

"Oh, now she a woman. Just the other day she was a bitch and some of everything else."

"Well, whatever, nigga. Pour me out at the house."

KP drove and thought about his next move. He wanted to stop by the salon to make the public apology, but thought against it for the mere fact that that's probably where they were waiting on him to show. There and his home and when remembering the words his wife said about him not having to leave, he knew he wasn't about to sleep there. "I'm going to chill at your place for a couple of days, Q."

"You what?"

"They don't even know where you live. We good."

Q looked in the side view mirror and sighed. "This is the second time you put me in some shit like this, man."

"Yeah, well, this the second time I listened to your ass too."

Raymond answered his phone on the second ring. He spoke briefly with Dell about the things he had going on with him and to hear that Camille was willing to invest a mil in their business, he inquired about the properties she found interest in.

"You just acquired that house and now you're already talking about selling it?"

Dell cleared his throat and told him, "Hell, if she pull up with the amount I threw out there, she can have this motherfucker."

"How much was that?"

"Five-seven at the least."

"So, you think King's the one pushing the folder?"

"There's no doubt in my mind. She's just the face he's using to make it happen."

"Well, as soon as Diamond handles her end, we're sending the boys in anyway, so it really don't matter."

"I just wish it was done sooner than later and by the looks of it, Camille is separating herself from King."

"Yeah?"

"From the looks of it. I could also tell that she was stepping out from under him."

"You come to this conclusion, how?" Dell sorted through some papers he was handling, found a list of San Antonio properties and told him, "'Cause there are many ways she could have done that without you."

"Just trust me, Raymond. I got this."

Raymond closed his files, placed his phone on his desk and sat back in his recliner. He'd done business with Dell long enough to know when the guy was holding information from him and if he was right, Dell was definitely holding back the fact that he and Camille had something else going on, other than some interest in a property. There was no way Dell was going to sell the home he just bought. It was his pride and joy and they all knew it.

"I'm surprised he hasn't at least called you yet," Datrina told Silvia once they were done looking at the invoices.

"He will," said Silvia. She looked over at Chris who was still seated behind her desk as if he owned the salon.

"What you looking over here at me for? You told me to leave it alone and that's what I'm going to do." Chris looked at Datrina and smiled.

"You ain't got to be looking all crazy. I'm not tripping on you anymore." Silvia walked over to Somolia and opened her arms. "You a real bitch, but you still my sister. Both of y'all my sisters and we're not about to let this shit come between us. We've been making money with men and without them and it's not going to stop now."

Somolia hugged her friend and told her, "I'm sorry, Silvia. I really am."

Chris looked at Datrina and asked, "Am I missing something here? I knew something was off the moment I walked through the door, but all this soft core shit y'all got going on—"

"Somolia sucked KP's dick while we were in Miami," Datrina blurted out, stopping him mid-sentence and causing him to look directly at Silvia.

"He did what?"

Before either of them could respond, Chris was out of the office door and despite the protest from both Silvia and Datrina, he was on his way. This wasn't the first time this exact same situation occurred, but this time it wasn't about to go unanswered.

Diamond sat and listened to King and the reasons he gave for wanting something more with her. She sat and listened to him explain his differences between love and lust. She watched his expressions, how he lit up when he spoke about her, and the enthusiasm he displayed when talking about helping her with a career she wanted nothing to do with. She could see that he actually was a humble soul. Never once did he speak about this street exploits. He never once bragged about his status or position in the game they both played or the women he ran through. Hoping to take things up a notch, Diamond stopped his speech and told him, "Tell me about the game and this life you're running from."

"It's not that I'm running from the game, Diamond. I just prefer you do something other than this. There's no need in both of us being consumed by the consequences of it."

"But what if this is something I want to do?"

"I'll continue to advise you against it and if need be, I'll even support your other endeavors."

"You just don't want me getting caught up in the drama that's sure to come with it, huh?"

"Exactly. Exactly."

"I might even have to get someone set up to get them out of the way."

"What you mean by that?"

Diamond shifted in her seat and told him. "There's no way you're going to grow in this game, without having to do something to rid yourself of certain competitors. People play the game for keeps and when you pose a threat on a grand level, they coming for you. Plain and simple."

"There's very little room for error in the game, Diamond. When you start looking at the moves everyone around you is making, you lose sight of the ones you need made. I've never stepped on another man for trying to provide for his. I've never shot skates on a nigga a day in by life. I have everything I have because we came together and thought. We formulated, strategized and executed, we put our team together and didn't allow nothing to come between it. Your team is only as strong as the weakest member, Diamond. Remember that. Now, as for Camille, that's a different story. I'm scared to ask her of some of the things she's had done."

"So, Camille's a boss too?"

King laughed and said, "She's the boss if you was to ask her or Buddy."

"Who's Buddy?"

"That's another story in itself."

"What about him. You trust him?"

"I trust that he'd protect her with his life. So yeah, I do trust him. "

Diamond pressed a series of buttons on the remote and continued, "You think he'd set someone up for her?"

King laughed. "Not at all, he's way past that. He looks after her and the dealings she has. When you see Camille, you see Buddy and if you don't see him, just know, he's seeing you."

"Buddy sounds like a straight-up killer."

"Well, he'll definitely fit the bill."

King looked up at the clock and when seeing they had only two hours before their dinner reservations he told her, "We've got two hours, what you want to do until then?"

"Really, King, Really?"

"I'm not talking about anything like that, Diamond. I really want to hear more about you for some reason you don't like that subject."

Diamond thought about just that and smiled. She'd been more there most of the day and was yet to tell him anything about her or her goals, her aspirations or her dreams of becoming the next queen pin. "I'll tell you what, let's go for a spin."

She grabbed the keys to her Bentley and stood.

"I'll drive," he offered.

"Naw, I got it. You want to know about me, then I'm going to show you.

Camille was climbing out of her Porsche when King and Diamond were making their way to the Bentley. She'd heard more than she wanted about the woman and to see her there with King, reminded her of the day she met Nava.

"Don't rush off on my account," she told both of them, while walking in their direction.

"We're just going for a spin before dinner, is all." King nervously looked from Diamond to Camille, then from Camille to Diamond.

"So, Camille, being that I've heard so much about you, the introduction is actually, this is awkward, but I'm Diamond and it's a pleasure to finally meet you." Diamond extended her hand.

"As is the same with you, Diamond." They shook, held each other's stare without blinking.

It was King that interrupted their face-off, not wanting any drama to unfold and when seeing them looking at each other the way they were, he didn't know what was next.

"You are beautiful," Camille complimented the woman before her.

"Well, you know what they say about beauty, but thanks. You're holding a little something yourself."

"Umph-umm," King cleared his throat in an attempt to break the stare down for the second time. "Do I need to leave or what?"

Camille laughed, looked towards him and said, "There just might be a day for that, King."

Before Camille disappeared into the house, the black Dually pulled around the rear of the house, and the driver parked and climbed out.

"King?"

"Hey Buddy, what's up?"

"Another day, another dollar."

Buddy looked at Diamond and nodded.

She nodded back, climbed into the Bentley and pressed the ignition button. With this being the first time seeing Buddy himself, and the first time she understood the role he played, she questioned herself. Why was it that Dell knew nothing of him, but seemed to know everything about King and the people he associated himself with?

"Put your seatbelt on," she told him before zooming up the drive and out of the gate."

Camille watched both of them from the patio window. There was definitely a different vibe received when she net Nava and if she wasn't mistaken, Diamond was just as much of a tomboy than she ever was.

"What do you think about her, Buddy?" Camille asked as soon as he walked into the living area.

"Hard to say, Boss Lady. She's like you almost, hard to read at first glance. She's not like Nava though." Buddy shook his head. "Nothing like that bitch."

"She's definitely not some broke bitch, huh?"

"Not driving that, she ain't."

Camille thought about the brief moment she and Diamond shared. There was something about her she couldn't put her hand on and when thinking about their trip to Miami, she had a pretty good idea what it was. Whatever the case though, she was going to be sure about it, whether King was or not.

Chapter Twenty-One

After making a couple of calls, Chris was more than sure KP would be shacked up with Q for a while. He called KP twice already and knew he was dodging him by not answering and that only angered him more.

He called Q's cell.

"Yeah?" Q asked, without questioning the blocked number on his screen.

"Where's KP?"

Q looked over at KP and frowned. He'd seen him send a couple of calls straight to voicemail and now that Chris was calling his number looking for him, he knew who that caller was.

"Um, I think he went to the house," Q lied.

"I'm at his house and he's not here, Q."

Q elbowed KP and asked Chris, "You're at his house right now?"

"Parked right out front waiting on him."

"I, um, I—"

"Where he at, Q? Them niggas are looking for him and I'm trying to get at him to let him know what's up"

"Oh, here he is right here." Q shoved the Samsung to KP and told him, "He's trying to help you, nigga, here."

"Hey, Chris, what's up?" KP answered.

"There's six niggas out here looking for you, man, and I need to throw them."

"I'm on my way to Q's, man. I'm going to be over there for a while, like you said."

Chris umphed to himself. It was just too easy. "You got money on you?"

"Yeah, I just hit a lick, so I'm straight for a while. Why?"

"I'm going to need you to lay low at Q's for a while."

"Well, we're pulling onto his street right now."

Chris sat and watched as KP's Ford bent the corner at the top of Q's street and shook his head. He knew for a fact if and when he did come for him, it would be the easiest hit he'd ever done. Despite

KP crossing the line with Silvia and the real reasons Chris was posted now, he felt sympathy for the man. His first mind was to physically do a little harm to him, but he gave Silvia his word he wouldn't. Then, he thought about appointing someone else to do the honors and act as if he had nothing to do with it but knew she'd see through it eventually.

He instead had another plan. As soon as they pulled into Q's driveway, Chris climbed out and walked towards them with his pistol drawn and calling Silvia at the same time.

"Totally Awesome, Silvia Pierson speaking. How can I help you?"

"Hey Silvia, has he called you yet?"

"Not yet, where are you?"

"Making that stop by the mansion, so I can drop this money. What's up?"

"Oh, the way you ran up out of here, we thought you were going to do something stupid."

Chris held his gun to KP's face with one hand and laughed into the phone using the other. "I have other things to do than get in the middle of what y'all got going on."

"Well, no, he hasn't called yet, but he will."

"Alright then, I'm going to get at you later."

Chris pushed his phone into his pants pocket and told KP, "Now, here's what we're going to do. You're going to call Silvia and you're going to tell her it's not working and that you're tired of competing with all of her ex-boyfriends. You're going to tell her you need some space and time away to sort some things out." Chris looked from KP, whose mouth was still agape, to Q who still had his palms raised as if they were being robbed at gunpoint.

"And put your damn hands down, nigga, ain't nobody even talking to you."

"Come on, Chris, are you serious, man?"

"You either do it like this or you burn, nigga. You fucking up our system now, nigga, trying to fuck Somolia out of all people again. I thought we were past this shit, KP."

"We are, man, I wasn't trying to fuck her I just let her—"

226

Chris cut him off and said, "Make the call, KP, I don't have time for this shit. You fucking up our money now. What the fuck you think was going to happen when Silvia and Somolia get to tripping and they go their separate ways? Somolia knows too much to be harboring ill feelings for Silvia and you know this, we talked about this shit before."

"I know Chris, I know, man."

"You fucked Somolia before, nigga?" Q looked over at his friend incredulously. "When was this?"

"Not now, Q. Not now, homie."

"You fucked my girl, nigga?" Q watched his friend for the sign and when seeing him without answers, he told him, "Man, that's fucked up, nigga."

"Make the call, KP!" Chris told him sternly.

"This was years ago, Q, you tripping. She wasn't your girl then."

"Why you ain't never told me no shit like that?"

"Niggas ain't running around here screaming news of how they fucked Somolia."

"But you—"

"Q! Will you please shut the fuck up and go in the house or something?"

Chris watched as KP hesitantly pulled out his phone and speed dialed Silvia. He nodded his encouragement and slowly placed his gun to his side.

KP couldn't believe the mess he'd gotten himself into and was hoping like hell that Chris wasn't about to take him anywhere. If nothing else, he knew that would be the last ride he had. He knew Chris as well as what Chris did and instead of making a bad situation worse, he made the call.

Silvia and Datrina went over a few more things once Somolia left the office and after telling Silvia that Diamond was spending more and more time with King, Silvia only shrugged. "She knows what she's gotten herself into. She knows what she has gotten herself into, Datrina, and she's set on seeing it through, so…"

Silvia looked down at the vibrating phone and when seeing her husband's face, she rolled her eyes and sighed.

"What do you want, Kevin?"

"Silvia."

"Um-hmm."

"Hey, look. I think we need a little time apart so we can sort through things on our own terms. It isn't working between us and before we become anything other than cordial with each other, I think—"

"Whatever you do is fine with me. Kevin, and you're right. I do think we need some space to sort through some things. So, it's whatever."

"You know I love you and that I'm sorry, don't you?"

"Yeah, just a hell of a way to show it." Silvia looked up at Datrina and shrugged.

Hearing the drama unfold, Datrina pulled out her phone and GPS'ed Chris' phone and when seeing he was nowhere near the McClendon mansion, she showed Silvia and said, "Chris is with him as we speak."

Silvia closed her eyes and smiled. She told KP, "You got some money on you or what?"

"Yeah, I just cashed one of my little ass checks."

"Well, tear your ass and tell Chris I said the mansion is on the other side of town." Silvia hung up and smiled at Datrina. If it wasn't Antonio, it was Chris that felt she was his responsibility. "KP's soft ass gonna end up getting stepped on sooner or later and it's me that's going to have to protect his dumb ass."

KP held his phone out so Chris could hear Silvia's words. He was hoping it would deter him from any uncivil action and when seeing Chris close his eyes, he knew something had been averted.

"She knows you're here, Chris."

"Datrina."

"She must have looked at your shit on the GPS app shit."

"Whoever designed that shit needs to have their ass kicked."

Chris began walking away but turned, faced KP and told him, "The next time you touch Silvia, I touch you. End of discussion."

***

Diamond pulled into the canopy under the loft where she was staying and parked the Bentley coupe. She made the drive to Fort Worth as fast as she always had, and being that she didn't have to drive out to the mansion, they had the time.

"Here we are at my humble abode."

"How many tickets have you had this year, Diamond, or should I be asking, this month?"

"Zero." Diamond smiled, grabbed her phone and climbed out. She was going to show King what he'd been wanting to see for the longest.

"By the way that cop got behind us, I could have sworn he was about to pull us over," he added, "you were going way over the speed limit."

Diamond smiled, she prayed like hell the officer didn't pull her over, because not only did he know her full name, but he was sure to ask about Antonio McClendon and that was not something she didn't need at the moment. "I guess he had other things to do besides harass a couple in a Bentley."

"Yeah, I guess so."

Diamond led him through the security gates and after punching in Chris and Datrina's code, she walked him into the two-story loft.

"Wow, Diamond, this is beautiful," he told her, while doing his very own walk through.

It was now that Diamond was glad she listened to Datrina and placed a bunch of group and personal pictures throughout the apartment. With most of them being pics of Diamond in a variety of sports apparel and her hair in cornrows, she knew questions would follow.

King picked up one of the pictures on the smoked glass end table and asked her, "Is this really Dax Prescott and Jason Whitten?"

"Hell, yeah, I have a few of Zeke around here somewhere."

She looked through her e-mails and missed calls on her laptop.

King smiled and laughed when looking at most of the pics of Diamond. He pointed. "I know this woman, Diamond, I just can't place her."

"Um, yeah." Diamond thought back to the back to the fact that most people in the Metroplex knew or knew of Silvia Pierson and knew that she was Antonio McClendon's cousin. "That's my beautician. She goes with me when I travel. Her and the dark-skinned chick in the other pics."

"That's where I've seen her before. Miami. She was with you."

Diamond rolled her eyes at the ceiling. She'd brought him there without thinking and now that he was piecing together a puzzle of his own, it wasn't in her best interest at all. She pointed at the clock and told him, "We might need to get going if we're going to keep our reservations."

Those words brought King back to his here and now. He'd lost himself in her world and when thinking of the surprise he had for her at The Cheesecake Factory, he smiled and told her, "Yeah, I'm hungry as hell too."

Diamond knew how Antonio always got her mind on other things with small surprises and by allowing her to do things he normally wouldn't. Seeing the position she put herself in and the wheels spinning in King's mind, she tossed him the keys to the Bentley and told him, "Let me see what you working with."

"What exactly are you trying to say, Diamond?" King laughed. He followed her to the door and before either of them walked through, he kissed her and smiled. "I need to step my game up, huh?"

"If not, I'm going to blow past you." Diamond walked out, climbed into the passenger's side of the foreign luxury car and laughed. Those were definitely words she didn't mean to speak.

Dell was sitting in his favorite area of the mansion, when three guys walked in and took up seats at various sections of the room. He offered each of them a drink of their choosing and once all was settled, he got down to the business at hand

A Drug King and His Diamond

"I appreciate you guys coming on such short notice, but I have some things in play. I want you all to be up on game before the time comes. As of this moment, we have a player on the inside of King's circle. The intel is exactly what we need and once it's confirmed, we're going to move and when we move, so does he. This is going to be as clean as possible but in any case, it's going to happen. There's ten thousand dollars in the envelopes I gave you upon your arrival, and another forty thousand dollars waiting for you after King has been disposed of."

"What's the hold up?" one guy asked.

"Just make sure it's worth every bit of our projected figures," said the second guy.

"Is this person on the inside trustworthy or what?" said the third guy.

Dell took a sip of the cognac he was drinking and nodded. It was time to make a move and all he needed now was for Diamond to provide the layout.

"Two weeks tops, guys. Be ready in two weeks." Dell stood, his gesture at dismissing the group and once everyone was leaving, he walked out onto his second floor terrace and raised his glass.

"To a King," he proposed the secret toast. "To a King," he agreed.

***

Silvia quietly thought about the move Chris was making and really couldn't say too much about it, Yes, KP was her husband, but if this is what it took to keep him from meeting a very untimely demise, then this was what she'd approve of. She and Chris talked about the very things Antonio would have done if he ever found out that KP had put his hands on his cousin. And, more than likely, it wouldn't have been Chris to perform such duties in the first place. For now, she'd allow Chris' discipline for KP.

"That damn Chris is something else, girl. I should have known his ass was behind it. As soon as he hung up, KP's ass calls talking all kinds of shit about needing space."

231

"That's what made me see where Chris really was. You know how he feels about you and Diamond, and you know the things he'll do for the both of you."

"Yeah, that's why I try to keep Diamond in check about the things she does. She's now starting to understand that her actions and inactions not only affect her, but those that love her."

"Well, if you ask me, we might need to be worried about the things she's doing with that man, King. All she does is talk about him."

"Deception isn't without attachment, you know that, right?" Silvia thought about the words she just spoke and found herself standing at the window of her office looking out at the lot of her salon. She was hoping that Diamond would be able to do just that. Detach herself from King, as well as detach herself of the guilt that was sure to follow. Silvia had been in this game years before her younger cousin and knew personally what it meant to have to live with a guilt of having someone killed.

Chris anticipated the call from Silvia for more reasons than one. He pulled to the rear of the mansion, unloaded the duffle bags from his truck into the storage space, and walked the cash to the vault Antonio had built in the floor of the mansion. This was where the cash would be until Diamond had it cleaned, and now that he was looking at over two million in cash of her personal money, he felt that should happen sooner than later.

With nothing more to do for the rest of the day, he texted Diamond to let her know that things were straight, jumped in his Calloway Corvette and went for a spin. There were some things he wanted to discuss with Dell personally and a phone call wasn't about to do.

Chapter Twenty-Two

The line on the outside of The Cheesecake Factory was out the door and halfway around the building. As soon as they pulled up, Diamond looked at King and before she could protest, he said, "I got this, Diamond."

As soon as the car stopped, one of the valets rushed to the passenger side and opened Diamond's door.

She frowned, hesitated and then took his hand. That was going to be one of the things she wouldn't miss once this was over.

"Welcome to The Cheesecake Factory, ma'am," the guy told her, before pulling her out of the coupe.

King threw him the keys and said, "Kengyon Johnson."

"Yes, sir."

Just as he made it on the other side of the car where Diamond waited, another guy walked up. "Right this way, Mr. Johnson."

"After you, babe."

Those within hearing distance would have definitely thought, by the way they were dressed, their matching outfits, their closeness and the smiles they wore, they were a couple. The inside of The Cheesecake Factory offered both ambiance and a choice in seating. Diamond walked through the outdoor patio area and was hoping King reserved them a table outside, because of the scene alone. She liked the set-up and when she and Antonio did the restaurant thing, he always made sure they were seated on the patio, if not a balcony.

"Right this way, Mr. Johnson."

They followed the young guy outside and to a table in the corner, away from the traffic and to the rear of the patio.

Diamond nodded her approval, allowed the guy to pull her seat out and thanked him. She looked back to where the desserts filled one entire side of the room and bit her bottom lip. For reasons of her own, keeping her figure was a must, despite wanting to indulge in an assortment of sweets.

"It sure smells good out here."

After being seated and handed menus, King looked over at her and asked, "Do you have an idea of what you'd like?"

"I'll just order what I normally do when I get out like this."

"You have no reason to be shy around me, Diamond. You want to get your fat girl on, that's cool with me."

"My fat girl on? You must be thinking about that Nava chick or someone else."

"You know what I'm saying, Diamond. You can eat like a snail if you want, but I'm hungry for real."

King waved the waiter over and told him, "I'm going to give you three hundred dollars to make sure me and my wife straight for the rest of our meal."

"Oh, I'm your wife now?"

"I believe in speaking things into existence." King looked Diamond in her eyes and told her, "One day you will be."

"Really?"

"Yes, really."

"And what makes you so sure of something like that, King?"

"'Cause, I'm going to do everything within my power to make it happen."

"And what if there's someone else believing in the same things you are?"

King took a sip of the water before him, looked over the rim of the glass and told her, "May the best man win."

"And that's the way you look at it, may the best man win?"

"Well, here's the thing, Diamond. There are times when I play for keeps and when there's something I want, I do what it takes to get it and if there's a cost, I'm paying it."

Diamond thought about the fact that her brother was sitting in a federal facility because of the principle and that very act. As far as she was concerned, there was nothing else to talk about. King had to go. As much as he reminded her of her brother with the things he did and said, or even the ways he made her feel, he had to go.

King nodded at the youngster, handed him his menu and asked Diamond, "You ready?"

"As ready as I'll ever be." She handed the guy her menu and told him, "I'd like the Caesar chicken salad, a side of sliced kiwi, and a Sprite with water."

"Will that be it, ma'am?"

Diamond looked towards the desserts and smiled. "Yeah, I do think that'll do."

"And you, Mr. Johnson?"

"Um, I'll take the pink salmon, steamed veggies, bourbon potatoes with cheese sauce, some of the sesame seed rolls, a citrus mimosa and a couple of slices of that caramel fudge cheesecake afterwards." He smiled at the waiter, looked across the table at Diamond and asked, "What?"

"I know you're not about to eat all that, King. That's enough for two people right there."

"Well, I guess you're about to find out, because I already know. I might even try some of them boneless wings they have now."

"Boneless wings?" Diamond looked around for the waiter.

"I see now, I'm going to have to fatten you up, Diamond. You already sexy as hell, but with a few more pounds, you'll be shutting some shit down for real."

"Oh, so I'm not good enough for the famous King right now?"

"And who said something like that? You are perfect just the way you are, Diamond, and you know that."

Diamond smirked, looked past him at the couple that walked by, thought about some of the things her brother continually said about her finding a man and settling down, and that once she found true love she'd be willing to give up everything just to keep it. She then thought about her trip to Miami and the life she saw being lived. The opulence, the power, the money and very status she wanted for herself, queen pin. There was no way she'd be able to live like that, working a nine to five and worrying about if some man was staying true to her. She'd seen Silvia and KP go through it time and time again and knew that wasn't something she wanted to continually go through.

"You should fear marriage, King. It goes against the lifestyle you live, as well as the principles you live by."

"I want to be able to give you the world. Diamond, I want to be able to afford you that Bentley coupe, as well as any and everything else your heart desires and this lifestyle is one of the only ways it can be done."

"Yeah, well there are other ways, King, and putting me in the game is one of those ways."

Once the platters were served, King picked over his salmon and thought about Camille. She was the same way years ago and saw the world through very similar eyes. He always felt there were other things Camille could do, but instead he gave in and created a monster of a woman he called his best friend. He'd made the mistake once and refused to do it a second time.

"Listen, Diamond, I know guys have come in your life promising this and that, only to come up short, but I want you to know that I do want you in my life and I want better for you. I have money, Diamond. In fact, I have lots of it because of this game, but what I don't have is someone to share it with. Someone to care for and more than anything, someone to love me the way I'll love them."

"Sounds as if you've rehearsed that line several times," Diamond told him, hoping to change the vibe and the atmosphere around them.

"I'm serious, Diamond, I'd give you the world. I really would. You deserve it."

"And how would you know what I deserve? Kengyon, you barely even know me, but you're ready to sell your soul and give your life for me, do you really expect me to believe some shit like that?"

"Then try it. Try me, Diamond. You lose nothing and I stand to lose everything. So, just try it."

Diamond could see sincerity in his eyes. She could hear the determination in his voice. With a list of things she needed to know about both him and his operation, this night would be the night she found them and if she had to make a few promises of her own, that's what she was going to do. Tonight, she'd do what needed to be done.

The following morning...

After showering and preparing himself for the day, King made a few calls in the hopes of purchasing a couple of tickets for the Dallas/Houston football game. Being that Diamond was such a fan of the sport, he was going to surprise her as he did last night at The Cheesecake Factory, when he had the live entertainment come in and sing to her. He loved the look on her face when they approached and asked her name and right afterwards, sang one of the songs she favored.

With Camille and Buddy making the rounds needed, he had all the time in the world for Diamond and the things she wanted to do. Not only did he drive her home, she insisted he keep the Bentley and return it this morning. He'd already texted her to let her know he'd be by in a couple of hours and was now about to have the Bentley detailed. Another surprise he felt she deserved

"You practically spent the night with the woman, Kengyon, and now you're back in the saddle again?" Camille had been following him throughout the house and when hearing of his plans for the day, she felt he was doing a little too much too soon.

"I have the loaner car and since I have to return it to her, we might as well spend some time together."

"Does she even know about these plans you made for the both of you, King?"

"She will soon enough."

"You're being clingy, King. Women don't like that. Let her initiate some things. It's not like she's some broke bitch."

"That she's not. She has a very nice apartment, Camille, and if I didn't know any better, I would have sworn the woman was married or at least had a boyfriend somewhere."

"And how do you know she doesn't?"

King walked past Camille and headed for the kitchen. He told her, "We're damn near together all day, on the phone just as long, and I'm sure that if there was another man in her life, he'd be entitled to some of her time. Wouldn't you think?"

Camille followed him into the dining area, picked up the glass he just sat on the ivory and wood dinette table and walked it back in the kitchen. "Women are more situated than men, King, and we know how to move without being moved, King. For all we know he might be out of town or something. Why is it you're just now able to visit her living space? Why hasn't she invited you before now?"

"She might have been embarrassed, Camille. It isn't like she's living like us."

Camille watched him ramble. Shook her head at the way he was misplacing items and asking her if she'd seen this and that. She could see that his mind was elsewhere and as bad as she wanted him to see just that, she held her peace. And, just as she'd promised, she was going to stay out of his business.

Diamond was standing on the stairs by the time Chris pulled under the canopy of the apartment. She told him and Dell all about the things she'd found out about King, and the things he had going on during their conversation earlier this morning. It was just something that happened, with Chris going to Dell's home and discussing plans for King.

She'd just read the text King sent her, talking about he'd be through in a couple of hours and knew she didn't have too much time to go over certain things with Chris. She wanted him to get a feel of the man himself, and just the way she was introduced to his bestie, Camille, he would be introduced to her bestie, Chris.

"Hurry up, nigga, with your slow ass."

Chris was seconds behind her and once they were in the apartment, he told her, "The nigga probably didn't even sleep last night."

"He's going to have plenty of time for that soon enough."

"So, what's up? What this nigga talking about now?" Chris walked over, fell onto the suede sectional and threw his leg over the arm of the couch.

"Nigga, get your leg off my Emmitt Smith jersey!" Diamond hurried to push him and smooth out her furniture. "Crazy ass."

"Oh, I forgot, you gave up the mansion to move in here. This is your new home now."

"Yeah, for now. This little ass place got me feeling like I'm in jail or something."

"Don't start that shit, Diamond. Just because you can run around your shit, swim, park eight cars and a bunch of shit you don't even do, don't mean you're gonna talk bad about the spot. This is a real home, not some amusement park."

Diamond laughed when hearing him compare their living quarters because just the other day, his girl was talking about upgrading their living conditions. She also thought about the words King spoke about his own house being made a home, and even included her in the making of it.

"Yeah, well, my shit is going to be bigger and better than my brother's real soon."

"And where you plan on living?"

"Might move to Miami or something."

"Yeah, right. So, Hurricanes Harvey and Irma can have a few kids to play with all your shit? I doubt it."

"That's fucked up, right? I'm glad we left that motherfucker before it blew in." Diamond thought about Sergio and the palace where he held their meeting, wondered if it was still standing and whatever happened to the tiger cubs he had.

"So, where you and this nigga going now?"

"Brunch. You know I got to keep this nigga close."

"Let you tell it, yo freaky ass might have even given him some pussy." Chris looked at her and frowned.

"Jealous ass nigga, ain't nobody sucking my shit for free."

When seeing Chris' expression, she couldn't help but laugh 'cause King had been paying for something ever since they were in Miami. "You know what I'm talking about, clown."

"Yeah, I do."

Nicole Goosby

Chapter Twenty-Three

KP and Q had been arguing most of the night and even came close to blows several times. For him to have spare time to mess with Somolia was something Q couldn't get past, because they were supposed to be tight and there was nothing not shared between them, so Q thought. Not only was Q tripping on KP's involvement with the said crush he'd been having on his wife, Q even went as far as telling KP they damn near kissed and if it wasn't for Antonio's popping up, they would have.

Through the course of the night, things spilled from both of their fountains and neither could believe the other.

"If I ever find out you fucked my wife, I'm going to kill your ass. You know that, right?"

Q had decided to make both of them a small breakfast and with all the things said last night, KP sat and watched him.

"I told you I didn't, nigga, so leave it alone."

"I'm serious, Q, if—"

"If nothing, let me find out you was trying to fuck Somolia."

"Nigga, that's back before she got fat."

"That bitch was always fat, nigga. She's been the same size since she was born."

"She's just pretty as hell, man. She be looking up at a nigga."

Q laughed, spooned a serving of eggs on his plate and handed KP the handle to the pan. "Here. Ya police ass might as well serve a nigga too. You the reason we hiding out now."

"Naw, if you would have kicked her ass a long time ago, she wouldn't have never ran off and screamed in the first place."

"See, there you go with that shit again." KP laughed, grabbed the pan and began spooning himself a serving.

"I still can't believe you made Somolia suck your dick while you got that rash, nigga."

"Fuck you too, Q. Fuck you too."

***

Silvia pulled up to the shop at the very same time Datrina was pulling up in Chris' Corvette. For the past few days, she'd been popping up in all kinds of cars and trucks belonging to both Diamond and Antonio, and was boasting about the life they lived.

Not only could she and Chris afford the very things she took a liking to, she was offered them. Her wanting to live the low-profile life was what Antonio advised both of them to do and with Chris being his right-hand, it was best for the entire Circle. And, this was the reason Antonio took the fall himself. Silvia climbed out of her Porsche and waited for Datrina to park the Corvette.

"You looking good in that car, Datrina. You really are."

Datrina climbed out, wearing a pant suit she'd gotten while they were in Miami, a pant suit King paid over seven hundred and fifty dollars for.

"Thanks, girl. Chris is going to have to let me have this one. You know how many niggas pulled up on me already, this morning alone?"

"Let that be the reason, Datrina." Silvia led the way into the salon. "Have you heard from Somolia yet or what?"

"Not yet." Datrina checked her phone for a text from their friend and when seeing none, she texted her.

"We need to get both her and Diamond a man, girl, 'cause they on some more shit," Silvia told her, before making her way to her office.

"Well, I wasn't the one that told you this, but Diamond has a man and she's about to fuck him off." Datrina gave her friend a prosaic look and rolled her eyes.

"I hope not."

"Remember what I told you, Silvia. She can play that role all day long, but I know what I'm looking at when I see it, and the girl can't stop talking about him."

"Well, that may have been the case, but after this, she's going to realize there are things she has to separate while in this game, as well as there are things she'll never be able to."

King pulled into the Bentley dealership and parked around by the service center. He was sure they'd be able to accommodate his request, being that the car did belong to them at one time or another. Before he was able to climb out of the coupe, a couple of servicemen walked towards him and asked, "Are you here for the annual or what?"

King looked around at the selection of cars out and told them, "Naw, I was looking to get it detailed this morning."

"Well, um, you'd have to make those arrangements in advance if you want the full details."

"Um," King pulled out five hundred dollars and told them, "and, how much would that cost?"

Seeing them look at each other, then back towards the service center, he knew he was on to something and seeing the shorter of the two reach for the key, he handed over the money.

"Thanks guys. It'll mean the world to me."

While the Bentley was being driven off, King took pleasure in walking through the lot himself. He'd always admired the handiwork of the Bentley and Rolls Royce brand, but never really thought about owning one himself, until he saw Diamond pull up in the pearl white coupe.

"Sir! Sir, excuse me, sir!" one of the guys yelled from across the lot.

King turned, faced the service guy and asked, "What's up? Is there a problem with the car?"

"Um, no, sir. I, um, we, the technicians found something in the trunk's side compartment and I'd like to inform you, before we continued with the servicing."

"What is it?" King, wearing a questioning expression, followed the guy to the garage where the Bentley sat. He knew he hadn't added or taken anything from the car and was hoping Diamond hadn't either. All he needed was to be blamed for something he knew nothing about.

"Um, right this way, sir."

By the way the rest of the guys were looking at him, he knew something was either broken or missing and more than likely, he'd be the one to pay for its repairs.

"Look right here, sir."

King's eyes widened when seeing the very thing that alarmed the service guys. Inside the trunk's side compartment, hidden under a custom panel, were rows and rows of U.S. currency. From the looks of it and from King's firsthand experience, there had to be over a couple hundred thousand dollars, if not more.

"We just wanted to make sure you were present while we serviced the car." One of the guys laughed and told him, "We could only imagine what you would have done had any of it come up missing."

"And I don't need a hit squad looking for me," said another.

King played the situation as best he could. He laughed. "I appreciate you guy's honesty." He began reaching into his pocket. "I know it's nothing compared to what you all stumbled across, but here's three hundred apiece. I forgot all about that money being there," he lied.

For the next hour, King watched intently as the crew gave the Bentley a thorough cleaning. On top of the cash that was found in the trunk, they found receipts above the driver's visor, papers confirming full-coverage insurance and several items of women's clothing, along with a pair of signature Chanel-framed shades. He at first thought the car belonged to a boyfriend of Diamond's, but when seeing Silvia Pierson's name throughout the documents, it allayed his anxiety.

He started to call Diamond to inform her of what was found, but decided against it, not wanting to worry her about something he had under control and more than likely, something she knew nothing about. As soon as the keys were handed to him, he headed for Fort Worth's Echo Heights.

After being filled in with the play, Chris asked her, "You really ready to do something like this, Diamond? This kind of shit stays with you for a long time."

"Me being away from my brother for God knows how long is also some shit that's going to stay with me. I'm not about to let this nigga enjoy the hell out of his life, while my bro is in some box for the rest of his."

Chris walked towards the kitchen and said, "Once you walk down this street, Diamond, ain't no turning back."

"I don't plan on it, Chris. I'm embracing this shit. The way you do it, is the way I'm going to do it."

Chris lowered his head and closed his eyes. There were definitely things he'd done and would do again and there were also things he'd done that he regretted to this day. And, those were the things that haunted him at times.

"Money ain't everything, Diamond."

"Yeah, well, that's what they took from me, so I'm taking it back."

"Speaking of money, did you ever take that issue out of the trunk and put it in the vault?"

"What money?"

Chris' brows raised. "The money you had in the side com-partment in the Bentley?"

Diamond thought for a minute and told him, "Aw, I forgot all about that shit. It wasn't nothing but two hundred and twenty thousand dollars. I leave that shit there for my rainy day fund." Diamond shrugged as it was nothing.

"That nigga might be on his way in the opposite direction with ya shit." Chris laughed, walked over to the patio and looked towards the entrance of the complex, looking for the pearl white coupe.

"That nigga ain't got no business in my shit like that anyway."

"And if it is missing, we'll get it right back."

Diamond opted for the black, shoulder-length wig with the green highlights. She applied a coat of matte green lipstick, blush with a hint of glitter, and asked Chris, "How a bitch look?"

Chris paused, tilted his head and told her, "Like you're about to charge this nigga by the hour."

"I'm for real, Chris." She walked towards the huge mirror behind her bedroom door.

"Hell, I am too. All you need on now is some thigh-high boots and one of them plastic mini dresses." He followed her eyes to the bed where her clothes lay and laughed. "Hell, naw!"

"Nigga, that outfit cost a bitch over three thousand dollars, the hell you talking about."

"Well then you need to charge the nigga that, 'cause that's the first thing that's going to run across his mind."

Diamond shot Chris the finger and when hearing the doorbell chime, she pushed him towards the door. "Make yourself useful."

Datrina and Silvia were engrossed in the conversations around the salon when Somolia came strolling in. They'd decided to give her some space, after they'd texted her several times each and received no call or text in return.

"Look what the dogs done brought home," Datrina told the group when seeing her.

"Good morning to you too, Datrina," Somolia greeted and went to her station to set up.

"It's about time you showed your face." Silvia walked over and gave her their usual hug.

"Raymond kept me up half the night," Somolia told them as if it was a routine thing they all knew about.

"That bitch lying, y'all," said one of the women present. "I saw her shit parked outside the clinic this morning."

When hearing those words, Datrina and Silvia looked at each other before breaking out in laughter. That was more feasible than her claim of Raymond being the reason she was late for her client.

"Followed by a follow-up," Somolia added before saying, "I'm just hoping you have some money today, Carroll, 'cause if not, I'm confiscating my wig, bitch."

"Ohhhh, listen to her, y'all, she must have found out she got something," Carroll shot back.

"Yeah, whatever."

Silvia looked from Somolia, to Datrina, to the other women that seemed to have been listening intently to the things said between Somolia and her client. She hadn't told anyone what transpired between them, but also knew that didn't mean it wasn't discussed among others that walked in and out of the doors. One sure thing at the salon was that if it was something to know, it would definitely be found out there. And, hoping she could save her friend from the rumors and making of them, she changed the subject. "Have you spoke with Dell yet or what? The last time I talked to him, he was talking about opening up more Totally Awesome Hair Salons and thought you and Datrina would be more than interested."

"Why haven't you told anybody about that, Somolia?" one or the other women asked.

With that, Silvia looked over at Datrina and winked. It was that easy when done before the conversation got good, and things were said that shouldn't have been.

After ending his call with Raymond and few of the guys he employed, Dell found himself unlatching the brass hooks from around the edges of the grand piano he showcased in his favorite living area. He ran his fingers over the stacks of hundred-dollar bills, inhaled the fragrance of the currency and closed his eyes. This was what it was all about. In this location alone, he had over two and a half million in cash and if things went accordingly and Camille came up with the five point seven million he was asking, he'd be that much richer. He'd surpass the wealth Antonio was rumored to have and being that he had been looking at the numbers his boss had been pulling in for a few years now, he felt his assessment of things were spot-on.

The two hundred and fifty kilos of cocaine had already arrived and was distributed throughout the Dallas, Houston, Austin and surrounding areas. He even had the hundred Camille spoke of purchasing. With the one point two million she was bringing to the table, it would be added to the rest of the money King was leaving. As much as he wanted to be present when the hit went down, he knew it was best that he kept his distance. Just in case.

In two weeks, he'd have killed two birds with one stone, or should he say, Diamond.

Dell thought about the position he placed himself in and sighed. He had to rid himself of the problem as soon as possible and with a hundred kilos to put in play, he dialed Camille's number. If it took him going to Dallas to get back that advantage, it was only a few minutes away.

"Hey, Camille, I'm ready. I'm on my way there now," he told her as soon as she answered the phone.

Camille had just stepped out of the shower when her phone lit up. She was expecting a call from King, but instead saw Dell's contact and after answering and hearing he was on his way, she lied and told him, "I'm in Kansas at the moment, Dell." It might have been early in the day, but Camille was always up on game and to hear that Dell was headed her way, there had to be reasons she was sure benefitted him.

"I need to see you today, Camille. I have the product with me as we speak."

"Well then, I'll have someone meet you at the Public Storage around the corner from your house in about one hour."

Before he was given the chance to respond, she ended the call and tossed her phone on her bed and shook her head.

"Dammit!" Dell yelled, hearing the call had been ended and he was still without the advantage he sought. "Bitch!"

Chris walked to the door and decided to play a little game with the man named King. He swung open the door and frowned.

"May I help you?"

"Um, yes, I'm looking for Diamond. Is she here?" King tried to look past him.

"And you are?" Chris opened the door wider, allowing him to see slightly past him.

"Kengyon, Kengyon Johnson." King extended his hand and said, "You must be Chris. Diamond talks non-stop about you."

Chris' frown was replaced with a smirk, then a smile. "Come on in, King."

King handed him the key to the Bentley and told him, "I had it serviced and detailed this morning and it's ready to be returned."

"Serviced and detailed?" Chris closed the door behind King and pointed.

"Yeah, I wanted to surprise Diamond by doing so." He low-ered his voice and leaned in so only Chris could hear, "You know how it is, man."

"Do you care for a drink or anything?" Chris walked towards the kitchen area and shook his head.

"Thanks, but no thanks. Me and Diamond have plans."

Chris returned with a bottle of water for himself and sat on the suede sectional, closest to the Emmitt Smith jersey. He took in King's attire as well as his mannerisms. This was his first time meeting him personally and he was nothing like he was rumored to be, but then too, Chris knew how it was when guys wanted to impress.

He noticed off the top that King was slightly shorter, had a medium build and looked to have kept himself in shape. If need be, Chris knew he could take him easily.

"You know Diamond is like a sister to me, right?" Chris took a swig of the bottled water, glanced in the direction of the hallway, then back to King. A gesture that should have told King this part of the conversation was private.

"Yeah, she talks about you quite often, it's as if I've been knowing you just as long as I've been knowing her." King smiled and told him, "I'm not out to hurt Diamond in any way, Chris. I'm really feeling her and would like a chance. I know how it is when your best friend dates a guy and I know the role we play when feeling them out. And if there's a test I need to undergo, then," King paused, looked Chris in his eyes and told him, "I'm all for it."

Chris laughed, shook his head and told him, "Not at all, King. Diamond does what Diamond does. There's no screening on my end, but just know this. When you cross her, you cross me and only then will we have a problem."

King nodded in agreement. "That's understood, homie."

"And, in case I never get to see you again, it was nice to finally meet you."

"Oh, and before I forget, the service guys found a huge amount of cash tucked off in the trunk and I made sure nothing and none was taken."

Chris frowned, and was about to say something, but Diamond walked into the living area.

"I thought I heard your voice." Diamond half-smiled, looked from King to Chris and asked King, "I hope he's not giving you a hard time?"

"Oh, no, we were just sharing a few thoughts with each other." King stood, smiled and nodded. He told her, "You are a Barbie Doll, Diamond. Every time I see you, you present yourself as a different person."

Diamond smiled, looked over at Chris and rolled her eyes. "Thank you, King."

"You are absolutely stunning."

Diamond walked center room, modeled her appearance and did a spin she'd been practicing. "You really like?"

"There's no doubt about that."

Chris sat back and gauged their interactions. He saw the way King looked at her admiringly, instead of with lustful eyes. He never once complimented Diamond on her figure or the way she wore her clothes, as did most men when approving of their next conquest. He watched him continually smile at the words she spoke and the way he stood, instead of sitting. He now saw why Diamond knew so much about the guy so fast. She had him wrapped around her finger and King wasn't trying to hide it at all.

"Well, here's the keys to your 'Vette, Diamond, I'm about to go and return the Bentley." Chris stood, extended his hand towards King and told him, "Nice meeting you, King, it really is."

"Likewise, Chris. Maybe we can get together for the women in our lives one day."

"Sounds like a plan." Chris walked past King and told Diamond, "Walk me out to the car, right quick."

Diamond followed him and once they were downstairs, she asked, "What's up?"

"The nigga found the money, Diamond, so—"

She cut him off. "How?"

"That nigga will turn the world upside down for you, Diamond. He's one of them niggas that will tell you everything. All you got to do is ask him, Diamond. All you got to do is ask him." Chris hugged her, opened the door to the Bentley and climbed in.

"I'll get at you later, Chris." Diamond turned and headed back upstairs. Chris had never steered her wrong and she was sure he wasn't turning back now.

"Is everything all right?" King asked her after she'd come back inside.

"Yeah, he just made me promise not to give you any pussy."

King asked her, "Is that what he thinks I want from you?"

"Do you?" Diamond met his gaze and looked for anything other than the sincerity she'd seen in him.

"It's not about what you can give or offer me, Diamond. It's about me giving you all of me, the best of me, and nothing but that. If the day comes to where you feel as if I'm worthy of your love, then so be it. If not, then that's the chance I'm taking."

Diamond closed her eyes and exhaled. She was about to bank everything on an assessment Chris made. "Have you ever heard of a guy named Antonio McClendon?"

King smiled. From the conversations they had and the game she knew, he as well as Camille, felt she knew more than she was letting on and hearing her inquire about the kingpin, it all started coming together for him. Diamond was Antonio McClendon's trophy.

"So, that's your boyfriend?"

Diamond looked at him with disgust. "Have you heard of him or what?" Her tone was more forceful this time.

"Yes, I've heard of him, who hasn't? But, I don't know him personally, if that's what you're asking." King could see she was as serious as she'd ever been and if she thought that would be a factor that pushed him away, it wasn't.

"What do you know about him?"

"Um, well, he's respected in the game and he's the reason a lot of people are on now. I've heard tell of the many doors he's opened in the game."

"Have you ever heard about him being in the way or doing anything foul?"

King thought for a second and slowly began shaking his head, "Not that I know of, why?"

Since it was now out there, she wanted to make enemies with his enemies and if necessary, allies with his allies.

"That nigga fucked over me a while back. Had me host several events for him and skipped out on the bills he accumulated. I'm glad his ass got locked up."

"I hate to hear something like that, Diamond, but you can't let something so small consume you. You've got to be a stepper in this game."

"But, he was in the way of my money, King. I had to do something. But, the game got to him first, I guess."

"That just goes to show you that you don't have to be the one to lower standards. Look at you now, you're modeling at some of the top places, you got money in the bank, and you're still able to make something happen. You were the bigger person, Diamond and because of that you're still standing."

Diamond felt his words, but more than anything, they reminded her of the things Antonio told her himself. If she was to close her eyes, she would have sworn her brother was standing before her with his usual speeches. "Well, you hungry or what?"

"And, if there's anything I can do to fix what he broke in your life, I'm here, Diamond. I'm here for as long as you want me to be." King reached for her and feeling her fall into his embrace, he squeezed her, kissed the side of her head and held her.

"Is that as tight as you can squeeze a bitch?" Diamond closed her eyes and felt for his heart. It was now she prayed she wouldn't regret the decision she was about to make.

Chapter Twenty-Four

That next day, Chris was standing next to his truck when Silvia arrived. Datrina and Somolia had already opened the shop and were going about their day, talking about the latest story and instead of entertaining them, he waited outside.

As soon as Silvia pulled into her parking space, he jumped in and told her, "Let's hit a couple of blocks right quick."

"And the day begins," she told him while backing out.

Chris checked his phone, made sure there were no business dealings calling and sat his phone on the dash of her Boxster. It was a few things he wanted to run by her before the end of the day.

"What's on your mind, Chris?" Silvia pulled into traffic and once her salon was in her rearview, she slowly turned on the next block.

"I finally met King yesterday." He looked over at her.

"And?"

"And, the nigga really feeling Diamond. He really is."

"Okay, and?"

"And, I think she's starting to feel him too."

Silvia glanced in his direction, thumbed the buttons on her steering wheel and smiled. "So, now you're thinking you gonna lose your best friend?"

"It doesn't have anything to do with me, Silvia—"

"Then what does it have to do with, Chris? Because Diamond knows what she's getting herself into and she's not backing down."

"That's just what I'm talking about, Silvia. The woman is wrapping herself in this role and she's starting to believe this nigga."

"That's a good thing, right?"

"That's what I'm trying to figure out."

"Well, just let her do her thing, Chris. It'll be over within a couple of weeks."

"Dell already trying to move, huh?"

"Yeah, that's a done deal and money spent."

Chris looked away from Silvia and looked out of the passenger side window. His gut was telling him to pull Diamond somehow, but the wheels were turning and the last thing he wanted was for King to see through Diamond's façade and turn the table against her. He also knew that she wasn't about to listen to him alone. What he needed was to get a step ahead of even her.

"I'm going to see Antonio. Alone."

"She's fine, Chris, Diamond is stronger than you think she is."

"Diamond's strength is in doing unplanned, off-the-wall shit, not love and the woman seems to be diving, Silvia. Fast."

"Yeah. You tripping now. That woman ain't even thinking like that."

"I know Diamond, Silvia, and I know what I'm looking at when I see her."

"Well then, she's going to have to get over it, 'cause what's done is done. It's just a matter of time now."

Chris nodded in agreement and said, "Yeah, it's just a matter of time now."

Q had come up with all kinds of excuses not to go to work and the one that had KP tossing his keys back on the counter was when he said, "That nigga would have killed you if Silvia hadn't caught on to him."

"Hell naw, me and Chris alright." KP walked into Q's living room and fell on the couch.

"Alright? Niggas don't pull heat on they patna's and demand they fake they own death and shit."

"Ain't nobody faked no damn death. Where in the hell you get some shit like that from?" KP turned and just stared at him.

"That's what that fake-ass call was about, he was going to do your ass and have her thinking you just up and left because of the things y'all going through."

"Shut the fuck up, Q. You've been watching too many of them bootleg DVD's, nigga."

"Nigga, the shit you got going on need to be on a DVD some-where. We could sell this shit." Q walked past him and pointed. "Think about it."

"What I need to be thinking about is a way to get back in my house, in my bed and with my wife."

"And that's that. This nigga tell you not to go home to your own house and you don't. I've been telling you to get out of my shit and you won't. What the fuck is wrong with that picture?"

"Just letting the shit die down, is all."

"That nigga Chris might be the one fucking Silvia. You ever thought about that?"

KP threw his head back and rolled his eyes. There was no telling what would fall from Q's mouth and as always, and there was no telling what he'd believe.

"They damn near like brother and sister, fool! They ain't doing shit. Ain't no way in the world."

"See, that's why it's so easy for them to do it, no one will think better of it."

"Naw, I don't believe no shit like that, so come up with something else."

"That's why the nigga always be there, KP, and why you think he tripping like he is about you slapping your own damn wife, huh?"

"Because they family, nigga."

"Or they fucking. Hoes be on some slick shit too, nigga. That's why I play they ass like I do." Q fell onto the couch next to his friend and leaned towards him. "No one would ever think they was fucking around, because they acting like they family. We used to do that shit way back when."

"You need to lean your ass back over there, smelling like your lips been sewed together for about a month."

"I bet you wish you could say that about ya wife's pussy."

KP swung at Q twice, missed him and started to swing again.

"I'm gonna knock your ass out, nigga. Keep talking about my wife if you want to."

Q hopped up and was squatting at the corner of the couch, smiling at KP when he told him, "That nigga probably knocking her off right now."

KP grabbed his phone, dialed Silvia's number and shot Q the finger. "Ain't nobody fucking my wife."

Silvia was in the middle of making a wide U-turn when her phone rang. "Get that, Chris."

Chris reached over, grabbed her phone and answered, "Hel-lo?"

Datrina was looking towards the parking lot just as Silvia was pulling back into her space and when seeing Chris jump out and head towards his Durango and Silvia about to walk in, she told Somolia, "Head's up, girl. Something's up."

"Silvia, is everything alright?" Somolia asked when seeing the expression she wore.

"Yeah, yeah, it's all good."

"Yeah, right. What happened now?" Datrina asked, knowing better.

"KP just called me, talking about me and Chris fucking around or something like that."

"He said what?" Datrina asked with a frown of her own.

"KP said something like that?" Somolia chimed in.

"He was talking all loud and crazy when I got the phone, so I just hung up on his stupid ass."

Datrina shook her head and said, "So, now Chris is going to go find him?"

"Hell naw. Chris got some more shit on his mind right now."

"What the hell is KP tripping on? Damn!" Somolia cried. She had been feeling like the things that were happening, were her fault to begin with.

"Ain't no telling. He's at Q's, so you know how that goes."

"Well, that answers everything right there. Q's messy ass always in the middle of something."

When hearing Somolia's comment, all present laughed. Silvia said, "He ain't the only one, Somolia. Not at all."

King was awakened by the sounds of loud music and a tapping noise he couldn't recognize. He groggily raised himself, wiped his eyes of sleep and started to head to his bathroom. He had a couple of stops lined up for the day and afterwards, he and Diamond were going to hang out a bit. They'd spent most of the day before together and King even surprised her with a twenty thousand dollar shopping spree at the Galleria. What surprised the hell out of him was when Diamond shelled out fifteen hundred for a pair of three-carat diamond earrings for him. Never the one to be outdone, he looked for things and ways to reward her continually.

He was just about to step into his walk-in shower when Camille walked into his bedroom.

"You're still alive?" She greeted him with raised brows.

"Morning to you too, Camille."

"I thought we were going to dinner last night?" Camille stood in the doorway with her arms folded, which was a gesture he knew spoke of her disappointment.

"I really forgot, baby and I'm sorry. Let me make it up to you." He walked towards her and tried to kiss her forehead.

"Don't put your lips on me, Kengyon Johnson, I'm serious."

"Oh, you tripping like that?"

"It's more than apparent as to who's tripping, Kengyon. You showering this woman with money already and you missing dinner with me. Yeah, it's clear when it comes to who's tripping."

"Well, do you mind if I take a shower? I have things to do today, Camille."

"What, she ran off right after the shopping spree or what?"

King sighed, pushed past her and said, "She hasn't gone anywhere. Camille. I told her that I had some business to take care of early in the day and that we'd get together later."

"I think you're fucking up. King. I really do."

"I thought we talked about this, Camille, and I thought we both agreed you'd allow me to handle this."

"It looks as if you're doing a hell of a job at it also."

King undressed, set the water's temperature and told her, "Chill out, Camille."

Camille grabbed his arm. "Are you really that hard up for some pussy, King?" She began removing the sports bra she wore. He watched her.

"Is that what this is all about? Huh?" Camille stepped out of her leggings, removed her panties and stood inches from him.

"You tripping, Camille. You taking this shit too far now."

"You putting pussy before me now. Well, here, here's some pussy right here, King!"

King stepped in the shower and closed the door behind him. He could tell Camille was hurt and being that this was her second time addressing him in such a manner, he told her, "Nothing is coming between us, Camille, and you know this."

"You setting yourself up for failure with this bitch, King. The game we in don't allow this shit, nigga, but here you are, putting both feet in for some stupid reason. You need some pussy that bad, you can pay for the shit. You ain't cheap and I know a ton of bitches that will throw some pussy at you for a fraction of the amount you spending on this Diamond bitch."

"She's not a bitch, Camille. She's really alright, once you get to know her."

"See there you go, defending her, just like you did that bitch Nava."

King adjusted the jets on the showerhead, angled it towards his neck and closed his eyes. "Is that why you did what you did to her?"

"What?"

"Nava. Is that why you ran her off?"

"The bitch lucky she's still alive, King. She saw a win and played the cards you gave her. You did that."

"Yeah, well, Diamond is different. She's nothing like Nava at all."

"At least you knew Nava's name. You're running around here acting like you in love and you don't even know the woman's full name, King. Are you serious?"

"We're getting to know each other, Camille, and this is how you go about it."

Camille hit the glass doors that separated them, scaring King, telling him, "Not only does she know everything about you, you keeping my name in your mouth. I don't play that shit, Kengyon! I'm in this shit because we made promises to each other. We—"

King cut her off, snatched open the shower door and pulled her inside. Before she could protest, he pushed his tongue into her mouth and pushed her against the Italian-tiled wall.

"Stop, King!"

King ignored her and began parting her legs with one hand and with the other, he held her by the chin. He kissed her deeply and when feeling her spread her legs, he pushed two fingers inside of her.

Camille moaned, looked him in his eyes and wrapped her arms around his neck. "I love you, King," she whispered. "I love you."

"I know, Camille, I love you too." King kissed her lips, pushed her now wet hair from her eyes and pushed himself from her. He told her, "But, I'm in love with Diamond."

Camille's gaze met his and they looked deep into the other's eyes. They stayed this way for seconds, before King said, "I'm in love, Camille." King smiled.

Camille backed away from him and stepped out of the shower. She grabbed a towel, gathered her workout clothing and left. She'd known Kengyon Johnson all her adult life and she knew when he was talking just to be talking, and she also knew when he was talking about the way he felt. She knew this was one of those times.

Diamond had been up for the past two hours. She'd already spoken with Chris and told him the things she had planned for the day. She was looking over some of the things King bought her the day before, but was remembering the time they spent together. The things said and the promises he made her. She thought about the fact that their time together would be short and she'd actually miss him. The words her brother spoke rang louder than any she ever wanted to hear.

"When you find it, you'll want to give any and everything just to keep it." Diamond knew she'd developed feelings for King, but that was it. And, those feelings could easily be separated and even replaced and that was what she was banking on.

After putting together her ensemble for the day, she grabbed her phone, went out on the terrace and called Dell. He'd left her several messages and now that she had some time to herself, she dialed him.

Dell was beaming, money had been coming in from the shipment they had distributed days before. Raymond had already begun cleaning parts of the money.

They were going to invest and things were looking better than he expected. He thought about the call he made to Camille in an attempt to re-schedule the drop at the Public Storage facility minutes away from his home and being that he was unable to do that, he had to go out and deliver the hundred kilos to a group of guys he knew nothing about. Camille definitely had him in a position he didn't favor at all.

He looked down at the one million, two hundred and fifty thousand in cash Camille had delivered in her stead, thought about the six-hundred-thousand-dollar loss and began adding it to the two and a half million he had there in a in the huge grand piano. Dell shrugged.

He'd taken a loss before and was more than sure he'd bounce back soon. Just as he was placing the last of the cash in the interior of the grand, his phone chimed. "About time," he told himself and when seeing the huge diamond his screen displayed, he smiled.

"What's up, Diamond? Tell me something good."

"You were right, Dell. The work was sent to the house. He received a call while we were out and Camille was upset about him not being there or something, by the sounds of it."

"Did you see where he keeps his money?"

"Yeah, he keeps it at his Ravinia home. He has a couple of safes throughout the house, but the main one is in a vault-like safe across from the pool outside."

Dell laughed. "Are you sure about this, Diamond? I don't want the guys going in there blind. I, we damn sure don't need them leaving and burning any cash they couldn't find."

"Yeah, I'm sure. He showed me every bit of three million there alone. Then, there's the safe in the hallway, he keeps a nice amount there also. The drugs are usually kept in the storage space he had built out by the woods."

After being filled in on all the things Diamond discovered, he began doing a preliminary count in his head and when seeing the numbers himself, he asked her, "And, what of Camille?"

"She's here most of the time, but she does have her own spots. I really don't know too much about her business, except that she brings money here all the time."

"Okay, well, I'm going to keep you informed. You're doing a great job, Diamond. Soon, you'll be that much richer and that much closer to the vision you have. Just don't lose focus, Diamond."

Dell concluded his call, stood and inhaled as deep as he could. This was the life for him.

Nicole Goosby

Chapter Twenty-Five

Diamond stepped into a color-blocked, Versace jumpsuit, a pair of black strappy heels, and grabbed her signature Chanel shades.

She decided against a wig and pulled her hair back into a high-crowned ponytail and allowed it to flow down to the nape of her neck. She admired her thin, petite frame and thought about something King said about her gaining a little weight. She smiled at the thought. Somolia had called her two days straight to remind her it was time to get her hair done, and that was a stop she did plan to make sooner than later.

After pulling five thousand dollars from the pocket money she kept, she grabbed the keys to her Corvette and was about to head out the door when her phone rang. Seeing the unfamiliar number, she frowned before answering. "Hello?"

"Diamond?"

"Yeah, what's up?"

"We need to talk, like yesterday."

"And who is this that feels as if we need to talk?" Diamond asked, still not recognizing the small and calm voice.

"This is Camille. I'm at King's home on Ravinia. Can you come?"

"Um," Diamond looked at the time on her Rolex watch and told her, "I'll see you shortly then."

After texting Chris and telling him of a change in plans, Diamond pulled out of the complex and headed for Dallas.

***

Camille stood at the glass doors of the patio and just watched King and Buddy load the rental car he was about to take to Oklahoma. She'd made several arrangements for herself and felt a talk with the one woman King favored more than her was now paramount.

"You sure you don't want to ride with me?" King yelled from the rental.

263

"Not this time. I have an appointment shortly and I can't miss it."

"Well, we'll be back later. If anything should come up that needs my attention, get at me."

"Will do." Camille watched both of them climb into respective cars and pull out of the drive. She checked her watch and headed back into the bi-leveled estate.

***

Chris stood when seeing Antonio being escorted into the visitation room. He'd do the attorney thing. He followed the CO's with his eyes and once they'd left them to themselves, he smiled.

"That shit works, huh?"

"It better work. I paid five hundred dollars for this visit."

"Yeah, well, I'm glad I was able to pull you out of that damn cell for a while anyway."

"Actually, I was writing."

"Writing what?"

"A book."

"You're writing a book? Hell naw."

"Yeah, I'm serious. I don't have shit else to do and I might as well do something productive."

"What's the title and what is it about?"

"Well, as for the title, I haven't named it yet because the publisher might decide to change my shit and I'm writing about us."

"Publisher? Man, we can publish our own shit, nigga."

"Yeah, well, I know you ain't here to talk about no publishing, so what's up?"

Chris pulled the briefcase he brought up and pulled out a stack of papers, making it look as if Antonio was going over some material.

"Ya sister done dialed in on this nigga, homie."

"Oh yeah?"

"Hell yeah, the nigga showed up at the spot the other day."

"The nigga knows where I live, Chris?"

"No, no, no. Diamond moved into the place Datrina and I live and she gave us the mansion."

"She did what, nigga?"

"Yeah, you didn't know I bought the mansion from her?" Chris smiled, watched his boss go from overexcited to extremely calm in a matter of seconds.

"Nigga, I thought you were serious."

"Yeah, well, I think ya sis is getting serious with this dude."

Antonio McClendon laughed. "Oh yeah?"

"You know how the girl feels about that Bentley you got her for her birthday, right?"

"Right."

"Well, she let the nigga keep her car, man. The nigga took it to get detailed and they found her little stash in the back."

"Yeah?"

"She gave the nigga some game about the car being loaned to her or some shit, but she wasn't even tripping."

"It's not a problem there, is it?"

"No. The nigga was more worried about her tripping than anything. She's spending more time with him than she does with…"

Chris' voice trailed off at the thought of the words he was about to speak and instead of continuing, he only smiled.

"You jealous, Chris? You got a girl, nigga."

"It's not that I'm jealous, Antonio, I just don't like her getting too attached to this dude, man."

"We just might have to accept that, Chris. She's destined to find somebody."

"Not this dude though, man. Not King."

"We said the same thing about Silvia and KP, and about you and Datrina, and you know I had my eyes on her."

"Yeah, you did, didn't you?" Chris thought back to when Antonio did things to win Datrina. His only flaw was that he had a bevy of women at his beck and call, whereas Chris was always the loyal one that gave himself to one woman only. Trust outweighed money, and his loyalty overshadowed the promises Antonio tried his best to keep.

"I had to accept that, homie. Not only that, but I'm cool with it."

"Yeah, I know, but—"

"Diamond was always the one that played on both ends of the court, Chris. She's liable to score on either end. The reason I okayed that shit was because Diamond sees things differently. She's going to make mistakes, but she has to learn in the process, Chris and she's learning, homie."

"I just don't like her getting too deep off in this shit."

"She's never been the shallow one, Chris, so just sit back and relax. It's too late for anything else."

To see Antonio as calm as he was put Chris in a better place mentally and that was the reason he nodded. It was now under-stood without being said and with it being between him and Antonio McClendon, it wouldn't be said.

***

"So, what are you going to do?" Q broke the silence around them. Ever since KP came to his realization that Chris might have been the one sexing his wife, he had no words to speak and Q called, but gave him the little space he could provide.

"That nigga been playing me all this time. Me and Datrina."

"That's fucked up too, man." Q shook his head in disbelief and asked, "You think Datrina knows about it?"

"I really doubt it, because she wouldn't accept no shit like that."

"I wouldn't be surprised if she did though."

KP frowned. "Why would you say that?"

"Look at it. The woman just not too long ago got that convert-ible Pontiac and shortly afterwards, they give her a Calloway Cor-vette and then take her to Miami and buy her all kinds of shit while they were there."

"Man, Diamond bought that car for Chris, and Chris was the one that insisted Datrina go to Miami in the first place."

Q twisted his lips and said, "Listen to yourself for a minute. You're steady talking about Chris' shit, remember, he was the one telling you to chill out while they were in Miami. He was the one answering the phone while they were in Miami, and when they came back from Miami, it was only Chris and Silvia. If you can't see that shit, nigga, you stupid as hell. It's always been Chris and they paying Datrina off, so she won't see the shit."

Kevin thought about the things his friend mentioned, thought about the timeline and the so-called coincidences. "I'm going to call Datrina and blow they shit up."

"Should have been done that, clown ass nigga."

Datrina held her phone up when seeing that the caller was none other than KP. She waved Silvia over and motioned for the other women to quiet themselves, 'cause she was about to let all hear what he had to say. Silvia even warned her that he'd eventually call with all kinds of questions he felt she should have the answers to and now that he was, they were about to have a couple of laughs, and she was sure of it.

"Datrina Ellis speaking," she answered as if she didn't know who the caller was.

"Um, Datrina?" KP asked in a hushed tone.

"Yeah, who is this?" She looked towards Silvia, who was rolling her eyes at his antics.

"This KP, can you talk?"

Datrina lied, "Yeah, what's up, KP?"

"Don't say my name! I don't want no one to know you're on the phone with me."

"Oh, uh, it's cool 'cause I'm in the office restroom anyway. What's up, KP?" she asked, noticing his uneasiness.

"Listen to me, Datrina, 'cause I'm about to tell you some shit I found out."

"What, what is it, KP?"

"I think Chris and Silvia are fucking around behind our backs."

"What!"

"Shh, don't trip, just listen to me."

"Why would you say something like that, KP?" Datrina looked around the salon at the other women, seeing a couple of them with their hands over their mouths muffling laughs, and others look on in awe, she began smiling also.

"This shit is going to sound crazy but me and Q put the shit together."

"Q?"

"Yeah, he's really the one that was able to see the shit 'cause I was blinded by love or some dumb shit."

"Well, what is it then, KP? Spit it out."

Datrina and the rest of the women there listened intently to KP and Q's claim while suppressing laughs, coughs, and everything else that threatened to expose the fact that they were listening. And instead of interrupting him with questions just as asinine as the words that spilled from his mouth, she only threw in a, "Umph," here and a "What you say," there.

And, when he got to the part about explaining the reasons Silvia and Chris came back ahead of her and Diamond, and that Diamond was also an integral part of their so-called secret, she told him, "I don't know, KP, I don't think she knows about it. At first, you was saying that she was fucking with Dell and even Raymond, then you said she was messing with the guy in Miami. Damn, KP."

"I, um, I might have been wrong about all them, but that's how they threw a nigga. I never expected for it to be Chris."

"Why didn't you kick his ass, KP?"

"Kick whose ass?"

"Chris' ass, if you knew all this shit, why didn't you kick his ass then?"

"Now you trying to get a nigga killed. He was damn near about to kill me yesterday after me and my own wife had a fight. The nigga had a gun to my head and everything."

"He did what, KP?"

"I'm serious, the nigga pulled up on a nigga like Jason Bourne or something. When we pulled up, he was already sitting across the street waiting. How in the hell he know we was coming here, Datrina huh? How in the hell he know that?"

"Let me just let me think about all this, KP."

"And don't tell Silvia shit, because she ain't going to do shit but start lying about the shit. Q had to help me figure the shit out, 'cause she had me too fucked up."

Silvia had heard enough. She grabbed the phone from Datrina and yelled into the mic, "Get your dumb ass off this phone, KP, and since you got Q helping you figure shit out, tell him to help you figure out how to get that rash from between your ass, nigga! Calling up here with that bullshit. Stupid ass, nigga!"

She ended his call, handed Datrina her phone and headed for her office. That was enough for the day and being that it would be the topic of salon conversation for weeks to come, it wouldn't be the last she heard of it.

Before Diamond was able to turn into the drive-in at King's Ravinia mansion, the black gates opened, allowing her entry. It was evident her arrival had been expected and when rounding the corner at the rear of the house, she saw Camille standing at the bottom of the stairs of the pool house. She could tell Camille must have been lounging around, because she wasn't draped in her usual dress of designer labels. Diamond parked alongside the 911 Porsche, looked out at the woman wearing the unbuttoned kittenish romper with nude heels and smiled. She definitely loved the way Camille dressed.

"Glad you could come on such short notice," Camille told her.

"You caught me just as I was walking out of the door." Diamond closed the driver's door to her 'Vette and followed Camille inside.

"Would you like something to drink, Diamond?" Camille offered.

"Um, I'll take water."

"How about something to boost the mood?" Camille smiled, walked towards the kitchen area and looked back at Diamond.

"I beg your pardon?"

"I have some of the best cocaine in Dallas, and an assortment of pills and even a little heroin, if that's what you prefer."

"Thanks, but no thanks, Camille. I don't move to that kind of music, unless it's making my accounts do so."

"Well, I just thought I'd offer. Most of the women King brings around has a habit, if not two."

Diamond sat on the corner of the sofa and crossed her legs at the ankle, accepted her water from Camille and told her, "I do have habits, but doing drugs isn't one of them." She shook her head at the ambiguity of the statement. "Not in that fashion anyway."

Camille sat across from her and took a sip of her drink before saying, "I'm going to get straight to the point with you. Diamond, that's just the way I am."

"I like it like that, Camille." Diamond sat her drink down and gave her undivided attention.

"Do you have any idea of what King is to me?"

"Some."

"He's all I have, Diamond. He's my man, my brother, my best friend and my girlfriend at times." Camille rolled her eyes to add emphasis. "It's been me and him for a while now and being that he was such a" Camille searched for the right word and said, "benevolent spirit, he tends to attract and bring around needy women that have agendas, ulterior motives and beauty he can't seem to see past. This is where I come in, with his best interest at heart, with an agenda of my own and motives totally opposite than the ones they have."

Diamond nodded, took another sip of her water and sat it down. Camille continued, "And here we are, Diamond. So, now I must ask you, why are you here? Why now?"

Diamond watched her and could see that she was really on edge, but was trying to remain as calm and professional as she could. Camille reminded her of Silvia. And, this would be one of those conversations she'd have with her.

"You know why I'm here, Camille, and since we're having this talk, let's do just that."

"With that being said, first question. Why doesn't King know your name?"

"He spoke of wanting me to disclose certain things about me when I'm ready."

"But, you're ready to spend his money at the drop of any syllable that sounds like shopping?"

"I have my own money to do that. King has been more than generous, to say the least."

"But yet, you make no attempts to stop him."

"Why should I?"

Camille sighed, shifted her posture and told her, "I'm also a woman that has her own money and for me to accept such efforts on their behalf, it's because I have an ulterior motive and because it's a part of the game I play. King wants to help me with this modeling thing. He insists on showing me that he cares about me and the things I have going on."

"Then why is it so hard for you to do the same, Diamond?"

"Um, you know nothing about me, Camille."

"Neither does King."

"But, I'm the open book. I'm somewhat easy to read." Diamond took another sip of water.

"Not for King, Diamond. Beauty is his weakness and I'm more than sure he's told you as much."

"He has."

"Yet you still use it as an advantage?"

"Advantage for what? My career, money, what?"

"Maybe it is your career, maybe it's for extra money. You are the only one that knows, but what I do know is that there's a plethora of things you're keeping from King for a reason. You're here for a reason and I want to know why."

King walked into the living area and smiled. "I thought that was your Corvette I saw exiting the freeway and being that I accidentally left my phone, I decided to turn around to intercept you if I could. I had a feeling you were coming here." He walked towards Diamond, who stood, and kissed her lips. He nodded at Camille.

"I just wanted to surprise you upon your arrival." Diamond lied and looked right at Camille, whose smile proved they now shared a secret of their own.

"Yeah, well, come ride with me right quick. Buddy's waiting."

"How can I say no to that?" Diamond stood, gathered her shades and phone and followed King outside. "Thanks for the company and the water, Camille."

Camille followed, caught King and Diamond as they crossed the pool area and told him, "The two of you should do, King. I need Buddy for other reasons."

Hearing his summons, Buddy climbed out of the truck and nodded at Camille. The order had been given.

"But I need for him to—"

Camille cut him off. "I have more pressing issues, Kengyon."

"I have to—"

It was now Diamond's turn to cut him off. "I got you. King."

"You sure about this?" King watched Diamond and Camille's silent exchange.

"Oh, yeah, I got you." Diamond climbed into the rental car and strapped on her seatbelt. "Let's go."

King began, "There's drugs—"

"Let's go, King," Diamond told him in a more commanding tone.

King climbed into his Lexus truck and slammed its door. He knew the card Camille was playing and knew it would be something they discussed later.

Camille waved at both of them and told King, "Be careful."

With enough cocaine in the trunk of the rental to sentence her for years, Diamond pulled out behind King, adjusted her seat and rearview mirror and was on her way. There was nothing to talk about, no instructions to be given. This was what she did and for her King, this was what she'd do.

Chapter Twenty-Six
One week later

It had been days since Camille and King last spoke and it was not the best decision she'd made in a while. She felt by her not speaking or visiting the house, he'd eventually come around to see things from her perspective, but it only caused him to confide in Diamond more. She'd called him early this morning to inquire about a business transaction she had lined up, but hearing Diamond answer the phone, she hung up. There had to be something she could do to get King to see things before it was too late, because she was more than sure Diamond had that ulterior motive they briefly spoke of.

She had been keeping a low profile for a week now and when remembering some of the scant details about the things King actually knew about the woman, Camille felt a trip to Fort Worth was overdue. "You ready, Buddy?"

"Always, Boss Lady."

She walked out to the passenger side of Buddy's Dually, opened the door and climbed in. It was just something about pulling up with Buddy that unnerved people and if this is what it took, then so be it.

"Where we headed, Boss?"

"Fort Worth." Camille pulled up the salon's address on his pop-up navigation screen and once the salon's location was known, Camille pointed. "That's where we're headed, Buddy. Got to see what little Miss Diamond really has going on."

Buddy pointed the Dually northbound and told her, "Yes, ma'am."

***

With Silvia having errands to run, both Somolia and Datrina opened the shop and got the ball rolling. It had been a week since the call from KP and it was still being talked about when regular clients came in and for the ones out of the loop, they were quickly informed. One of the main reasons was because Somolia knew that as long as there was something else to talk about on the floor, she wouldn't be the focal point of the subject matter.

Q had stopped by a time or two and they knew he was just doing so to see what kind of vibe he could pick up on. The first time he showed his face, he was met with stares, frowns and questionable expressions and he even tried to plead his case, but things were heard as well as believed and when he began explaining, no one believed him.

Somolia was walking a set of barrel curlers to her station when Datrina asked her, "Can you imagine another Totally Awesome Hair Salon opened up somewhere?"

"Yeah, and you'd be running it, because it ain't nothing but a big ass headache."

"Tell me about it. You see what Silvia has to deal with."

"The only good thing about it would be the money, but that's only half of the business. The other half consists of all the BS that comes in and out of the salon."

"Don't forget about the drama, the drama queens and everything else."

Datrina waved her off. "You ain't heard nothing I said, Somolia. Nothing at all."

"And, when is Diamond supposed to be bringing this King by the shop so we can meet him? I've been hearing about him for a while now."

"Well, you need to be talking to Diamond about that, besides, I don't think she'd want you ogling over her man anyway."

"Her man? When did this happen?"

"I wasn't the one that told you, but um, he is that into her, even though she refuses to believe it."

"Girl, please, Diamond is Diamond and having a man is the last thing on her mind. Believe that. That woman is about some money right now and truth be told, if I was in her shoes, it would be mine too." Somolia snapped her finger in a prosaic manner.

"Whatever the case though, she spends the days with him and if that's not something you do with your man, then what is?"

Somolia smacked her lips and added, "At least Chris ain't with her all day, every day anymore."

"Shut up, Somolia, Don't even start that shit."

They all laughed.

The bell dinging above the door halted the laughter and when seeing the huge guy entering, Somolia turned, looked him up and down and asked. "Can I help you?" He had to have been the biggest man she'd ever seen in her life and this caused her to both stare and frown.

"Um, yes, I was looking to get another color going with this." Camille pointed to her hair as if it was a pain.

Seeing Somolia stuck in her trance, Datrina walked around to where Camille stood and examined her 'do. "What exactly are you looking to do, because your hair is perfect and looks to have been recently treated." Datrina pulled at the coils of Camille's hair and looked her over. There was something so familiar about her. She looked at her facial structure, her thin nose, high arched eyebrows and into her hazel-green eyes. "You're pretty as hell, you know that?"

Camille smiled. "So I've been told."

"Here have a seat and let's see what we can come up with."

Somolia subtly walked past Buddy to get a better feel of his height alone. He made her feel like the woman she was and at the same time, scared her. His menacing look, silent but so powerful presence, and the size of him all intrigued her thoughts and watered her mouth. Somolia swallowed hard, looked up at him and asked, "Can we talk?"

"You'd have to ask him." Camille nodded at the big guy, sat back and crossed her legs.

"Hi, I'm Somolia. I…"

"Nice to meet you, Somolia." Buddy's voice alone caused her to step back and when he extended his hand, she became frozen with fear.

"He's not going to hurt you, unless he feels threatened for whatever reason." Camille laughed when seeing the common reaction of those that encountered Buddy.

"Um," Somolia extended her hand also, saying, "It's nice to meet you also."

"They call me Buddy."

"Buddy?"

"Yes, ma'am."

Somolia looked back at Datrina and the rest of the women present and told them, "I like it when they call me that."

"Girl, you just like when they call you, period," one of the women told her.

"Would you like me to trim you up while you wait on your girl?"

Somolia knew they weren't an item because of the way he watched her, but she decided to do a little fishing to see if he did have a significant other.

"She's not my girl. That's my boss lady."

"Boss lady?"

"Yes, ma'am."

"So, what's up? I won't charge you anything with this being your first time."

Each of the women looked at Somolia as if she was crazy and when seeing the stares, she inquired, "What?"

"Where the hell is he going to sit, Somolia?"

Somolia turned, faced Buddy and bit her bottom lip. "I might have to climb this one."

"Yeah, you would climb up on something," Datrina told her, before rolling her eyes and facing her newest client, Camille. "Where do I know you from?"

"It might have been at one of those symposiums or some-thing," Camille answered.

"Symposiums? Naw, I haven't been to one of them in so long."

Camille cleared her throat and continued, "I was under the impression you worked with models and the like."

"The only models I've worked with are those that walk up in here acting like they are," said Datrina.

Somolia laughed and said, "That would be Diamond."

"She's one of them," Datrina told Camille.

Camille uncrossed her leg and placed it over the other. "I thought Diamond did model professionally."

"That woman refused to model and she has all the potential. I don't understand her at all," Somolia chimed in.

"She's just taking it slow right now. I'm more than sure if she keeps hearing it, she'll buckle down and get with it," said Datrina.

"Last I heard, she was buckling down with some guy we haven't, well, I haven't seen yet." Somolia looked towards Datrina and smacked her lips.

Datrina eyed Somolia and said, "She'll bring him around when she's ready. You know how she is."

Camille sat and listened to the tale of Diamond and the fact that she was a beautiful woman many wanted to be. She sat and listened to how spoiled she was and had been for as long as they could remember.

In the course of the whole gist, Camille got to know about the Bentley coupe Diamond's brother bought her as a birthday gift, the convertible Diamond herself bought for Datrina, both the Calloway Corvettes she recently purchased and the three-million-dollar estate she lived in alone. It wasn't until the third mention of the name, did she realize that they were referring to Diamond when they spoke of the name, Chanel.

To hear so much about Diamond and so little about modeling, Camille couldn't help but think of all the reasons she'd have to lie about something of that nature. She couldn't help but see an ulterior motive. She had money, lived a lifestyle many envied and could have any man she wanted. Why her King? What did Diamond want with her King?

By the time Camille was handed the mirror and spun around to where she could see the finishing touches, she was looking at a totally different woman.

"I like this," she told herself. She looked at Buddy for his approval and when seeing him smile, she knew she was on one. "I definitely like this color."

"The honey-blonde normally does it with women your color and the kinky coils you got going on, gives it the volume it needs. Not to mention, the color of your eyes," said Datrina.

"Mm." Camille smiled, snapped her fingers, gaining Buddy's affection from Somolia and asked, "How do I look?"

"Always beautiful, Boss Lady. Always."

"Tip the woman for me." Camille climbed out of the swivel chair and headed for the door. She'd found out more than she needed and now that she had, she had business elsewhere.

Buddy reached into his pocket and pulled out ten crisp hundred-dollar bills and handed them to Datrina. He smiled. "Keep the change." Before ducking under the top beam of the door, Buddy looked back at Somolia and told her, "I'll be expecting that call sooner than later."

"And I'll be expecting your return as well." Once the door closed behind Buddy, she looked at Datrina and told her, "His dick has got to be huge."

Datrina replied, "You know what they say about them big ass men. Big man, small package." They laughed.

Somolia looked towards the parking lot and said, "Not in my experiences."

"Hey," Datrina looked around the salon and asked, "Did anybody catch her name?"

"Yeah, Boss Lady," they said in unison.

Diamond accepted the gold-rimmed flute from Dell and looked down into the glass. "You know I don't fuck with alcohol, Dell."

"I know, I know, Diamond. I just wanted to have a drink with you, is all. You've been a major player for us already and I want to be the first to tell you we appreciate it. We would have never gotten a foot in Kengyon's camp, if it wasn't for you."

"Yeah, well, I'm just wanting to make sure everything is good on my end, 'cause I have some plans in the works myself." Diamond walked out onto the front porch of Dell's mansion and looked out across the manicured lawn, towards the six-foot hedges that aligned the Italian-styled driveway. She thought about Sergio's beachfront estate and wondered whatever became of it after the hurricanes.

"I'm going to want to look at a few beach-front properties when this is over with," she told him before taking a sip of the bubbly.

"Whatever you need or want, Diamond. That's what this is all about." Dell pointed at the scene before him. "You have to do what it takes to live, Diamond, and you have to set your own standards, and hold yourself to them."

"Yeah, well, at least I won't have to live under my brother's shadow for too much longer."

"Um," Dell swallowed and continued, "then there's that. With this move, we'll no longer have to do any of that."

"I was even thinking about moving."

"What do you mean, out of the mansion or out of Fort Worth?"

"Thinking about moving towards San Antonio to be closer to my bro for as long as he's in there. It's kind of lonely at the house without him." Diamond smiled, her thoughts taking her to memories of Antonio and the fun they used to have, the things they used to do and the things they promised to do together.

"I'm more than sure we can find you something nice out that way and at a breathtaking price."

"I'll be running back and forth, so I might as well keep the house here also."

"Yeah, I heard that Datrina's taking a real liking to it."

"Really?"

"That's just what I'm hearing." Dell laughed. "It's hard to not like that house, Diamond."

"Well then Chris needs to spend some money on one."

"You and Chris are the real breadwinners for the Circle, Diamond. The two of you have been bringing in numbers faster than me and Raymond can work them. With you expanding to San Antonio, I'm more than sure those numbers would double, making us all that much richer."

"Us? Who is us, nigga? San Antonio is going to be mine, right?"

"Um, yeah, but you'll still be a part of the Circle and all, so…"

Diamond looked back towards the mirror tinted doors of Dell's home and told him, "I'm going to make my own way, Dell. I'm not trying to do the Silvia thing, having you guys kick me a little something once a month, or no shit like that. I'm trying to be bigger than this shit. In a few years, I want to be sitting on at least twenty-five mill and that includes properties, vending, construction, and whatever else. I want you niggas to work for me."

Dell laughed, squeezed Diamond's shoulder and told her, "Sounds as if you have it figured out."

"Pretty much."

"So, instead of working as an associate with the Circle, you want the Circle to work for you?"

"What's wrong with that?"

Diamond pulled out of Dell's estate and drove past several homes in the Las Colinas area. She'd told Chris many times she didn't understand the reasons they paid dues to the Circle, but still waited on the very people to make things happen for them. She felt if she paid dues, she should be able to make things happen. She'd visited Dell today to get a better understanding of the system her brother had in place. Not being able to come to the terms they set, she asked for the half a million-dollar advance and to hear the many excuses given about why she should consult with the Circle as a whole, her mind was made up. She and Chris would do their own thing. He'd keep their contacts in Fort Worth and Dallas and she'd take Austin and San Antonio. The Circle could have and keep the clientele they had now.

She pulled past an estate that sat off in a plateau-like setting and thought about King. Thought about the times she spent with him, laughed when hearing Chris' jealousy and shook her head when thinking of Antonio's assessment of her non-existent love life. Diamond then realized she hadn't had sex in months. She'd spent the night with King days ago and sex was the last thing on either of their minds. Feeling her phone vibrate in her pocket caused her to jump and swerve. "Shit!" She pulled her phone from her pocket and answered, "What?"

"Young Diamond?"

"Sergio?"

"How's the day, Young Diamond?"

"Yeah, where are you? I've been worried."

"I'm well, I'm well."

She could hear him laugh while speaking. She wondered about the nature of his call, because she'd given Silvia the two hundred thousand a while ago.

"How'd you get my number?" she asked. Diamond pulled over to the curb and threw the car in park. Her near collision with a curb and streetlight pole unnerved her.

"I had a couple of calls made and they all led to Silvia and she—"

"She violated the code, that's what she did." Diamond smiled. "But, I'm glad she did. I've been thinking about you. How's your home?"

"The one in Miami?"

"Yeah, that one."

"Well, Young Diamond, it was never a home, only a house and it was destroyed, as I knew it would be."

"But, wait, where are those tiger cubs? What happened to them?"

"Ah, young Diamond, I still have them. They're around here somewhere. The longer they live, the bigger they get. They're huge."

"Send them to me. I don't want them to go to any zoo for adoption."

"Remember our talk about outgrowing our situations?"

Diamond thought about her meeting with Dell. "Yeah, how can I forget? I'm going through it now, Sergio."

"Well, just know that you've the ability to choose what's next, young Diamond."

"That's becoming something harder to do now." Diamond exhaled, looked across the way at the secluded home and said, "I'm glad you called. I really am."

"Sounds as if you're needing a word of reason."

She listened to him cough, clear his throat and cough again.

"You smoking or what?"

"Cuban, a habit of mine."

Diamond filled Sergio in on the happenings surrounding her, without giving away too much information. She told him about her need to expand, as well as her need for independence. She listened to him cough, clear his throat and cough again.

She listened to the game from a more experienced perspective and had to agree with most of it, despite it being totally against the things she did and the way she viewed them. He continually talked to her about longevity and security, about love and loyalty and most importantly, about life. He told her how fortunate she was to have lasted as long as she did. Told her to never take today for granted and in order to prosper beyond her wildest imagination, she had to take chances and at times, they would even be the ones that went against the order.

"A house can easily be lost and replaced, Young Diamond, but a home will be and mean so much more. You buy houses, but build homes, young Diamond."

By the time they ended their call, Diamond had a better vision of the one she had for herself. Sergio's illustration was bigger, better, and offered her much more. "You can't fear living," she told herself, before pulling away from the curb and heading to the one place she wanted to be more than anyplace else, Dallas.

Chapter Twenty-Seven

After hearing about her meeting with Dell and the talk she had with her supplier, Chris knew it was just a matter of time now and he wanted her to stay far away from King as possible. Since neither of them was sure of the date when Dell and Raymond would send the team, or the orders they were given, it was in her best interest. It wasn't until now that she told him there was a change in the plans the Circle had, and she needed for Chris to ride with her decision.

"You're sure about this, Diamond?"

"Yeah, I'm on my way there now."

Chris looked at his watch and told her, "Just wait for me, Diamond. I'll go with you."

"I've got to do this myself, Chris."

"I don't think that's a good idea, Diamond. If the nigga trips out, then what?"

"That's a chance I'm willing to take, Chris. He's shown me some things I didn't see at first, didn't want to."

Chris sighed. He was forty-five minutes away from Dallas and knew he wouldn't get there in time and if things went awry, she'd have no one to back her play, and in the game they were in, things didn't always go according to plan. "Just wait for me, Diamond. Shit."

"Some shit I have to do on my own, and this is one of them. I love you, nigga, and if anything should happen to me—"

Chris stopped her, "Listen to me, crazy-ass woman. Just wait for me. I'm forty-something minutes out, Diamond. Don't go up in that nigga's shit, dealing with shit like that alone, I'm telling you."

"If I don't call within the next hour or so, you know what it is, Chris."

It was evident the words he spoke weren't even being heard, and instead of praying for something he knew wasn't about to happen, he asked her, "Do you have your gun on you or what?"

"Yeah, it's in the compartment."

"Take it. Use it if you have to, Diamond."

"I got this, nigga. Chill!"

Chris heard the disconnecting buzz, threw the phone on the passenger side of the Durango and peeled out of the McClendon Estates. He floored the Durango. He had to get to Dallas.

***

Q walked out of his bedroom to find KP sitting at the kitchen table with his head down. He knew KP had been trying to call Silvia and when seeing KP's cell phone faced down on the table, he figured he'd made more unsuccessful attempts. It had been a week since he'd heard or even spoken to his wife and he was missing her like crazy. He and Q went by the house to get most of his things while she was at work, hoping she'd find out how serious he was and go out of her way to get him to come back, but that wasn't the case at all. This wasn't how he told KP it would be. It was nowhere near the way he promised.

"Sitting over there drooling on the floor ain't going to fix nothing, nigga." Q pushed one of the chairs, pushing the table as he did so.

"You fucked my life off, nigga," KP mumbled.

"What?" Q bent at the waist to hear him.

"You heard me," KP looked up with bloodshot eyes and told him.

"You fucked my life off, nigga!"

"Nigga, fuck that. Fuck that shit. It was bound to happen sooner or later."

"Even if it ain't Chris, it's somebody."

"It wasn't anybody. You got me running around here chasing ghosts and shit."

"Take your ass home then, nigga. I ain't got no knife to your neck, making you stay here."

"I ought to kill your ass, Q. You need to let me kill your ass."

Q backed up, looked for something to arm himself with and said, "If I put your ass out, you're going to be living in that damn truck you got out there. Hell, I ought to just bust you upside your punchbowl ass head and get the shit over with." Q raised the salt shaker above his head and told KP, "Just lay your head down right quick. It's going to take me about fifteen tries, but I'll put ya lights out for ya."

"I miss my wife, Q. I miss my wife, man."

Q sat the salt shaker down and leaned against the counter. "Don't do yourself like this, man. You got me feeling like I lost a bitch."

KP pointed out, "You ain't never been married, but you have all the fucking answers for the shit that happens in a marriage."

"Nigga, I'm a counselor. People come to me with their problems all the time. I help people. That's what I do." Q beat his chest, gesturing the confidence either he had in himself or the confidence others had in him.

"I need for you to go talk to her again, Q. Tell her that I'm about to kill myself. At least we'll see if she really cares for me. Call her, call her and tell her, Q." KP looked at him with pleading eyes. "Call her, nigga!"

Q grabbed KP's phone.

"Use yours. If she sees my shit, she might not answer." KP said, before snatching his phone from Q's hand.

Silvia listened to Chris ramble about what he felt Diamond was about to do. With his words and sentences being jumbled and run together, she could only catch bits and pieces of what was being said. Before she could question him of his whereabouts, he ended the call.

"Chris! Chris!" she yelled into the phone.

"What's up, Silvia?" Datrina asked, hearing Silvia yell his name.

"The hell if I know. He was going off about something Diamond did or was about to do. I couldn't understand three words that…"

The ringing of her phone halted her explanation. "Chris!"

"Hey, Silvia, this is Q."

"Q?"

"Yeah, ya husband's best friend. I don't know where Chris is. I was calling to tell you about KP."

"What about KP?" Silvia frowned and looked towards Datrina and shrugged.

"He's about to kill himself. The man loves you, Silvia, and he said—"

"Q, I don't have time for this shit right now. If that stupid ass nigga wants to kill himself, tell him to hurry up, so I can claim his life insurance policy."

Silvia hung up, looked at Datrina and the rest of the women and told them, "Q called, talking about KP's going to kill himself and some more stupid shit."

"What if he's serious, Silvia?" one of the women asked.

"Then he'll beat me to the punch, because if he ever puts his hands on me like that again, that's exactly what's going to happen to his ass."

Another woman told Silvia, "Girl, just call that stupid-ass nigga and tell him to sit his ass down somewhere. And, tell him to stop listening to Q's dumb ass."

"What good is that going to do? I'm tired of his shit anyway. Q ain't did nothing wrong. When a nigga believe his friends over his wife, then that's who he needs to be with. I wouldn't give a damn if I lied or not."

"You go then, Silvia," said Datrina.

"The power of the pussy!"

"The power of the pussy!" they all said in unison.

***

Q lowered his phone and shook his head.

"What she say, with your Batman boots-wearing ass?"

"The first name that came out of her mouth was Chris and it sounded as if she was more concerned about him than you."

"What she say about me killing myself, stupid ass!"

"She said hurry up, so she can claim that insurance policy."

"Stop lying."

"Motherfucker, you asked me what she say and I told you."

"She ain't said no shit like that, 'cause I don't even have no insurance policy on me."

"Well, you do now."

***

Diamond tried calling King twice, then remembered he might have left his phone again, or was actually taking care of some business somewhere. She personally knew what it was like to be distracted by a phone call, 'cause she'd damn near wrecked her car with that very distraction. She turned onto King's street and drove past the other secluded houses, until she came upon the black gates with the huge lion in its center. Instead of being buzzed in, she drove down the winding driveway to the rear of King's home.

On the way over, she rehearsed the very things she'd say. She'd tell him all about Chanel McClendon. She'd tell him the real reason she came into his life and the exact things she was helping people put together, because of him. Diamond was there to tell him that she wanted nothing more than to be with him. To take that chance in life.

She looked for either of his cars, but there were none there. Not even his Escalade trucks, which were normally always there. Diamond then looked towards the glass doors past the pool. She slowly climbed out, the frown on her face complimenting the feeling she was now having.

Diamond walked through the patio doors, nothing. She walked from the living area to the kitchen, nothing. There was nothing and no signs of there ever being anything but. It was like her time spent there was a figment of her imagination, like it never existed, as if it never mattered. "King!" She could hear her call echo through the halls and living area, no longer muffled by the furniture, the African, the expensive entertainment system he loved showcasing. Not even the promise of this being the house he wanted to make his home.

Diamond walked every inch of the bi-leveled home and found nothing, no signs of King and no signs of anything of him. She turned, made her way back downstairs and was about to call him, until she noticed the single rose and a card on the marbled counter. The huge diamond centered on its cover pulled her in its direction. She picked up the rose, looked around, hoping he'd appear from some corner in some attempt to surprise her, as he'd done a time or two before and when seeing and hearing nothing, she opened the card and read,

Diamond,

To finally think I had found that one person to spend the rest of my life with. That one person I was willing to throw caution to the wind for, then realize that it all was just a twisted and delusional dream I somehow refused to let go of, it hurts.

It really does. To walk away from that which I've tried so hard to build, from the very things that I've given my all for was something I never wanted to do but had to.

I thought what we had was special, Diamond. I thought, for whatever reason—that the feelings I had for you would be enough. That you'd someday feel the way I've been feeling from the day I first saw you. You were that one, Diamond. You were the king's jewel every man wanted, the very one we'd somehow die for. All I wanted to do was love you, but I now see love wasn't enough.

Take care, Diamond,

King

Epilogue

King was standing in the bay window of Camille's studio home. He periodically glanced at the people that walked by below him. His thoughts were of Diamond. The woman he knew only as Diamond. After hearing Camille's warnings because of the things she found out for herself, he had no other choice but to heed her advice. Not only that, but the movers were already clearing his home of its furnishings, despite his protest. Camille was in control and with the loyal monster of a man alongside her, her orders held the most weight.

He couldn't believe the woman he loved would be the end of all he dreamed. His Diamond, his weakness and eventually, his demise. King thought of the times he spent with her and refused to believe they were lies. He refused to believe Diamond was anything other than the woman he fell in love with. He looked down at his phone, saw Diamond's contact and read the text:

Standing here, I'm more than sure you feel just as alone as I do. I came here to tell you that in the beginning it was a game, that it was something I felt I had to do to live and move on. I never expected to meet Kengyon Johnson. I never expected to fall for someone I didn't know, but life has its way of bringing people together as well as tearing them apart. For me to say I never meant to hurt you would be a lie, because in the beginning that's all I wanted to do. You took so much from me and I thought I needed to take just as much from you. I never in a million years thought I'd be willing to let go of everything that held me up just to be held by you but this is where I am now. I do love you, Kengyon, and I will find you. I will find that love I lost. I will find my King.

'Til that day,

Chanel McClendon

Camille walked up behind King and read the text from behind. She watched him. Saw him smile, spied him frowning a couple of times and even saw his eyes fill with tears. She reached around and grabbed the phone from his hand.

"We have to get rid of this, King."

"I know it. I..."

Camille hugged him from behind, kissed his shoulder and said, "We're going to be okay, Kengyon. I promise you that."

"I love her, Camille."

"No, you loved her. You hear me, King? Look at me." Camille turned his face to her, looked into his eyes and smiled. "You'll find it one day."

"I did find it, Camille. Now, I'm hoping it'll find me again."

King turned, realized he was alone and told himself, "She's going to find me. She promised."

The End

<u>Coming this March!</u>

Bred by the Slums 3/25
By Ghost

Blood Stains of a Shotta 2 3/31
By Jamaica

Nicole Goosby

BOW DOWN TO MY GANGSTA

By **Ca$h**

TORN BETWEEN TWO

By **Coffee**

BLOOD STAINS OF A SHOTTA **II**

By **Jamaica**

WHEN THE STREETS CLAP BACK **II**

By **Jibril Williams**

STEADY MOBBIN

By **Marcellus Allen**

BLOOD OF A BOSS **V**

By **Askari**

BRIDE OF A HUSTLA **III**

By **Destiny Skai**

WHEN A GOOD GIRL GOES BAD **II**

By **Adrienne**

LOVE & CHASIN' PAPER **II**

By **Qay Crockett**

THE HEART OF A GANGSTA **III**

By **Jerry Jackson**

LOYAL TO THE GAME **IV**

By **T.J. & Jelissa**

A DOPEBOY'S PRAYER **II**

A Drug King and His Diamond

By **Eddie "Wolf" Lee**

IF LOVING YOU IS WRONG... **III**

By **Jelissa**

BLOODY COMMAS **III**

SKI MASK CARTEL II

By **T.J. Edwards**

BLAST FOR ME **II**

RAISED AS A GOON V

By **Ghost**

A DISTINGUISHED THUG STOLE MY HEART **III**

By **Meesha**

ADDICTIED TO THE DRAMA **II**

By **Jamila Mathis**

LIPSTICK KILLAH II

By **Mimi**

THE BOSSMAN'S DAUGHTERS 4

By **Aryanna**

Available Now

(CLICK TO PURCHASE)

RESTRAINING ORDER **I & II**

By **CA$H & Coffee**

LOVE KNOWS NO BOUNDARIES **I II & III**

By **Coffee**

RAISED AS A GOON I, II & III

Nicole Goosby

By **Ghost**

LAY IT DOWN **I & II**

LAST OF A DYING BREED

By **Jamaica**

LOYAL TO THE GAME

LOYAL TO THE GAME II

LOYAL TO THE GAME III

By **TJ & Jelissa**

BLOODY COMMAS I & II

SKI MASK CARTEL

By **T.J. Edwards**

IF LOVING HIM IS WRONG...I & II

By **Jelissa**

WHEN THE STREETS CLAP BACK

By **Jibril Williams**

A DISTINGUISHED THUG STOLE MY HEART I & II

By **Meesha**

PUSH IT TO THE LIMIT

By **Bre' Hayes**

BLOOD OF A BOSS **I, II, III & IV**

By **Askari**

THE STREETS BLEED MURDER **I, II & III**

THE HEART OF A GANGSTA I & II

By **Jerry Jackson**

CUM FOR ME

CUM FOR ME 2

CUM FOR ME 3

An **LDP Erotica Collaboration**

BRIDE OF A HUSTLA **I & II**

THE FETTI GIRLS **I, II& III**

By **Destiny Skai**

WHEN A GOOD GIRL GOES BAD

By **Adrienne**

A GANGSTER'S REVENGE **I II III & IV**

THE BOSS MAN'S DAUGHTERS

THE BOSS MAN'S DAUGHTERS II

THE BOSSMAN'S DAUGHTERS III

A SAVAGE LOVE **I & II**

BAE BELONGS TO ME

A HUSTLER'S DECEIT I, II

By **Aryanna**

A KINGPIN'S AMBITON

A KINGPIN'S AMBITION **II**

I MURDER FOR THE DOUGH

By **Ambitious**

TRUE SAVAGE

TRUE SAVAGE II

TRUE SAVAGE **III**

By **Chris Green**

A DOPEBOY'S PRAYER

Nicole Goosby

By **Eddie "Wolf" Lee**

WHAT ABOUT US **I & II**

NEVER LOVE AGAIN

THUG ADDICTION

By **Kim Kaye**

THE KING CARTEL **I, II & III**

By **Frank Gresham**

THESE NIGGAS AIN'T LOYAL **I, II & III**

By **Nikki Tee**

GANGSTA SHYT **I II &III**

By **CATO**

THE ULTIMATE BETRAYAL

By **Phoenix**

BOSS'N UP **I , II & III**

By **Royal Nicole**

I LOVE YOU TO DEATH

By Destiny J

I RIDE FOR MY HITTA

I STILL RIDE FOR MY HITTA

By **Misty Holt**

LOVE & CHASIN' PAPER

By **Qay Crockett**

TO DIE IN VAIN

By **ASAD**

BROOKLYN HUSTLAZ

A Drug King and His Diamond

By **Boogsy Morina**

BROOKLYN ON LOCK I & II

By **Sonovia**

GANGSTA CITY

By **Teddy Duke**

BOOKS BY LDP'S CEO, CA$H

TRUST IN NO MAN

TRUST IN NO MAN 2

TRUST IN NO MAN 3

BONDED BY BLOOD

SHORTY GOT A THUG

THUGS CRY

THUGS CRY 2

THUGS CRY 3

TRUST NO BITCH

TRUST NO BITCH 2

TRUST NO BITCH 3

TIL MY CASKET DROPS

RESTRAINING ORDER

RESTRAINING ORDER 2

IN LOVE WITH A CONVICT

Coming Soon

BONDED BY BLOOD 2

BOW DOWN TO MY GANGSTA

A Drug King and His Diamond

CPSIA information can be obtained
at www.ICGtesting.com
Printed in the USA
LVHW051504231121
704247LV00010B/1091